MARS
MALICE

Also by Amanda Flower

Amish Candy Shop Mysteries

Assaulted Caramel

Lethal Licorice

Criminally Cocoa

Premeditated Peppermint

Botched Butterscotch

Marshmallow Malice

Amish Matchmaker Mysteries

Matchmaking Can Be Murder

MARSHMALLOW MALICE

AN AMISH CANDY SHOP MYSTERY

Amanda Flower

KENSINGTON BOOKS
www.kensingtonbooks.com

KENSINGTON BOOKS are published by

Kensington Publishing Corp.
119 West 40th Street
New York, NY 10018

All Kensington titles, imprints, and distributed lines are available at special quantity discounts for bulk purchases for sales promotion, premiums, fund-raising, educational, or institutional use.

Special book excerpts or customized printings can also be created to fit specific needs. For details, write or phone the office of the Kensington Sales Manager: Attn.: Sales Department. Kensington Publishing Corp., 119 West 40th Street, New York, NY 10018. Phone: 1-800-221-2647.

Kensington and the K logo Reg. U.S. Pat. & TM Off.

First Printing: June 2020
ISBN-13: 978-1-4967-2203-4
ISBN-10: 1-4967-2203-5

ISBN-13: 978-1-4967-2206-5 (ebook)
ISBN-10: 1-4967-2206-X (ebook)

10 9 8 7 6 5 4 3 2 1

Printed in the United States of America

For Alicia Condon

ACKNOWLEDGMENTS

By the time this novel releases, 2019 will be a memory, and it was a crazy year. So many wonderful things came together for my writing career, and a lot that would have been impossible without my super-agent, Nicole Resciniti, and my wonderful editor, Alicia Condon. You have both been a dream to work with, and I hope to live up to all the faith you have put in my work.

Thanks, too, to the entire team at Kensington, especially my publicist, Larrisa Ackerman, who goes the extra mile every time.

Even though my writing has taken off this year in unexpected ways, it has been daunting to write as much as I have in the last twelve months. Very special thanks to friends Mariellyn Grace, Delia Haidautu, and Alexandra Coley for keeping me sane, to my family, Andy, Nicole, Belle, and Andrew, for being understanding, and to David Seymour for weathering the ups and downs of an exciting but crazy time in my life.

Finally, thanks to my Father in Heaven. I could not do this without you.

CHAPTER ONE

"This is supposed to be the best day of my life!" Juliet Brody wailed in the small library inside the large white church in Harvest, Ohio. She wore a pink and white, polka-dotted silk robe and hugged her comfort animal, black and white, polka-dotted pig Jethro to her chest. Jethro, who was about the size of a toaster, stuck out his tongue, and his eyes rolled in their sockets as his mistress gave him another mighty squeeze.

Carefully, I reached for Juliet's arms and loosened her grip. The pig let out a gasp. I didn't tell her that she'd almost squeezed Jethro to death. If I did, it would send her into another bout of hysterics, and that wasn't something we needed when she was going to be walking down the aisle in an hour to marry Reverend Simon Brook, who was the pastor of the church we were in.

She looked at me with watery eyes. "Oh, Bailey, you are so kind to me, but what am I going to do looking like this?"

"This" was a huge chunk of hair missing where her bangs should have been. The young hairstylist responsible, Dylan Caster, stood a few feet away hold a curling iron in her hand with a hank of Juliet's blond hair hanging from it. The strands wrapped around the iron appeared to be a little crispy. The scent of burnt hair filled the room.

"Dylan," I said, "can you unplug the curling iron?"

"Oh, right." She yanked the cord out of the wall. "I'm so sorry," Dylan said for the fourteenth time. "I didn't expect Jethro to be there."

Dylan was in her late teens and a beauty school student who went to Reverend Brook's church. To keep the congregation involved in the wedding, he and Juliet had decided to hire as many church members as they could to handle all the various jobs that a wedding requires. I was willing to bet Juliet now wished they'd picked someone other than Dylan to style her hair.

Not that I completely blamed Dylan for what had happened. Jethro was equally at fault. Unbeknownst to the beauty school student, Jethro had been hiding under the end of Juliet's robe, and when Dylan came around the front to curl Juliet's bangs, she stepped on his hoof. The pig squealed bloody murder and took off. In the process, he scared Dylan, who had Juliet's bangs wrapped around her curling iron. Dylan screamed and jumped back, taking a big chuck of Juliet's hair with her.

Juliet sniffled. "It's not your fault, Dylan. These things happen."

I smiled at Juliet. It was just like her to try to make the other person feel better even when she was so distraught. It was a gift she had bestowed on her son, Sheriff Deputy Aiden Brody, as well.

I was the maid of honor in Juliet's wedding. I had only known her for a year when she'd asked me to fill that role, so I had been more than a little surprised at the request. However, when she said it was due to the close connection between our two families, I couldn't refuse. I was the best candidate because everyone else I was related to in Holmes County was Amish, and an Amish person would not be allowed to be the maid of honor in an English wedding.

Aiden was the best man. What made it even more interesting was that he also happened to be my boyfriend. As quirky and silly as his mother could be, I had to thank her for raising such a wonderful son. I also suspected that Juliet hoped to nudge Aiden and me toward the altar by making us stand side by side at the wedding. I'd like to think she wasn't that calculating, but I also knew how much she wanted us to marry. It wasn't as if she had been secretive about her hope.

"We can handle this," said my best friend, Cass, who was in Harvest by way of NYC for the wedding. As Cass had said, she wasn't going to miss a wedding that had Amish ushers and a pig ring bearer—not for all the chocolate in New York, which was actually saying quite a lot because she was the head chocolatier at JP Chocolates in New York City, the most famous candy shop in all five boroughs, or at least that was what founder Jean Pierre liked to say.

Although resigned to making it work, Cass shook her head and whispered to me, "It's not looking good. She has a bald spot on the front of her head."

"We have to do something," I whispered back.

Cass glanced at Dylan. "She's not going to be any help. The poor girl looks like she's afraid she will be sued."

"If it was any other bride, she might be," I whispered back. "She took out a lot of hair."

"You know, Juliet," Cass said in a louder voice, "I was just thinking that with those glorious polka dots, your wedding dress needs something other than a traditional veil. You need a hat!"

Juliet used her free hand to dab at her eye with a tissue. The other hand still had a vise grip around Jethro's middle. "A hat?"

"Yes! This might be a blessing in disguise, because it gives you a reason to wear a hat," Cass said.

"You think I should wear a hat?" Juliet asked.

"Of course! All the royals do it, and I have been seeing brides in hats more and more in NYC. It's on trend."

"But we need a hat," I said. I had no idea where we would find the perfect hat to match Juliet's dress in the next fifty minutes, when she was due to walk down the aisle . . . not that I was counting or anything.

"I have a pink hat at home. It was my mother's," Juliet said. "It's in a hatbox in the closet. It has pearls and feathers on it. It has quite a broad brim."

"That sounds perfect!" Cass said. "A broad brim is just the thing—and who doesn't want a little pink at a wedding?"

I grabbed my phone from the librarian's desk in the corner of the room. "I'm texting Aiden right now to ask him to grab it. Where is it in your house?"

"It's in a flowered, round hatbox in my master

closet," Juliet said. "It's on the top shelf. He can't miss it."

I relayed the information to Aiden, and he texted back right away that he was on it. *I love that guy.*

There was a knock on the library door. "Juliet?" Reverend Brook's voice came through the door. "Is everything all right? I thought I heard screaming."

"Don't let him in!" Juliet cried. "It's bad luck for the groom to see the bride before the wedding, and he can't see me with my hair like this! He will think I'm hideous."

"No, he won't. You know that's not true. You could walk down the aisle with a patch over your left eye and a Mohawk. He wouldn't care," Cass said.

I opened the door and peeked out.

The reverend, who was already in his gray linen tuxedo, wrung his hands. "Is everything all right? I thought I heard someone scream."

"Perfectly fine." I smiled. "Why don't you go check on everything for the ceremony?"

"Right," he said, as if he was happy to have some sort of direction. "I'll do that."

He wandered away. I glanced back at Juliet. As soon as the hair crisis was averted, I needed to hurry over to Swissmen Sweets, the Amish candy shop I owned with my Amish grandmother, Clara King. I was doing double duty today. I was the maid of honor *and* the wedding cake designer. Juliet had been very specific that she wanted two things on her cake: polka dots—her favorite pattern—and marshmallow icing. I wasn't too worried about the polka dots, but that marshmallow icing had kept me up at night.

The wedding reception was being held outside on

the village square, and it was hot and humid, typical
for July in the Midwest. The temperature was already
over eighty and it was eleven in the morning. I was
afraid the cake's icing would melt and the whole
thing would slide off the table in a mushy heap. If
Juliet was this upset about her hair, I didn't want to
know how she would react to a giant wedding cake
puddle. Thankfully, I had my grandmother and our
two shop assistants, all of whom were Amish, working
on the cake. The Amish were used to keeping things
cool without the benefit of electricity. I hoped they
had come up with some good ideas while I was inside
the church.

Cass poured us iced teas, and the four of us took a
few minutes to settle. My best friend kept up a steady
flow of chatter and questions, talking about the
weather, the beautiful flowers—daisies, lilies, and
roses—Juliet had selected to line the church pews
and decorate the altar. When conversation lulled,
Cass asked about Jethro. Juliet *loved* to talk about
Jethro.

Juliet calmed down and let Dylan do her makeup.
While she was distracted, Cass disposed of the piece
of fried hair in the small bathroom off the library.
Dylan laid out the eye shadow, mascara, and eyelash
curler. Seeing as how the polka-dot pig had caused
the hair debacle, I thought it best to hold on to
Jethro to avoid any more mishaps. I had the toaster-
size pig under my arm when there was another
knock at the door.

I hurried to the door and opened it a crack, which
was just enough space for Jethro to stick out his
snout.

"Is the best man allowed to see the maid of honor before the wedding? Is that bad luck?" Aiden asked with twinkling, dark brown eyes. Like Reverend Brook, he was wearing a tuxedo, but Aiden's was powder blue, and his blond hair was brushed back from his face. He was so handsome, it took my breath away for a moment.

"Not as far as I know," I said.

"Good." He held up the flowered hatbox.

I took it with my free hand. "Thank you for this. I hope the hat is as pretty as your mother described it. I don't think I can handle any more tears today."

He laughed. "If it's the hat I remember, it's quite pretty, and because it was my grandmother's, it will work for something old, right?"

I raised my brow. "I see you are up on your wedding traditions."

He grinned. "I want to make sure I'm ready when our wedding comes around."

I stared at him, unable to speak.

"Bai!" Cass shouted from the room. "Kiss Hot Cop goodbye and get in here with that hat. We have thirty minutes until showtime!"

Aiden chuckled and gave me a quick kiss on the lips. "Now, let's get my mother married off so we can enjoy some of that delicious marshmallow frosted cake you made, okay?"

"Will do," I said, still reeling from his previous wedding statement. I really didn't want to worry about what that meant at this moment in time.

CHAPTER TWO

I now knew what it felt like to be a cupcake. With Juliet satisfied that her mother's pink hat covered up the hair disaster, I felt free to sneak over to Swissmen Sweets to check on the cake one last time before the ceremony. I was cutting it close, but I had to see for myself that the cake was ready. Thankfully, the candy shop was just across the square from the church. I ran out of the church door, and my lavender and white, polka-dotted bridesmaid dress puffed out around me as I skipped down the church steps.

A little boy playing on the square pointed at me. "Look, Mommy, she's dressed like a cupcake."

I put my head down and ran around the gazebo. Thankfully, I had thought to wear my sneakers to dash to the candy shop. No, they didn't go with the tea-length dress, but at least I could make a quick yet poufy getaway from my cupcake humiliation.

I stopped at Main Street for an Amish buggy before continuing across the street to my shop. There were four children in the back of the buggy, and they all stuck out their blond heads to take a look at me. I gave a finger wave. They smiled and waved back. As the buggy continued on, I could hear them talking excitedly in Pennsylvania Dutch to their parents. I didn't know the Amish word for cupcake, but I was pretty certain I heard *kuche*, which meant cake. That was close enough.

When the buggy passed, I made a dash for the shop. Right before I went in, I made the mistake of looking to my right. Esther Esh stood outside the Esh Family Pretzel Shop scowling at me, but then again, that's all she ever did when I was around.

I didn't have time to worry about Esther, though. I had exactly ten minutes to check the cake and then run back to the church to walk down the aisle ahead of Juliet. Cass had promised to be waiting by the church door with my heels.

The moment I stepped into Swissmen Sweets, I felt comforted. The sweet smell of vanilla, caramel, and, of course, chocolate permeated the front room of the candy shop. An Amish shop in every way, it was clean but with no frills. There were several blond wood tables around the room with ladder-back chairs where customers could sit and enjoy all the delectable treats on the wooden shelves behind them.

There was every kind of candy available, from licorice to lemon drops and everything in between. However, the crown jewel, if there could ever be such a thing in a plain Amish business, was the glass, half-domed counter, which was filled to bursting with fudge and chocolate-covered delights of every flavor. There were even chocolate-covered marshmallows in that case, which was surprising when I considered how much marshmallow it had taken to ice Juliet's cake.

"What are you wearing?" Charlotte Weaver, my twenty-two-year-old cousin and shop assistant, was standing behind the half-domed counter with her mouth hanging open. Charlotte had fair skin and red hair, and for the last few months she had been straddling the fence, trying to decide whether she wanted to be baptized into the Amish faith. She was currently a practicing Amish, but not a baptized one. She had started her *rumspringa* years ago, and I knew the Amish district and my grandmother, also her cousin, were becoming anxious to see her make a decision.

I looked down at the gauzy dress. "It's my bridesmaid dress. I don't want to talk about it."

"I thought *Englisch* clothes were strange, but . . ." she trailed off.

"Yes, I know, I look like a cupcake."

Charlotte cocked her head. "I was going to say a purple lily pad, but cupcake works."

I didn't know which was more insulting, being called a cupcake or a lily pad.

"I can't stay long to chat. I just ran over to check on the cake before the ceremony."

Charlotte smiled. "The cake is fine. Cousin Clara and Emily are in the back, putting the last touches on it."

I gave a sigh of relief. I didn't know what I'd do if the cake flopped. Juliet was counting on my ability to make a "wondrous cake," and had told everyone who was coming to the wedding that I was baking it. If it didn't go well, it would certainly be my last venture into wedding cakes and could affect the reputation of my other sweets, too. If the cake went well, weddings could become a lucrative side business for the shop, with the proximity of the village church. I would always be a candy maker and chocolatier first—like my BFF Cass, I'd gotten my start at JP Chocolates in New York—but I would be willing to continue making cakes for the right price.

"Oh," Charlotte said. "That new fire extinguisher you ordered for the kitchen was delivered." She pointed to the large, narrow box behind the counter.

"That's good news," I said. "I'll hang it up after the wedding."

She nodded, and I stepped into the industrial kitchen. While the front of the shop was rustic, with pine floors and furniture, the kitchen at Swissmen Sweets was all business. It had a white-tile floor, stainless-steel countertops, and industrial-size mixers, refrigerators, and convection ovens. In the middle of the room was a giant, stainless-steel island where we did the majority of our prep work. On top of the island was the cake. It was a four-tier, pink and white, polka-dotted triumph. Charlotte and I had been up half the night icing it because I knew that I wouldn't have any time on the day of the wedding. Even so, this was the first time I had seen it all together. We had put the marshmallow icing on each tier separately before storing it in the refrigerator for the night because it would never fit in the fridge assembled. But now, with all three layers stacked up, the giant cake stood three and half feet tall. No one at the wedding was going to go without a slice of cake. Pink fondant polka dots decorated it, and a pink fondant ribbon wove around it to the very top, where it was tied into a perfect bow.

It was quirky and elegant, the perfect wedding cake for Aiden's mother.

The cake was surrounded by large blocks of ice set in plastic tubs. It looked as if it was surrounded by an ice fort.

"It's like an old-fashioned icebox," I said.

"It's not that old-fashioned to us. There are Amish who still keep their food cool in root cellars," *Maami* said.

I blinked at her. "Really? I can understand that they wouldn't have electricity to run appliances, but I would have thought that at least the fridge would be run off a propane generator."

My grandmother smiled. "That is the case for most, but it's up to the local bishop to decide what technology a family is allowed to use."

How well I knew that. Everything in Amish life seemed to come from the bishop's mandate—from how a woman dressed and where she could work to what technology she could use.

"The cake looks great," I said, unable to keep a note of relief from my voice. "Are you sure you will be able to get it over to the tent after the services? It's huge!"

"Do not worry, Bailey," *Maami* said. "We have it well in hand. Several men from the district will be carrying the cake over right after the wedding."

I sighed. "It looks like you have everything under control. I should have expected this." I tried to smooth the ruffles in the many layers of my dress.

"I've never seen a dress like that," said Emily, our

other shop assistant. Emily was close to Charlotte's age, but she was fully committed to Amish life. She had been baptized into the church years ago and had married a local Christmas tree farmer a few months earlier. She also happened to be Esther Esh's younger sister. This was one of the many reasons that Esther didn't care for me. She thought I had stolen Emily from her when I offered her a job at Swissmen Sweets.

But the truth was, I never offered Emily a job. She asked me for one and told me how much she wanted to get out from under the authority of her sister and her brother, Abel. Also, the older Esh siblings hadn't wanted Emily to marry. In order to have her own life, she had no choice but to leave her brother and sister behind.

"You look like an upside down summer poppy. We have some in our garden at the Christmas tree farm," Emily said with her customary smile.

I smiled. "So far, I have been compared to a cupcake and a lily pad and now a poppy. Of those three, I will take the poppy. It's the most appealing."

Emily smiled sweetly back.

"Don't you worry for a moment about the cake, Bailey," *Maami* said. "We have everything under control. By the time you reach the reception tent, it will be in place, with time to spare." She glanced at the battery-powered clock on the wall and cocked her head. "Now, shouldn't you be at the church?"

I glanced over and squeaked. "Got to run. You all need to get to the church, too."

"We are on our way," *Maami* said. "We were just about to lock up when you popped in. Now, go!"

I waved at them and thanked them for taking such

great care of the cake. Now I could enjoy the wedding without fear. As the maid of honor and the cake creator, I had taken every precaution I could think of to give Juliet the best possible day. There was no way anything could go wrong now. One mishap at a wedding was to be expected, but that was over and done with when Dylan burned Juliet's hair. All would be well now, or so I thought.

CHAPTER THREE

"Your shoes are right here," Cass said and waved at me from the corner of the entry to the church. The wedding guests were filing in, and the guest minister, who would preside over the cere-mony, was at the front of the sanctuary. The sound of the organ boomed through the building. I knew that in the middle of the service, Charlotte, who was also an organist, would be playing a hymn. Reverend Brook and Juliet wanted to involve as many people from the congregation and the community as possible.

Aiden, in his powder-blue tuxedo, waited at the door of the church to walk his mother down the aisle. Cass held my arm while I removed my sneakers and put on my heels.

Aiden wove around the guests filing into the church to stand next to us. "Wow."

It wasn't the kind of wow you wanted to hear from your significant other. It was the sort of exclamation someone made when they witnessed a car crash.

"She looks like a cotton candy machine exploded, doesn't she?" Cass smoothed her wrinkle-free dress. She was slim and sleek in her all-black tank dress and bright red heels. Her black and purple hair was perfectly styled and her eyeliner was on point. Don't tell Cass that you can't wear black to a wedding. Actually, don't tell Cass that you can't wear black anywhere, because that was all she wore.

"Well . . ." Aiden trailed off as if he was dumbstruck by my appearance. Then he said, "It's the kind of outfit that makes you believe there just might be unicorns out there."

Cass snorted a laugh.

I finished putting on my heels and let go of Cass's arm. "I'm pretty sure that was the look your mother was going for."

"Mission accomplished," Aiden said with a laugh. "You're a beautiful lavender and white puff. No matter what you wear, you will always be beautiful to me."

Cass handed over my bouquet. "Oh my gosh, Bailey, if that doesn't make you fall over dead in a swoon, you're a robot."

I was smiling but wasn't swooning. "There's no time to grow weak in the knees. We have a wedding to get to."

"You're right," Aiden said. "We should all head to our posts."

Cass saluted us and went into the church.

As she found her seat, the last of the guests, including *Maami,* Charlotte, and Emily, settled into theirs, and Reverend Brook stood at the front of the church with the other pastor, a man with a poor comb-over who might be pushing one hundred. Juliet had told me that the reverend presiding over the ceremony had been the former minister of the church until Reverend Brook took his place twelve years ago. I sure hoped the wedding would begin soon; the old reverend appeared to be on the verge of needing a nap.

The church was packed. It wasn't often the village minister got married, and it was an open community wedding, which meant that everyone in the village was invited. At least half of the people there were Amish. Reverend Brook was well-respected in the Amish community because he allowed the church building to be used for Amish functions. There wasn't a single person in Harvest who had a mean word to say about Reverend Brook, and the same went for Juliet. I couldn't say that about Jethro. People had a lot to say about that little pig. I suppressed a sigh as an usher walked the little bacon bundle over to me on a lavender satin leash.

The wedding party was small, consisting of the bride and groom, Aiden and me, and Jethro.

"You're taking the pig down?" the usher asked, as if he wasn't sure I was up to the task.

I waved the bouquet that Cass handed me. "Yep."

He shook his head, as if it was my funeral. "Get in line. It's almost time."

As if on cue, the organist started the wedding march. I wasn't surprised in the least that Juliet had chosen to go with a classic tune to walk down the aisle. She had been waiting for this day for so long and it was finally here. She would want everything to be perfect. Any bride would.

I looked down at the polka-dotted, potbellied pig.

"Let's do this," I whispered. "Make Juliet proud. Chin up. Tail high!"

He lifted his head and his tail sprang into action.

Jethro was wearing a lavender satin bow tie for the occasion. Part of my job as the maid of honor was to carry the bouquet, adjust Juliet's train, and walk Jethro down the aisle. I took the satin leash into my hand. In the pig's mouth was the handle of a small basket that held the wedding rings. When Juliet had first told me that Jethro would carry the rings in his mouth, I almost fell over. Even with the protection of the tiny basket, the risk of the pig losing the rings was high. However, this was one point of the ceremony on which Juliet refused to budge. Other than Aiden, Jethro was the most important being in Juliet's life. Of course he had to have a large and important role in the wedding. As Cass said, "Being best bacon wasn't enough; he had to be the ring bearer, too."

He stared up at me with his brown eyes as if he understood all my thoughts and turned his attention toward the front of the sanctuary. The little bacon bundle had his game face on, and I was happy to see it.

"Go!" the usher urged in a harsh whisper.

I hesitated, but Jethro took the usher's words as a command and moved out.

I tripped a little as I doubled my pace to walk beside him.

People smiled and chuckled softly as we made our way down the aisle. Truthfully, we went at a faster clip than was normal for this sort of thing, but I blamed Jethro for that. I liked to think the guests were chuckling at that pig with the lavender bow, but it could just as easily have been my cupcake dress arousing their amusement.

Despite the too-quick pace and my worries over the rings being lost, we made it down the aisle and stood a few feet away from the reverend. Jethro looked up at me.

"That'll do, pig, that'll do," I whispered, quoting from *Babe* with a smile. It was something I had always wanted to say to Jethro. However, because the little pig was a bit of a troublemaker, the opportunity had never arisen. Apparently, when Juliet needed it the most, the little oinker would come through with his very best behavior. I hoped it would continue through the rest of the ceremony and well into the reception. But I might be pressing my luck to ask for good behavior from Jethro for that long.

The music picked up and the congregation stood as Aiden and Juliet made their way down the aisle. They were a handsome mother and son, and Juliet was radiant. Cass had been right about the pink hat: It was both chic and somehow classic, and with the polka-dotted theme, it somehow managed to tie everything together. Juliet was beaming and couldn't take her eyes off Reverend Brook. I glanced at the minister's face and saw that he was watching her intently, too. His expression was happy but far more cautious than Juliet's, which I immediately dismissed as wedding jitters. No one in Harvest doubted Reverend Brook's devotion to Juliet Brody.

In front of the church, Aiden kissed his mother on the cheek, and then, much to my relief, he bent down and took the basket of rings from Jethro's mouth. When he straightened, he winked at me. I blushed.

"Welcome, one and all, to this joyous occasion," the presiding minister said into the stand-up microphone, but only the wedding party could hear him.

Reverend Brook helped the old minister turn on his mic, and there was a bout of awkward laughter.

"Oh," the minster laughed. "That is much better. Thank you, Reverend, for helping another man of the cloth in his time in need." He cleared his throat. "As I was saying, welcome to this joyous occasion of the marriage of Reverend Simon Brook and Juliet Brody. We, as a congregation, have seen their love and respect for each other grow over the last several years. There were whispers before the public announcements that they were together, but they were coy with us. Now, we can celebrate with great happiness their love and felicity in holy union."

I watched as Juliet and the reverend spoke the traditional vows of marriage. They lit the unity candle, and the ceremony was just about to come to an end when the back doors of the church, which the ushers had closed the moment Juliet was inside, flew open with a bang against the wall.

A woman in a tropical print sundress stomped down the aisle. Her dirty blond hair was tied in a messy bun on the top of her head, her skin pulled taut against her thin cheeks . . . Everyone in the sanctuary froze as she ran down the center aisle.

"Is this the time when you ask if there are any objections to this marriage?" the woman cried. "Don't you have to ask that?" Her voice was raspy, as if she had smoked most of her life.

The old pastor blinked. "We don't ask that question any longer. It's not really up to anyone else if two people should marry."

"I say they don't get to be married!" She held her right fist in the air and then pointed at Reverend Brook. "He doesn't deserve happiness after what he did. Did you tell them, Simon? Did you tell them what you did?"

Reverend Brook paled.

"Please, someone, do something about this disturbance," the old pastor said.

Aiden handed the minister the little basket that held the rings and waved to someone at the back of the church. Deputy Little, who was in his sheriff's department uniform, walked down the aisle. "Ma'am?" he began.

All the while, Reverend Brook looked like he was caught in the bright headlights of an oncoming train. All he could do was stare at the woman as if she was a ghost who'd come back to life to haunt him.

Deputy Little held up his hands in the same way I'd seen countless Amish farmers approach a skittish cow or horse. There were no sudden movements in either case. "Ma'am, perhaps this isn't the best time to discuss whatever grievance you might have with the reverend."

"The heck you say!"

The woman hadn't actually cussed, but that didn't stop the audible gasps heard through the church.

Deputy Little held out a hand. "Now, ma'am, we are going to have to ask you to leave."

The whole congregation leaned forward, eyes glued to the spectacle. I had to hand it to Deputy Little. He didn't have a whole lot of experience in hostile situations, as far as I knew, but he was treating this one like a pro.

"You don't get to ask me to leave. Ask Simon why I'm here. You didn't tell her about me, did you? What a cruel joke that she will have to find out on her wedding day—or is it a wedding day not to be?" she spat.

"Ma'am," Deputy Little said. He looked as though he was debating tackling her. I thought that was a bad idea, because the church was crowded and guests were likely to be taken down along with the intruder.

I glanced at Juliet, who stared at the woman openmouthed, as if she couldn't believe this was happening. My heart hurt for her; I hated the thought that this might be her clearest memory of this special day, a day she had awaited for so long.

"Ma'am," Deputy Little said again. "Come peacefully out of the church or I will have to arrest you for disturbing the peace."

She spun around to face him. Her back was toward the front of the sanctuary now. She then turned back to face the wedding party. She held up her fist. "Traitor!" the woman screamed and ran from the room.

After the church door banged closed with a resounding thud, the sanctuary was so quiet, you could hear a horse shake its bridle outside the building. No one moved. No one spoke.

Juliet gripped Reverend Brook's arm for all she was worth. "Don't stop. Keep going. Please. The wedding must go on. Please finish it," she said.

The old pastor blinked at her.

There were tears in Juliet's eyes. "Please."

The pastor looked to Reverend Brook, who nodded.

"I now pronounce you husband and wife," the retired minister said. "You may kiss the bride."

CHAPTER FOUR

After the ceremony and hundreds of photographs in the front of the church, the wedding party was finally released from what felt like forty days in a photo shoot desert, where Juliet did all she could to get photos of Aiden and me together at the altar. I think she was concerned more about getting those shots than the ones of her and Reverend Brook.

"Who *was* that?" Cass demanded as she met me at the foot of the church steps when I was finally able to leave the church building. She and I walked arm in arm to the large reception tent in the middle of the village square. "It was like a scene out of a midday soap opera, but with bonnets and buggies."

I knew what she was talking about. It was what everyone at the wedding was whispering about, the woman in the tropical dress who'd called Reverend Brook a traitor. I gave Cass a look.

She cocked her head. "Come on, you have to admit I'm right about that."

I smiled. "It was dramatic."

"No kidding. It gives me another story to tell Jean Pierre when I get back home. I swear, he doesn't believe half the things I tell him about Amish country. Who would? This place is as crazy as New York."

It was a fair question and statement. My life had become much more interesting and exciting when I left the Big Apple. Wouldn't you have thought the opposite was true?

"Do you know who that woman was?" Cass asked.

I shook my head. "No idea."

"She tried to stop the wedding. That's heavy stuff. Why would she call Reverend Brook a traitor?"

I shrugged, as if I wasn't wondering that exact same thing, which of course I was. It was all I could think about during the wedding party photographs. In the back of my head I prayed and hoped that Juliet hadn't made some kind of mistake by marrying Reverend Brook. "I guess it doesn't matter now that Juliet and Reverend Brook are married."

She made a face that told me she wasn't buying my nonchalance about the situation. "Maybe it's the New Yorker in me, but I don't think I would have gone through with the ceremony until I had some answers from my husband-to-be. If I was about to marry someone and a guest shouted in front of God and everyone that my almost-husband was a traitor, that would give me pause."

"I don't think that woman was a guest," I said. "I don't know who she was, and believe me when I say I went over the guest list with Juliet no less than a hundred times."

"So she was a wedding crasher, then. That makes the story even more interesting." Cass brushed her purple bangs out of her eyes. "I have even more material for

Jean Pierre. You know, if Amish country continues to be this interesting, he might just fly out to see it all for himself."

"I cannot imagine Jean Pierre in rural Ohio." I stopped at the edge of the tent.

"Stranger things have happened," my best friend mused.

Across the tent, Reverend Brook and Juliet greeted their guests as if nothing out of the ordinary had occurred. Juliet beamed at her new husband, but worry nagged at the back of my mind. I had told Cass that it didn't matter now who the woman was because Juliet had married Reverend Brook, but that wasn't entirely true. I had a feeling a person who went to the trouble of making a scene at a wedding wouldn't give up until she got whatever she wanted. But what was it that she wanted? She hadn't asked for anything in her outburst.

I shook the uneasy feelings aside and admired the tent. Everything was perfect. Twinkle lights hung from the cloth ceiling, giving the space an ethereal glow inside. Dozens of round tables with pink and white polka-dotted tablecloths surrounded the hardwood dance floor at the center of the tent. Pink and white roses in round vases perched in the middle of each table. Even with all the lovely decorations, my eyes went immediately to the cake. A whoosh of relief went out of me. My creation was at a place of honor by the head table, where Juliet and Reverend Brook would sit. It was perfect. As *Maami* had promised, the Amish men from her district had delivered it to the tent unharmed.

Mission accomplished.

Several guests came over to me and shared their excitement about the wedding, and I did my best to dodge the recurring question as to when Aiden and I were going to get married. It wasn't something I had an answer to. Both Aiden and I were very focused on our careers at the moment. As second in command at the sheriff's department under a disgruntled sheriff, Aiden had a lot of responsibility. At the same time, I was trying to grow my business at Swissmen Sweets, plus launch my new cable television show, *Bailey's Amish Sweets*, which would premiere in less than two weeks. Even thinking of the show's premiere made me nervous. I had seen the episode and was proud of it, and it had been well-received by early reviewers, but would anyone watch it? I didn't know. My producer insisted that there was a place for Amish candy on his channel, Gourmet Television, but I wasn't so sure.

We weren't engaged, but I knew Aiden and I would marry someday. I was almost sure we would, but *when* was a question that seemed to loom large in the wedding guests' minds. The other burning question was the identity of the mystery woman in the tropical dress. I didn't have an answer for that one either.

As the reception went on, I felt more relaxed about the surprise woman at the ceremony. Surely if she really wanted to make trouble for the new couple, she would have crashed the reception, too.

Aiden walked over to me. As if he could read my mind, he said, "I asked Deputy Little to keep a lookout for her. I'm not going to let anything else ruin my mother's day."

I didn't have to ask him who "her" was, and he didn't have to explain. It was the woman in the tropical dress, of course.

There was a hard set to his jaw. "My mother gave up so much and did so much for me. I just want her to be happy."

When Aiden was small, Juliet had left her alcoholic and abusive first husband, Aiden's father, in South Carolina. She'd traveled north, trying to get as far away from him as possible, and she'd ended up on the doorstep of Swissmen Sweets in Holmes County, Ohio, where my Amish grandparents had taken in Juliet and her young son. *Maami* and *Daadi* let them stay there as long as they needed. I imagined the Amish way of life must have been a shock to Juliet after coming from South Carolina, where there are very few Amish. Even so, she fell in love with the little village of Harvest and the people there. She decided to stay, and when he was an adult, Aiden decided to stay, too, and join the county sheriff's department.

Because of this, our families had always been close. At the time, I was a child growing up with my non-Amish parents in Connecticut. I was living a very New England life. I had no idea that my grandparents had people living with them above the candy shop. *Maami* and *Daadi* never thought to tell my parents about the Brody family. It wasn't the Amish way to brag about helping someone. It was just their way to help.

I learned about my grandparents' selflessness when I moved to Harvest about a year ago. That's when I met Aiden for the first time, too. I blushed at the memory. The first time I saw him, I had been so taken aback by his handsome appearance and his kind demeanor that I nearly choked on a piece of chocolate I'd been eating when he came into Swiss-men Sweets.

I touched his cheek. "That makes you the man I fell in love with."

He smiled. "Well, that is certainly an added benefit."

"There are other benefits, too. You're an amazing cop and son. It's hard to find anyone who doesn't like and respect you."

He laughed. "Okay, okay. I'm not in need of that much of a pep talk."

Charlotte cleared her throat. She was standing right behind us, and I hadn't even realized she was there. "Bailey, Juliet would like a photograph with you beside the cake . . ."

I smiled. "All right."

By the time I made it to the cake table, the bride and groom were already there. The photographer, yet another member of the church, was poised and ready to take the shot.

Juliet held Reverend Brook's hand. "The cake is beautiful, Bailey. It's more beautiful than I could ever have dreamed."

"Yes, Bailey," the reverend said solemnly. "Thank you for all you've done. We appreciate it."

"It was my pleasure," I said as I set out the large cake knife and two polka-dotted china plates I had found at a consignment shop the next county over. I knew Juliet would love them and I couldn't resist. "These will be here when we are ready to cut the cake."

The cake was beautiful. I had done all that worrying for nothing. My grandmother would have told me that worry was always for nothing and to just trust in God. If I did, all would be well.

Juliet didn't disappoint me with her reaction. "Aren't those plates just lovely?" She beamed. "Bailey, you really do think of everything!"

I smiled for the camera with Juliet and Reverend Brook, and then stepped away so the photographer could take more shots of just them with the cake. Juliet looked blissfully happy. I was so happy for her. No matter what trouble that wedding crasher had wanted to cause, there was nothing that could take the smile off Juliet's face this afternoon.

After the photo op, I walked across the tent to stand with Cass again. I smiled as I went. The inside of the tent looked just as Juliet wanted. The colors were lavender, pink, and green. The decorations and dishes set the tone for a country wedding, with burlap-covered Mason jars on every table holding lovely bouquets. But the people at the wedding were the most important piece to Juliet, and at least a third of them were Amish. The difference between the appearance of the Amish in their plain clothes and the English in their summer party dresses and tailored suits was never more striking. Despite those differences, they'd all come together for Juliet and Reverend Brook. I thought that said a lot about the couple, and the community of Harvest as a whole.

I waved at Millie Fisher, an Amish matchmaker from my grandmother's district just a little bit younger than my grandmother. She was sitting with her niece and her best friend, Lois. Lois, who had spiky red hair and wore a bright bubble dress, was decidedly not Amish. I hoped when I was Lois's age I would have the confidence to wear a dress like that.

Cass stood with me at the edge of the tent and

rubbed the back of her neck. "I'm going to have the smallest wedding ever. This was exhausting."

"You have any candidates for a groom in mind?" I wiggled my eyebrows.

She laughed. "You know what it's like to date in New York or, should I say, not date. All I do there is work."

I frowned. This was the first time I had ever heard Cass complain about working too much. Like me, she was a workaholic, and I thought that was what made us such good friends. Neither of us got hurt or upset when the other had to cancel plans if something came up at work. We both had drive and did what we must to get the job done. "You okay?" I asked.

She glanced at me. "I am. Weddings don't usually make me feel this way, but it could be because JP Chocolates seems to attract very particular brides."

"Bridezillas?" I asked with a smile.

She grinned. "I don't mind a bride knowing exactly what she wants. That makes things easier really, but sometimes . . ."

I chuckled, remembering some of those brides. I knew, too, that Cass was exaggerating. Not all the brides were bad. Just some of them. Honestly, the mothers of the brides were the ones I'd really learned to watch out for.

The mother-and-son dance was announced, and Aiden and Juliet went to the dance floor.

"You can always tell if a man is a good guy or not by how he treats his mom," Cass said. "That's what my Italian grandmother always said."

Then by any estimation, Aiden was a very good guy. Beyond him, I saw several of the Amish guests, including Charlotte and Emily, laughing and talking at a long table. Just past that table, I spotted a bit of tropical fabric. Could it be the woman from the ceremony? I didn't want to draw attention to her, not even to Cass, in case I was wrong, so I whispered to Cass that I needed to find a restroom and walked across the tent.

When I stepped out of the opening in the tent, I spotted the newly married reverend talking to the woman in the tropical dress by the gazebo. The woman erratically waved her arms in the air and seemed to teeter on her feet, and Reverend Brook put his fingers to her lips in an attempt to keep her quiet. My best guess was the woman was drunk. It was a wonder that she was still even able to stand upright. From my vantage point I realized she was much younger than I'd first assumed. She was likely closer to my age than Juliet's. I turned back into the tent to wave Cass over to me for reinforcement. Before I could, I glanced across the dance floor and saw the cake wobble.

I stared at it. Surely I had imagined the cake moving. I chalked it up to the paranoia I'd felt about the cake all week. There was nothing to worry about now. It was here in one piece and would soon be consumed by the hungry guests.

The cake wobbled again, and this time more than before. It shook, and dread seeped into my bones as it began to fall.

"No!" I cried, running as fast as possible toward the cake. I didn't know what I could do to stop gravity, but I had to try. I lunged the last few feet, arms outstretched in an impressive Superwoman impersonation, hoping to push the cake into place. But I was too late. As the cake toppled onto the grass in a heap, I couldn't stop my momentum. I tripped over my fluffy dress and fell on top of the cake. I lay in the midst of all that cake and marshmallow icing, wondering how my life had landed me here.

Jethro came around the side of the cake covered in marshmallow, pink fondant dots, and crumbs of chocolate sponge with a sheepish look on his face, and then he ate a mouthful of cake from my shoulder.

CHAPTER FIVE

Aiden knelt at my side. "Bailey, can you get up?"
"It would be really bad if a cake killed her.
With all the times she risked her life, that would not
be the way she would want to go out," Cass said.

I wiped marshmallow from my cheek but only suc-
ceeded in pushing it into my hair. That would be a
nightmare to get out. "I'm not dead. Can someone
help me up?"

"Aiden, you had better do this. My dress is designer, and I don't know what a dry cleaner can do
with marshmallow," Cass said.

Aiden helped me to feet, and I could feel the eyes
of everyone in the tent on me.

Maami and Charlotte appeared at my side. "You go
get yourself cleaned up, Bailey," *Maami* said. "We can
clean up the cake."

"Your dress is ruined," Cass said. "Then again, it's no
great loss. I love you, but now you look like a crushed
cupcake."

Juliet dropped the hand covering her mouth. "Are you all right, sugar?"

"I think so . . ." I trailed off when I realized she wasn't asking me if I was all right. She was asking Jethro. I should have known.

"Juliet, I'm so sorry," I said.

"It's not your fault," Aiden's mother said.

"I'll go over to Swissmen Sweets and make up a tray of sweets and candies for the guests. We have plenty to feed everyone," Emily said.

Juliet shook her head. "No need. These things happen." Despite her words, she looked like she might cry.

"Please," I said. "Let us do this for you. I feel just awful about the cake."

I felt bad about the cake, not just because it was another thing that had gone wrong at Juliet's dream wedding, but because everyone at Swissmen Sweets had worked so hard on it. Now there would be nothing left, and Reverend Brook and Juliet wouldn't be able to freeze the top tier to eat on their first anniversary either.

Juliet sniffled. "Do you have any of those chocolate-covered marshmallows at the shop? Those are my very favorite."

"I can bring you a whole tray," Emily promised and took off.

Juliet handed a napkin to me. I didn't know what good that was going to do. I accepted the napkin and tried to wipe icing off my arms, to no avail.

"Don't you worry about the cake, Bailey."

"Thank you, Juliet. You really are being so understanding," I said.

Juliet said with a smile, "I'd give you a hug, but

then I would be covered in marshmallow, too." She smiled sweetly at me one more time, then walked over to her groom, who'd just stepped back into the tent. There was no sign of the woman in the tropical dress.

"I'll just run home to clean up," I said, looking down. "I'll be back in no time."

"That's a good idea," Cass said. "I mean, I never thought it was possible to make your bridesmaid dress look worse, but you have done it. That's quite an achievement."

"Do you want me to go with you?" Aiden asked.

I laughed. "Don't be silly. Stay here and enjoy the wedding."

"I can drive you home," Aiden said. "It would make the trip quicker."

"And I would ruin the interior of your car." A piece of fondant fell from my skirt as if to illustrate my point. "I'll just walk home and be as quick as I can. This is your mother's day. I don't want you to miss a moment of the wedding."

"It has been rather eventful so far," he said.

That was most certainly the truth.

He glanced at his mother, who was hugging Reverend Brook for comfort. The pastor held onto his new bride, but his forehead was wrinkled in concern. Was it worry over his wife? Or was it guilt over something he had done with the woman in the tropical dress?

Aiden nodded at my mess of a dress. "I hope you didn't have any plans to wear that again. It's safe to say it's done for."

"I wasn't planning to." I laughed. "Actually, maybe Jethro did me a favor. Knowing your mother, she would want me to dig it out for a special occasion, like a future anniversary party for her and the reverend. This saves me from staging an unfortunate accident to avoid that."

"There is always dry cleaning. Despite what Cass said, the local dry cleaner has been able to work miracles in the past. She got tar out of my uniform . . ."

"Keep your voice down," I teased. "You will put the idea in your mother's head, and I would hate for the dry cleaner to have to wrestle with marshmallow in organza. It would be cruel."

Aiden chuckled, and then he became serious. "I could walk you home." He made one last attempt to accompany me to my house.

"Stay with your mom. This is her special day and she wants you by her side."

"I just worry . . ."

"Worry about me? Walking through the mean streets of Harvest?" I joked as I shuffled out of the tent.

"I just can't stop thinking about that woman who came into the church during the ceremony. I have Deputy Little trying to find out who she is," Aiden said.

"Did you ask Reverend Brook directly? She certainly seemed to know who he is."

"I did." He pressed his lips together. "He said due to pastor confidentiality, he couldn't tell me. Normally, I would have pressed him, but I didn't want to ruin my mother's day any more than it already was. But be sure I will find out before they leave on their honeymoon tomorrow afternoon what his connection to that woman is." He set his jaw.

I frowned and wondered if I should tell Aiden that I had seen Reverend Brook speaking with the woman outside the reception tent just before the cake toppled over. I decided to wait until the wedding was over, too. I didn't want to cause him any more worry during the remainder of the reception. But I had to admit that I was glad he was trying to get to the bottom of who the mystery woman was. I was dying to know.

"I'd better go; the frosting is starting to stiffen up. It won't take me more than thirty minutes to walk to my house, change into another dress, and come back." I lowered my voice. "Between you and me, I'm quite happy that I don't have to dance in this. I would have fallen on my face. I think the dressmaker used all the organza in Ohio to come up with this monstrosity. It's no great loss."

"So you paid Jethro to topple the cake and ruin your dress, is that it?"

My face fell as I thought of the once beautiful cake. "I hate to think of all the time *Maami* and the girls from the shop put into that cake, only to have it destroyed in a matter of seconds."

"You know your grandmother isn't upset." Aiden look back into the tent. "She's having a nice time, too."

"I know." I smiled. "It's nice to see her so cheerful. Ever since *Daadi* died, there's been this underlying sadness in her face. I'm glad to see she's happy now. She loves your family very much. She wouldn't miss Juliet's wedding for the world."

He kissed my cheek. "And I love hers, most especially her marshallowed granddaughter."

I squinted at him. "Is 'marshallowed' a word?"

"It is now."

"Aiden?" A woman of about thirty came out of the tent. She had beautiful red hair that fell to her shoulders in a movie star wave. Her dress was a sky blue the exact shade of her eyes. She smiled at Aiden in a way that made me uncomfortable. "Your mother sent me to fetch you. The two of you need to finish your dance."

"Thank you," Aiden said in a clipped way.

"And I hope you will save a dance or two for me as well." She smiled up at him. "For old times' sake."

Old times' sake?

The woman glanced at me in a measured way and went back inside the tent. I would be lying if I didn't say I thought she put a little more sway in her walk as she went.

I stood there in my cake-covered dress, but Aiden didn't explain who the woman was. I desperately wanted to know, and to ask him what old times' sake meant. He said nothing. Okay, I stored the topic away for a conversation at a later time.

"Go," I whispered.

He nodded. "Hurry back."

"I will." I watched him walk inside the tent. His mother waited on the temporary dance floor. She beamed at him. I hoped that the woman in the church would not make the smile waver ever again, but even I knew that was wishful thinking.

CHAPTER SIX

Leaving the wedding tent, Aiden, and the mystery redhead behind me, I hurried across the square and stopped on Main Street to wait for a minivan full of kids to drive past. They stuck their heads out of the van's windows when they spotted me, and I had a feeling that several of them snapped a photograph of me with their phones. I'd be trending on social media with the hashtag "exploded cupcake" before I even reached my house. It made me wonder how many people at the wedding took photos or video of the great cake clasp. It was unlikely I would ever be asked to make a wedding cake again; the entire village had seen what happened to Juliet's cake. Shaking my head, I knew there was nothing I could do about it. I just hoped that I'd ducked my head in time, so no one could see my face.

I passed Swissmen Sweets on Main Street and continued down to the corner of Apple. I had my head down. In my current state, I didn't want to make eye contact with anyone. I knew how ridiculous I looked. When I turned onto Apple Street, I saw the woman in the tropical dress again. She stood on the opposite corner with her arms folded, glaring at the proceedings around the reception tent. Part of me wanted to talk to her, ask her who she was and what she was doing here.

But how could I ask any hard-hitting questions and hope to be taken seriously when I looked like an exploded cupcake?

She began to walk, taking a winding path down the sidewalk. As if just putting one foot in front of the other was a difficult business. She stumbled toward the curb. My earlier impression, when I saw her with the minister, had been correct; she was definitely drunk. I knew she hadn't gotten tipsy at the reception. Reverend Brook had insisted on a dry wedding. There wasn't much dispute from anyone about it. He was the pastor of the church, and the many Amish attending wouldn't approve of spirits either.

Reverend Brook had spoken out many times about the troubles that alcohol caused. I knew the possible dangers of alcohol, but I wasn't against a margarita when I was back in NYC. At the same time, I respected my Amish grandmother enough not to talk about alcohol in front of her.

This woman needed help. I increased my pace to catch up with her. It wasn't an easy feat, considering that I had to shuffle to keep from tripping over the cake-covered dress.

When I was about ten feet away, she still gave no indication that she knew I was behind her. "Ma'am?" I asked.

She didn't even twitch.

A little louder, I asked, "Ma'am? Do you need help? Can I call someone for you?"

Still there was no response.

I said it a third time, and she fell on the sidewalk.

I forgot to worry about tripping over the dress and ran to her. "I'm so sorry I scared you."

She did look at me then, and I could see that her eyes were bloodshot. She opened her mouth as if she were about to say something.

Before the words could come out, a compact red car pulled up to the curb. A man jumped out, ignoring me, and began to yell at the woman. "What are you doing out here? We need to leave. Let's go." He was a brown-haired, short man wearing a muscle shirt and cutoff jean shorts. He was tan from hours in the sun, but I couldn't see the color of his eyes because they were behind aviator glasses.

"I'm not done yet," the woman said in a slurred voice. "You can go."

"I wouldn't have to if you hadn't made such a mess of things," he said.

"I told you it wasn't me. I would never do it."

"You can prove that by coming with me. It's time to go." He reached for her arm, but she jumped away.

"I don't need your help! I'm perfectly capable of getting inside a car."

I shuffled closer to them. "Can I help? Is everything okay?"

The woman spun around. "Who do you think you are, barging into a private conversation?" She made a rude hand gesture at me. "Get lost!"

"I–I–" I was completely taken aback. "I only wanted to offer my help."

"Help? What can you do to help? Look at you!" She barked a laugh.

The man scowled. "That's enough. It's time for us to go."

She glared at him. "I decide when it's time for me to go. No one tells me what to do. I put up with that for too long as it is."

He frowned. "Please. Let's leave now."

I tried one more time. I felt like I had to. "I can call someone for you." I took my phone from the pocket of my dress. The dress's one saving grace was that it had pockets. The phone only had a little bit of marshmallow icing on it.

"That girl is covered in cake!" the woman in the tropical dress chortled. "Cake!" With that, she opened the passenger side door and half-fell, half-sat inside the car. "Get away from us, Cake Girl." Then she laughed at her own joke, as if it was the funniest thing she had ever heard.

I stumbled two feet back from the car.

The man closed the door after her, glared at me, and then ran around the other side of the vehicle. He jumped in and sped away.

I stood there in my ruined dress in a state of shock. What had I just witnessed? Some kind of domestic dispute?

I wished I had thought to look at that license plate number, but I was too surprised by what had happened to react. I couldn't shake the odd feeling and decided it was time to call Aiden.

"Are you okay?" he asked as soon as he picked up.

"I'm fine. Still walking home. Listen, I just saw something strange." I related the story to him.

"That does sound alarming. Did she get in the car of her own free will?"

"Yes, but she was drunk or on something for sure. She could barely walk."

"Did you get a license plate?" Aiden asked.

I sighed. "I knew you were going to ask that, and I didn't." I went on to describe the car.

"It's okay. You were too upset to be thinking about license plates. I will put out an alert to be on the lookout for the car." He paused. "I will pull Reverend Brook away from the festivities for a bit to see if he can tell me more about her. If we knew her name, we might have better luck finding that car."

"You don't think I'm being an alarmist?" I asked.

"It's better to be an alarmist than sit by and do nothing." He paused. "Can you describe the man?"

I told him what I remembered of the man's appearance. "I'm sure if I saw him again, I would recognize him." I shivered, hoping that the uneasy feeling I had was simply the result of the woman's storming the church that afternoon. Maybe the man who'd picked her up was a friend. Someone who was helping her. I wanted to believe it, but I trusted my intuition that something about the entire encounter was very, very wrong.

There was no way I could track down the car, so I would have to leave that in the hands of the police. It wasn't easy for me. I would much rather put on my running shoes and figure out myself what was going on.

I walked the rest of the way home without incident. When I reached my driveway, my next-door neighbor, Penny Lehman, stood in her front yard with her mouth hanging open. "Bailey King, what happened to you? You look like you have been attacked by a giant doughnut."

I sighed.

Penny looked like she was Amish, but she was a member of the conservative Mennonite Church. That meant that she dressed like an Amish woman, all the way from her prayer cap to her black, sensible shoes, but she was able to use technology, drive a car, and have electricity in her home. She was short, with brown-and-gray hair, and put all the nosy neighbors I'd had back in the city to shame. None of them did surveillance as well as Penny.

"I had a run-in with a wedding cake," I said, hoping the conversation would end there.

Her mouth made an "O" shape. "It looks to me like the cake won."

"It most definitely did. It's nice to see you. I just need to go get cleaned up." As I hurried to the door, a piece of marshmallow fell on a nearby bush. I'd worry about that later. Or maybe Penny would. She was much more likely to clean it up before I got around to it.

I unlocked my front door and closed and locked it behind me before she could follow me inside. Penny had been known to do that. It was most uncomfortable when Aiden was visiting and she thought that was a good moment for a neighborly chat. Aiden and I never had much time to spend with each other because of his work as a deputy, and now that I was flying back and forth between Harvest and New York City, we had even less. Penny wasn't making it any easier.

I couldn't believe that the premiere of *Bailey's*

Amish Sweets was so close. I was nervous just thinking about it. I had been able to put the premiere out of my mind for the last week because of the wedding, but I knew concerns about the show would come creeping back in just as soon as the reception tent came down.

I let out a breath as I stepped farther into the house. The living room was sparsely furnished because I was hardly ever home. However, I had found a secondhand leather sofa to replace the love seat in the room.

While Cass was in town, I slept on the new couch and gave her my bedroom upstairs. The couch was a bit on the lumpy side, but it still beat the cot I used to sleep on when I shared a tiny bedroom with Charlotte above Swissmen Sweets.

Since I had moved into the house, I had done a few more things to make it more like a home. There were now some pictures on the wall, and I'd also bought a floor lamp.

There was a snuffling sound at my feet, and I looked down to see my large, white rabbit, Puff, hopping toward me. She was about five feet away from me when she stopped, sat back on her haunches, and looked up.

She shuffled a few more feet back, as if my appearance was just this side of frightening.

I groaned. "Not you, too? I thought at least my rabbit would show me some respect."

She dropped her eyes, turned around, and hopped back into the kitchen.

I went upstairs to defrost myself.

*   *   *

Later that night, after the wedding festivities came to an end, Cass and I walked back to my rental house. Other than the woman who'd stormed the church and Jethro taking out the cake, the wedding had been a great success. Despite all the mishaps, Juliet looked happier than I had ever seen her. That made all the wedding preparations I had undertaken over the last several weeks worth it.

In the middle of the night a storm rolled in and I was awakened by a crack of thunder so loud, I was sure the house was falling down around me. Puff pressed her nose up against my hand, which dangled over the edge of the couch. I could feel the rabbit trembling under my touch. I gathered her up in my arms and counted. "One Mississippi, two Mississippi."

Another crack of thunder and I hid with Puff under my blanket. Midwestern summer storms were worse than any I'd experienced in Connecticut.

I half-expected Cass to run downstairs from my bedroom and ask if we were under attack, but she never did. The earplugs she wore at night must really have done wonders. I might have to ask her where she got them to make it through the rest of the Ohio summer.

Eventually, Puff and I drifted back to sleep.

CHAPTER SEVEN

The next morning was Sunday, and it was my day off. Actually, it was my only day off because Swissmen Sweets was open six days a week. If I was in the village, I was at the shop every day we were open, but Sunday was my day. On Sundays, I spent time with Aiden if he was free. Being a sheriff's deputy, he worked seven days a week. Even when he wasn't on duty, he was still on duty, being the second in command at the department. His job was high stakes and stressful at times, and I wished he could slow down and enjoy life a little bit more. I would never ask him to do that, though, because I knew how much he loved his work and cared about the people of the county.

Even though I didn't have to go to the shop, I still had early morning duties. At the end of the reception, I had promised Juliet I would check the church to make sure everything was cleaned up before the service. She didn't want anything to bother Reverend Brook's Sunday morning service, not even her wedding.

As far as I knew, it was my last maid-of-honor responsibility. Well, perhaps that wasn't true. I was also going to watch Jethro while they were on their Prince Edward Island honeymoon. It was no surprise that Juliet was an *Anne of Green Gables* fan. I was, too. She'd promised to bring me a gift even though I'd told her it wasn't necessary.

At first she had planned to take the pig with her, but crossing international borders with what would be considered livestock was a big no-no, and she finally decided to leave Jethro behind.

The day after his wedding, Reverend Brook had promised to preach, and then he and Juliet were off. Church wouldn't start for two more hours. I didn't think the janitor was even there yet. It would give me enough time to make sure everything was perfect for the start of services.

When I reached the foot of the church steps, I immediately realized something was wrong. There was someone lying at the top of the steps. "Hello? Do you need help?"

The person didn't move or make a sound, and I ran up the steps. When I got there, I knew the woman was beyond help. There was a large gash on the back of her head and blood on the concrete landing.

She wore the same tropical sundress that she had worn to the wedding the day before. Something about seeing her in the same outfit made her fate seem even worse to me. Had the man who'd picked her up killed her? Had she never made it home at all, wherever home might be? I felt sick. I had had a bad feeling when she was picked up on the street by that driver. I'd reported what I had seen. Aiden had told his department. I didn't know what else I could have done. I didn't know the car, the driver, or the dead woman. Even so, guilt seeped into my heart. I felt that I should have done something.

I stumbled back down the church steps and removed my phone from the pocket of my shorts. "Aiden, you have to come to the church quick," I said before he even had a chance to say hello.

Aiden yawned. "Is it something with Jethro? I told you you shouldn't have agreed to watch him. You need to draw some boundaries with my mother now or you will be helping her out a lot. She means well, but she can be needy."

There was another yawn that gave me just enough time to say, "No, Aiden, listen to me. You have to come to the church. I found something."

"What?" He was wide awake now.

"You're not going to believe this, but I found another dead body." I whispered it because I couldn't even believe it myself.

Aiden said a word that would not be appropriate in any church, but considering the circumstances, it seemed fitting. I knew he was in as much disbelief as I, because . . . this wasn't my first time. In fact, it wasn't even my first time in this very church.

"Do you know who it is? Was it an old person who had a heart attack?" His voice was hopeful. I knew it wasn't because Aiden wanted anyone to die, but because he didn't want this to be yet another case of murder in the little village of Harvest. I wished I could tell him it was a heart attack.

"Aiden," I said, "it's the woman from the wedding yesterday."

"What woman?" His voice was sharp.

I knew he wasn't trying to be harsh with me. He was only seeking information. Even so, I flinched at his tone.

"I'm sorry, Bailey," he said. "Who is she?"

"It was the woman in the tropical dress." I paused. "And Aiden, I think she might have been murdered. The back of her head has a huge gash, like she was slashed or something." I took a breath. "What if that man who gave her a ride killed her?"

"We don't know that's what happened," Aiden said, fully awake now. "We don't know anything about how she might have died. You shouldn't blame yourself."

Maybe I shouldn't blame myself, but I did. I blamed myself for the entire situation.

"Good Lord!" a voice cried at the top of the church steps where I had left the woman. I looked up and saw the janitor, Sal, staring down at the body with his mouth hanging open. He was in his seventies, and Aiden said he had been the janitor at the church for as long as anyone remembered. Reverend Brook didn't want to let him go, so he hired a group of young Amish women to clean the building once a week. All the janitor really did was unlock the church on Sunday mornings and make sure the furnace or air conditioning was on inside, depending on the season. Sal gaped at the woman. "She's dead!"

I still had Aiden on the phone, and he yelled into my ear. "Who's that? What's he saying to you?"

"It's Sal," I said. "He just unlocked the front door of the church and found the woman there."

Sal stared down at me. "Did you kill her?"

"I did no such thing!" I couldn't help but feel offended by his question. "I don't even know who she is."

"I don't know who she is either, but she is certainly dead. My God, that is a lot of blood. You will excuse my language on a Sunday, but that's the truth. Looks to me as if she has quite a cut on the back of her head, too, like it was made with a sword even."

I frowned. A sword? I didn't think there were any medieval knights in Amish country. "Thanks, Sal."

"I'm in my car," Aiden said. I could hear the sirens from his SUV going at full blast. "I'll be there in five minutes. Don't leave the scene. Don't touch anything, and don't let Sal touch anything either."

"I know the drill," I said.

He sighed. "I know you do. I hate that. I'm going to call the department. Are you all right? Do you need me to stay on the line?"

"Do what you need to do, Aiden," I said. "I'm fine."

"Okay. I love you."

"I love you, too." I glanced at the woman's broken body. "Hurry if you can."

When I hung up the phone I noticed that Sal was bent over the woman. I hurried back up the steps. "Move back," I told him. "That's a police order."

"Are you the police now?" Sal asked.

"No, but I was just on the phone with Aiden, who is, and he said not to touch anything."

"I wasn't touching her," Sal said, seeming shocked by my words.

I sighed. "Fine, but you don't want to get anything on the body. That might link you with the crime."

Sal gulped and took a big step back. "I didn't kill anyone. I don't even know who that is." He paused. "Wait! Is that the woman who yelled at the minister in the middle of the wedding? My, that was a scene, wasn't it? I thought that Reverend Brook was going to faint dead away."

I had thought the same thing, but I didn't say so. Instead, I asked, "You were at the wedding?"

"'Course I was at the wedding. Who else was going to clean everything up when the ceremony was over?" He sniffed.

Not you, I thought.

"Not those Amish girls the minister thinks help me clean the church. I am the one with the janitor badge and have been for thirty-four years." He puffed out his chest to show me the brass janitor badge.

"I can see that," I said. "I still think it's best if we don't stand right over the body like this."

"We're going to have to do something about this mess." He wrinkled his puglike nose. "There's a bloodstain on the church steps. I won't be able to get that out of the concrete. There's a blood mark on the church now."

"We can consult with the police about it. They know people who have ways to remove stains like this." I knew, because I had seen it done before, when I discovered another dead body in the kitchen of Swissmen Sweets. There had been blood in the grout in the tile floor, and the specialized cleaning crew had been able to get it out. I hoped the same would be true for the church. I bit my lip and wondered if I should call Juliet to tell her. Would it be better for Aiden to reach the scene first?

Just then, I heard a high-pitched Southern voice call out behind me. "What on earth is going on?"

Apparently, I didn't have to decide.

CHAPTER EIGHT

Juliet and her new husband hurried across the parking lot toward the front door of the church. Usually, the minister went into the building through the back door, which was closer to his office, but they must have seen all the commotion and opted to enter from the front of the church instead.

The minister had lived alone in the parsonage on a side street off the square for as long as he worked at the church, and now it was where he and Juliet would live together. I hated to think this was what they would find on their first morning as husband and wife.

I steeled myself, knowing I would have to be the one to tell Juliet about the latest tragedy at the church. At least this death had not taken place inside the building, but I didn't think the reverend would see that as a stroke of luck.

Jethro trotted along behind the couple as if he didn't have a care in his piggy world. Now that Juliet was married to the reverend, would Jethro become a bit like a church mascot? Juliet had always been involved in the church. She was in charge of a quilting group and a member of the choir, and she was always the go-to person to help Reverend Brook no matter what was happening with the congregation. None of those roles would change now that she was the pastor's wife. In fact, she might have even more responsibilities, but I knew Juliet would revel in the opportunity. This was what she'd wished for so long. I was happy that her wish would finally be fulfilled.

"Reverend Brook—" I stepped in his path. "There's been an accident of some sort."

He tried to peek around me. "What kind of accident? Did someone fall?"

That was one way to describe it.

"Not exactly. I just found a woman at the church door." I paused. "She's dead."

"Oh no." The blood drained from Reverend Brook's face. "Is that . . . it can't be . . ." He walked up three steps and froze. Clearly, it was the person he was hoping not to see.

"That's the woman who interrupted our wedding," Juliet exclaimed. She scooped up Jethro and held the pig close to her chest. "Bailey, what on earth happened? Did she fall and break her neck? How can that be?"

I shook my head. "I don't know. I came to the church this morning as you asked me, to make sure everything was clean before the morning services, and I found her . . ."

"Wait," Sal said at the bottom of the steps. "You asked her to check that the church was clean? It's my job to clean the church." He folded his arms. "First you hire a bunch of Amish girls to clean and now you send some candy maker to check the church. The old pastor would never have insulted me like this."

I ignored Sal and went on. "I called Aiden. He and some more deputies are on the way."

"Good. Reverend Brook, please come down the steps," Juliet said, placing a hand on her husband's shoulder. "It will be too painful to see."

He nodded and walked down the steps. "Yes, dear. I think I'm in shock."

Juliet nodded. "Of course you are. You tried to help that poor woman and look what's happened. Please know it's not your fault. None of this is your fault."

Reverend Brook looked back at Sal and me at the top of the steps. "In a way, it is my fault. If I'm right, I'm responsible."

I desperately wanted to ask the minister what he meant by that.

Sal clicked his tongue. "They aren't married even five minutes and the little woman is already calling the shots. Let me tell you, now that the reverend has a wife, things are going to change around the church. I have seen it before. When a woman gets her claws into a man, everything changes. My ex tried to make that happen to me, too, but I'm made of stronger stuff."

"Sal," Reverend Brook said. "That's enough. I will kindly remind you that Juliet is my wife and should be treated with respect, as all women should be treated with respect."

Juliet's eyes shone as she looked at her husband. I could doubt a good many things in this life. I could not doubt that she loved the reverend, despite the

fact that a woman who'd accused him of being a traitor in the middle of his wedding ceremony lay dead
on the church doorstep.

Sirens approached. Aiden and his team would be
here any moment, which meant that soon I could get
out of the middle of the awkward conversation between the janitor and the pastor. I left them standing
at the base of the church steps as the police cars
pulled up.

Aiden jumped out of his SUV just as the tires settled in the gravel parking lot. "Bailey," he began.
Then he stopped short. "You called them?" I knew
"them" meant his mother and Reverend Brook.

"No one called us," Juliet said, coming to my side.
"We just came to the church a bit early because there
were a few things the reverend wanted to get done
before we left on our honeymoon. I can't believe this
is happening. We just got married," Juliet said. There
were tears in her eyes.

I hadn't seen Juliet this upset since Jethro went
missing for a few days last fall. But then again, this
was a dead woman, who'd accused Juliet's husband
of being a traitor, lying on the steps of the church
where he was the pastor. She had every reason to be
upset, and then some.

She swallowed. "How can I be so horrible? The
poor woman is dead. And the situation is even worse
because Reverend Brook tried to help her." She held
on to her husband's arm. "You tried so hard to help
her."

Reverend Brook was looking a little green.

"Oh, my dear." She touched his face. "She was a
troubled young woman. None of this is your fault."

Aiden watched his stepfather closely. I wished I could hear the thoughts that must be going through his head.

"Reverend," Aiden said. "Is this Leeza?"

Reverend Brook looked at the woman. "It is, and it's my fault that she's dead."

CHAPTER NINE

Aiden folded his arms. "I think it's time for you to tell me what was going on with Leeza. Now that's she's dead, your pastoral confidentiality doesn't apply."

Juliet placed a hand on the reverend's arm. "You can tell him, Simon. I know that it's hard to break your confidence, but you will be helping poor Leeza now if you share what you know with Aiden."

Reverend Brook pressed his hands together as if in prayer, and then he glanced at Sal. Juliet seemed to get the hint and said, "Sal, let's go in the back way through the church to make sure everything is ready for our service." She was already an exemplary pastor's wife.

"You're still planning to have church, then?" Sal asked. "With a dead woman on the doorstep? I'm not sure that's wise."

Reverend Brook straightened up. "Yes, nothing can get in the way of the worship of our Lord. We will have the congregation come in the back way. It will be a good opportunity to pray for Leeza and her family."

Juliet beamed at him as he spoke.

Sal shook his head, as if it were the most ridiculous thing he had ever heard. He followed Juliet around the side of the building as the crime scene techs swarmed around Leeza's body.

"Did she come to you at the church for help?" Aiden asked.

Reverend Brook shook his head. "No, I met her at the Holmes County Community Hall."

I frowned. All I knew about the hall was that it was a place to rent for events. It was popular for wedding receptions and baby showers. "At a party?" I asked.

"No." He took a breath. "Compassion for Crisis meets there once a week, and I've been volunteering for the last several months."

"Compassion for Crisis?" I asked.

He glanced at me. If Reverend Brook thought it was odd to find me poking my nose in on Aiden's interview, he didn't say anything. Neither did Aiden, for that matter. I didn't know if it was a good or bad sign that they took for granted I was there and looking for answers. I think it certainly said something about what my life in Amish country had been like.

"It's a nonprofit that's been around for a few years. The purpose of the organization is to provide counseling for people in crisis. The group approached me last year to see if I would be willing to give some of my time. I believed it was a good chance to reach out to the community."

"Is it for the Amish?" I asked, remembering there were other nonprofit groups in the county that helped Amish people who left the faith assimilate to English life. I wondered if it was former Amish who went to Compassion for Crisis. But then again, Leeza had most certainly not appeared to be Amish.

"It's for anyone. Participants can be Amish or English," the minister said. "But most of them have been English. I haven't counseled any Amish people." He took a breath. "There are five or six counselors who volunteer for the program on a weekly basis. No one needs to make an appointment to meet with us. A struggling soul can just walk in and we will do our very best to help him or her."

"What is the goal of the appointments?" Aiden asked. "Are you counseling one person for a long time?"

Reverend Brook shook his head. "No, most of the time we're directing people to resources they don't know are available to them, either for free or through their medical insurance companies. Many times, when people are in crisis, they doesn't know where to begin. We help with that. We aren't long-term counselors, but we can set them on a course to get the long-term help they may need."

"What was Leeza seeing you for?" Aiden asked.

The minister pressed his lips together, and again, I thought he wasn't going to answer Aiden's question. He took a breath. "I met Leeza at the end of April. She came in on a busy night, and I was the only counselor available, having just finished up with another client. When I saw her, she'd definitely had a little too much to drink. Her words were slurred, and she even had trouble standing up straight. Any time that happens, I make sure to ask the person if they have a ride home. I don't want someone in that condition getting behind the wheel of a car. She told me her friend was going to pick her up in an hour."

I wondered if it could be the same "friend" who'd picked her up on Apple Street the day before.

"Was she seeing you about her drinking?" Aiden asked.

Reverend Brook nodded. "She said that she wanted to stop and turn her life around, so she could see her family again. She claimed that they wouldn't see her until she made some changes."

"To her drinking?" I asked.

Reverend Brook nodded. "I assume that was the first step."

"What's Leeza's last name?" I asked.

The minister shook his head. "I don't know. I don't even know if that was her real first name. It was the name she gave me. We don't require last names, addresses, phone numbers, or any other details of our clients' life. We only find out those things if the person volunteers that information. Leeza was one who opted to share nothing." He paused. "I told her about AA and other groups that could help her. She didn't request more than that, so there wasn't much more I could do."

I rocked back on my heels. "If you were helping her, why did she crash the wedding?"

The reverend swallowed and wouldn't make eye contact with me. "It's hard to say."

Aiden folded his arms. "Take your best guess."

Reverend Brook frowned as two cars pulled into the parking lot. Two couples exited their cars and stared openmouthed at the police vehicle and the coroner's car at the front of the church. They were dressed in their Sunday best, ready for an uplifting message from Reverend Brook the day after his wedding. I was certain they weren't expecting to find something like *this* on a quiet Sunday morning. They started to come our way, but Juliet ran interception and guided them to the back door.

The reverend ran his hand down the side of his face. "This will be the talk of the village."

"Murder typically is," Aiden deadpanned. "Now, why did she come to the wedding? Why did she call you a traitor?"

"I don't know how she found me or knew who I was. As her counselor, she only knew me as Simon. The counselors are on a first-name basis with all our clients."

"Holmes County isn't that big," I said. "It wouldn't take much research for her to find out who you are."

He sighed. "I suppose not. I hate to think how she ruined Juliet's special day."

Aiden glanced at me, but I couldn't read his expression. I had so many questions about how these events must seem to Aiden. It was his mother's future wrapped up in this tragedy, and it was his *stepfather* who was the only link—and likely a suspect—in a woman's death.

"Reverend Brook," he began, "why did Leeza call you a traitor?"

He licked his lips. "I suppose I can tell you now. Recently, Leeza told me about some illegal activity she knew about, and I reported it to the police."

"Her illegal activity?" Aiden asked.

"I . . . I don't know . . ."

Aiden waited with his arms folded and stared at

Reverend Brook. It was the stance he used when interrogating suspects.

After a few minutes, his patience paid off and Reverend Brook cracked. "She certainly had a drinking problem. It was clear to me the moment she walked into the community center."

"That's not illegal as long as she didn't drive," I said.

"I know." Reverend Brook frowned. "She told me that she was involved with a man who was running an illegal still in Harvest Woods."

I blinked. "Like moonshine?"

"Yes," Reverend Brook said.

"Is it illegal to have a still?" I asked.

"Yes," Aiden said. "If someone is selling moonshine without registering with the feds and paying taxes, it's illegal. I assume this is the case."

Reverend Brook nodded. "And this is why I am responsible for her death. She was scared of that man, and I told the police about the still."

"You were the anonymous caller?" Aiden asked.

The reverend nodded. "The sheriff's department must have found the still, and he killed her in retaliation."

"Anonymous caller?" I asked, trying to follow the conversation without having all the pieces.

Aiden glanced at me. "About a week ago, the department got a tip that there was an illegal still in Harvest Woods. We've been looking for it ever since. Harvest Woods is dense, and the moonshiners know how to camouflage their stills. It takes a good eye and a lot of luck to find their operations. We got lucky finding this still."

"You found it?" I asked. "Did you make an arrest?"

Aiden shook his head. "Just confiscated the equipment. The people behind it must have gotten a tip we were on to them because they never came back." He turned to Reverend Brook. "Why didn't you tell the dispatcher who you were when you reported it?"

"I didn't want to worry Juliet, and I knew she would hear about it if I gave my name." He licked his lips. "And also, it wasn't a call I should have been making. Leeza told me this in confidence as her counselor. She was drunk at the time and may not have realized until much later what she told me. I breached her trust by calling the sheriff's department."

"She realized it by the wedding," I said, remembering the dramatic scene when she'd stormed inside the church in her tropical dress and called the reverend a traitor.

Aiden frowned. "The department has been looking for the person responsible for the still ever since we discovered it. Last night was the only night we haven't gone out."

"Because of the storm," I said.

He nodded. "Right."

"Sheriff Jackson took on this case personally," Aiden said. "There hasn't been a public announcement about finding the still because he doesn't want to tip off the moonshiners."

"If you weren't supposed to tell the sheriff's department about the still, why did you?" I addressed my question to the minister.

The reverend turned to me, and there was anger in his eyes that I had never seen before.

"Drinking is so awful. It destroys families and ruins lives. If I can do something to stop it, I will," he said with such ferocity that I took a step back. This wasn't the quiet, timid minister I knew. This was a man with an edge.

His anger faded. "Now, I must get ready for our Sunday morning service. The message today is particularly important."

"You're still going to preach?" I asked.

The reverend straightened his shoulders. "We will not let this evil person win by canceling church. The service will go on and we will pray for Leeza and for whoever did this to her." He marched off, and I was surprised Aiden let him go. Aiden's face was an impenetrable mask as he watched his mother's new husband walk away. Maybe he was hiding the fact that he was afraid Juliet had made a mistake marrying the clergyman.

I feared the same.

CHAPTER TEN

I wanted to ask Aiden his thoughts about the illegal still, Leeza's death, and Reverend Brook's behavior, but before I could do that, Deputy Little called him over from the top of the church steps.

Aiden gave me a half smile. "I know you have a thousand questions, Bailey, and so do I. I don't think we are going to get answers that will satisfy us any time soon."

I didn't think so either. I watched Aiden join Little and the crime scene techs at the church door. I couldn't see Leeza's body and was just as happy that I couldn't. The memory of it was something I wished I could forget.

My goodness, that poor woman. Again, guilt washed over me. Should I have interrupted her argument with that man? Should I have stopped her from getting in the car?

I felt something cold touch my bare leg and I jumped. Glancing down, I found Jethro looking up at me. The little pig seemed to have concern in his eyes, but I wasn't sure if that sympathy was for me or for himself because he'd missed his second breakfast due to the murder.

Juliet was a few paces behind him and looked as stressed as she had the day before when Dylan, the hairstylist, burned her hair. Juliet was still determined to hide the damaged hair. Today, instead of a hat she wore a strategically placed headband. It was polka-dotted, of course.

"I thought you went inside," I said.

"I did, but Jethro ran back outside. I came to fetch him." She smiled. "I think he wanted to make sure that you're all right. You know the little pig has a soft spot for you."

I stared down at Jethro, and he cocked his head. He was cute. I had to give the little oinker that, but I hadn't completely forgiven him for destroying my cake.

Juliet's eyes flitted in the direction of the church steps. "I just can't believe this. First that woman storms into the church and tries to ruin my wedding, and now she is dead on the church steps. How can this be happening?" She blinked back tears.

I didn't know what to say.

Juliet picked up Jethro and held the little pig tight. He kicked his legs. "What am I saying? I'm being selfish. That poor woman was dealing with her demons and now she is dead because of them. I should only feel sympathy for her and nothing else."

I patted Jethro's head. Considering what had happened, I decided to forgive him for toppling the wedding cake the day before. His crimes were minor when compared with murder.

Juliet wrinkled her nose.

"What is it?"

She snuggled Jethro close. "I feel awful that I'm thinking about myself, but . . ." She glanced at the steps again. "Does this mean the reverend and I can't go on our honeymoon?"

I winced. I hadn't thought about that. Other than the wedding, all Juliet had talked about for weeks was her honeymoon to Prince Edward Island. They were leaving for the airport right after church, or they would have if this hadn't happened. "You might have to postpone the trip."

Her face fell. "I know we must." She couldn't keep the disappointment from her voice. "We bought travel insurance. I hope this will qualify as a reason to postpone."

I hoped so, too, but I had never seen murder as one of the options to claim money back with travel insurance. Perhaps it could be filed under family emergency.

I prayed that Aiden would clear up the case quickly, both for Juliet's sake and to bring justice to Leeza. No matter what choices she'd made, or how rude she might have been to Reverend Brook or even to me, she didn't deserve an end like this. What bothered me the most was the feeling that I could have prevented all this if I had only interrupted her and that man on the street. I had to find her killer.

In the past, I had helped Aiden solve a murder case or two, but in those instances the murder always involved the Amish: Either the person killed was Amish or had a connection to the Amish community. I helped in those cases, sometimes with Aiden's blessing and sometimes not, because my grandmother was Amish and beloved in the community. That connection made it easier for me to find out information than it would be for Aiden, who, as a member of law enforcement, was distrusted on sight. From what I knew about Leeza, she had no connection to the Amish.

Juliet grabbed my hand. "Maybe you could help Aiden find the person who killed that poor woman?"

"Juliet, you know Aiden doesn't want me to help on his cases," I said, even though I had been thinking the same thing.

She shook her head. "He may say that, but he loves your help."

I was pretty sure he barely tolerated my help, but I wasn't going to say that to his mother. Instead, I asked, "What do you know about Leeza? I mean, I got the impression that Reverend Brook has told you some things about her."

She blinked at me, and then her face cleared. "Oh, see, you are listening to me. You are asking as part of your investigation. I knew you would decide to help."

I opened my mouth to protest, but before I could, she said, "I didn't know anything about Leeza, at least until last night. After the reception was over and the reverend and I were alone, I asked him to explain to me who she was and why she'd stormed into the wedding like that. I believed as his wife I deserved an explanation."

"You most certainly did, but . . ." I stared at her. "You didn't know who she was when you told the other minister to go on with the wedding?"

"No, I didn't know."

"And you were still willing to marry Reverend Brook without knowing who she was and what her accusations meant?" I asked. In my head, that sounded crazy. I would have at least postponed the wedding for an hour so I could get an answer from the man I was about to marry.

"I couldn't do that. That would make Reverend Brook think I didn't trust him, and I do trust him. I knew there must have been some sort of misunderstanding that had upset the woman, but I knew my husband could not be at fault. Reverend Brook is too good, too pure, to have done her any wrong."

I wanted to argue with her that no one was perfect, but I stopped myself. Instead, I asked, "What did he tell you?"

"He told me that he counseled her at the community center and she had a drinking problem. He guessed that she was drunk when she stormed the church. She was a troubled woman, and he told me that being a pastor's wife meant I would at times have to deal with other people's troubles."

I wondered if Juliet knew about the still. She hadn't mentioned it, and knowing Juliet as well as I did, I thought she would have told me if she had heard about it.

"He was just trying to help her," Juliet said. "And she acted out in such an embarrassing way." She squeezed her hands together so tightly, her knuckles turned white.

If Juliet didn't know about the still, I wasn't going to be the one to tell her.

"I can tell you think it was unwise of me to marry the minister after that disruption in the church yesterday."

I thought it was more than unwise; I thought it was crazy. But I kept those thoughts to myself.

The county coroner came down the steps of the church and nodded at me as he passed by. I knew him because of Aiden's job and because I wasn't a stranger to finding dead bodies. There was movement at the top of the stairs, and two crime scene techs picked up the stretcher bearing the body bag and started down the steps.

"Oh!" Juliet had to look away.

I did, too. Even though I couldn't see Leeza's face now, I would always remember what it looked like.

"Juliet, what is happening?" a high-pitched voice asked.

Juliet spun around, still holding Jethro to her chest.

The other woman looked familiar to me, but many people who went to Juliet's church did. She was petite and wore a cream-colored linen dress that I would wrinkle if I even dared to touch it. Her graying, strawberry-blond hair was sleek and fell to her shoulders. Over her right arm she carried a designer handbag, something that I would have seen every day in the city but was much more uncommon in Amish country. The name of the designer was on it for all to see.

Juliet's cheeks flushed. "Christine, there has been an accident."

"It looks like much more than an accident. Was that a body bag they put in the back of the ambulance? Is Reverend Brook all right? It would be just a shame if something happened to him the day after the wedding." She placed a hand on her cheek.

"No, no." Juliet set Jethro on the grass. "The reverend is fine. Sadly, a young woman passed away. My son and the other deputies are trying to find out what happened."

Christine's face cleared. "That is good to hear. If anyone can get to the bottom of this, it's Aiden. Kayla always says he's the one you can count on."

I frowned. The way she said that made me uneasy.

Juliet's eyes widened. "Yes, well, Aiden is a good man."

I cleared my throat.

"Oh my," Juliet said. "I'm sorry. Christine Kepler, I'd like you meet Aiden's fiancée, Bailey King. I'm sure you have seen Bailey around the church. She visits here often with Aiden."

I froze when Juliet said "fiancée." I wondered what I could possibly say to her at this point to discourage her from forcing a wedding on Aiden and me.

I recognized Christine's name from the wedding guest list. At the time, all Juliet had told me about her was that she was a member of the church. Most of the guests were church members. There was no reason for me to take special notice of her name. Maybe I should have.

Christine held out a hand to me. When I took her fingers, they were ice cold. "It's nice to meet you."

I dropped her hand as soon as it was polite.

"You and Aiden are engaged?" Christine asked in a sharp voice.

"No," I said, and glanced at Juliet. I didn't know how many times I had corrected her on this point over the last few months. The worst of it had been when my parents were in Harvest for Mother's Day. Both my mom and his had been determined to have Aiden and me engaged before my parents returned to Connecticut. I was grateful that we had been able to resist. Aiden and I would become engaged when both of us were ready and not a moment before. When that moment would come, it was hard to say.

The wrinkle in Christine's brow smoothed. "I'm so glad to hear that." She narrowed her eyes at Juliet. "You know that things are supposed to have happened a certain way."

Juliet's mouth made a little "o" shape, and I was certain I was missing something important. However, unless it had to do with Leeza's death, I didn't want to know. What I had learned during my year in Amish country was that gossip was a useful tool for gathering information, but it didn't always lead to the right information.

Juliet scooped Jethro up again. "I should go check on the reverend. Christine, I hope you plan to stay for Sunday services. Reverend Brook would like to continue. He's writing a special prayer right now for Leeza. He is such softhearted man."

"Yes, I plan to stay." She sniffed. "I attend every week, not like some others who tend to visit when it's convenient."

I raised my brow. Was that dig aimed at me? I wasn't a regular churchgoer. For the most part, I went on major holidays and when Charlotte played the organ.

"You run along, Juliet. I will be in in a moment. We are going in the back way, I take it." It was more of a statement than a question.

Juliet bit her lip. "Yes, that's right." She fidgeted with Jethro's collar, and I wondered what on earth was going on. It was clear to me that these two women had some kind of history. I didn't want to be caught in the middle of it. I had enough to worry about with my *Bailey's Amish Sweets* show hitting the small screen and my guilt feelings over Leeza's death.

Juliet shifted her feet, and Christine stared her down with one eyebrow raised. Finally, Juliet said her goodbyes and walked around the side of the church to the back door.

Hoping to get away from Christine, I muttered something about its being nice to meet her and took one step.

"Bailey, before you go—" Christine said.

I turned.

"I would like you to meet my daughter."

Behind Christine, the redhead who'd asked Aiden for a dance at the wedding approached us. Like her mother, she was dressed in an expensive day dress and heels, and here I was, in shorts and T-shirt. My dark hair was piled on the top of my head in a knot. I'd yet to take a shower. I'd thought, mistakenly, that I could run in and out of the church without being seen. That possibility had flown away the moment I found Leeza on the steps.

Christine's daughter stared up at the ambulances and sheriff department's cars around the parking lot. "What's happened?"

Christine wrapped her arm around the shoulders of her daughter. "There's been an incident," she said vaguely. "I'll tell you after church." Christine shook her head. "I knew something bad was bound to happen if Juliet and the reverend married. I didn't know that someone would die, but something was bound to happen."

"You think a woman was killed because of their wedding?" I asked incredulously.

"Well, I was at the wedding, and that woman *did* make a scene." She adjusted her handbag on her arm and turned to her daughter again. "My dear, here's someone you *need* to meet."

I was at least six inches taller than either woman and felt like an Amazon as I shifted back and forth on my large feet.

Cass's voice rang in my head. "Just always dress like you will be in a car accident. You don't want to look like a wreck when you are in the middle of one." Clearly, this wasn't a situation Cass would have found herself in, at least not with messy hair. I knew she was back at my little rental house, showered, dressed all in black, with her makeup on point. I should have sent her to check the church in the first place.

"Bailey, this is my daughter, Kayla." Christine beamed at the younger woman.

"It's nice to meet you," I said, wondering why Christine felt the need to introduce us at this moment, with so many police and crime scene techs milling about.

Kayla held out her hand. It was just as cold as her mother's. "Oh, you're the girl who fell in the cake!" She covered her mouth. "What a shame."

I ground my teeth.

"I'm so glad I finally got to meet you. I have heard so much about you. Aiden and I go way back."

That was the impression she'd tried to give me at the wedding. I knew that much.

I blinked. "You heard about me from Aiden?" I asked.

She nodded. "He said that you have been dating for a short time."

I frowned. Somehow she made "short time" sound bad. "It's nice to meet you. I always like to meet Aiden's friends," I said.

"We are friends. Very good friends," she added.

"That's nice," I said, thinking I was in the middle of a coded conversation and I didn't have the key to unlock the meaning of it. "I need to check with the deputies to see if I can leave. I have a friend of my own visiting me from New York, and she will be wondering what's become of me."

I started to leave again. This time, I didn't hesitate. I wanted to get away from Kayla and her mother. There was something about the two of them that didn't sit well with me. I spotted Aiden talking to the coroner. I knew he would be busy for a while and that wasn't a conversation I should interrupt. I found Deputy Little standing at the entrance of the parking lot, directing churchgoers to go in through the back door. I told him I was heading home so Aiden would know where to find me when he needed to record my statement. I was eager to return to my house to tell Cass what had happened. She wouldn't believe it . . . or, considering my track record, maybe she would.

I sighed. Today was supposed to be Aiden's day off, and we'd planned to spend the day taking Cass on a sightseeing tour of Holmes County before she had to fly back to the city after the Fourth of July. That wouldn't happen now. Aiden would be completely absorbed in the murder. He had to be to solve the case.

"Bailey!" a woman's voice called after me, and I turned around. I was surprised to see Christine Kepler walking briskly in my direction.

I stopped at the edge of the sidewalk.

She hurried over to me and took a couple of seconds to catch her breath.

"Are you all right?" I asked.

She waved my concern away. "I'm fine. I'm glad I caught you."

I waited.

"You won't say anything to Juliet or the reverend about what I said about their marriage back at the church? Kayla is quite upset with me about how I spoke."

I took a breath. "I won't say anything," I said. I wouldn't say anything because it would hurt Juliet, and she already had enough to worry about this morning.

"Thank you." She took a breath. "I just don't want anything I say or do to impact the relationships between our families. We have been friends for a very long time, and we are looking forward to being even closer in the near future."

I knew she wanted me to ask her what she meant by that, but I didn't give her the satisfaction. "That's good to know. I really should be getting home . . ."

"We are close and always have been since Aiden and Kayla decided to get married." Her lips curled into a cold smile.

"What did you say?" I whispered.

CHAPTER ELEVEN

"Oh," Christine said. "You didn't know that Aiden and Kayla were promised to each other?" She covered her mouth, as if she felt bad for revealing this information to me, but chances were, she enjoyed telling me this news. She knew exactly what she was doing. "It's been understood for such a long time. I would have thought Aiden or Juliet would have told you." She clicked her tongue. "It's not like Aiden at all to keep that from you. I'm sure he thought Kayla had moved on, and that's why he failed to mention it. She never did." She smiled. "Those two were meant to be together. Everyone believes it."

I stared at her as if she'd spoken to me in ancient Chinese. I couldn't make heads or tails of what she'd said. I had known Aiden for a year, and he'd never once mentioned anyone named Kayla in all that time.

"My daughter and Aiden were high school sweethearts and always had a plan to get back together after they sowed their wild oats. They went to prom together, you see, and promised each other before they left for different colleges that if neither had married by the time they were thirty-three, they would marry each other."

I blinked at her. Aiden's thirty-third birthday was in September, just two months away.

"Kayla went out of state for college, and she had some wild days." She bit her lip, as if the memory of that time was painful. "What got me through it was the knowledge Aiden would wait for her. She cleaned up her act and has a great career. Now, she's back in the village. I think she's realized what's truly important. Love and family."

I didn't disagree with her that love and family were important, but Aiden loved me. He was with me. He wasn't a single man who could keep that vow he'd made as a teenager.

Christine's eye shone. "Aiden Brody is a man of his word, so I know all will end as it should." Her face broke into a smile. "I won't keep you any longer." With that, she turned and walked back to the church, leaving me in the parking lot with my mouth hanging open.

I stumbled away from the church with my head reeling. It wasn't that I believed Aiden and Kayla would marry. I knew Aiden. I knew he would never cheat on me in any way, but at the same time, it would have been nice to know that an old girlfriend might pop up in our lives someday. He certainly knew about my tumultuous romantic history.

By the time I crossed the square and Main Street in front of Swissmen Sweets, I'd calmed down. I knew Aiden would have some kind of explanation for all this. I would just have to trust him. Unfortunately, it wasn't a conversation I could have with him any time soon. Solving the murder had to come first. I tried to put Kayla out of my mind at least for the time being. I thought about Juliet's comment that I should help Aiden solve the murder because we'd had so much success solving crimes together in the past. I had been a help those times because the murder involved the Amish. This time, it didn't look like that was the case.

"What sort of trouble have you brought to the community now?" a woman's voice asked.

I was so deep in thought, I hadn't seen Esther Esh walking up the sidewalk toward her shop. It was a warm summer day, so she wasn't wearing a bonnet. Only the required prayer cap covered the top of her head.

"Esther, I would have thought you'd be at church today." The words came out a little sharper than I intended them.

She looked down her nose at me. "We had church last Sunday, so today is for private study."

I nodded. I should have known that. Typically, the Amish meet for church every other Sunday at a church member's home. The host rotates every time. I should have known that Esther didn't have church that Sunday; she was in the same district as my grandmother. I blamed it on information overload in the last hour.

Esther looked past me at the church. "I can tell from your face you have brought more trouble to Harvest."

I swallowed. Ever since Emily had left her family's pretzel shop to marry and work for me, Esther had blamed me for everything that had gone wrong in the village. It was true that I had been involved in a lot of the trouble that had befallen Harvest, but I wasn't the source of it.

"Was it that woman?" she asked when I didn't say anything.

I sucked in a breath. "What woman?"

"The woman in the palm tree dress. She ran from the reception tent yesterday and walked up and down the street, shouting and causing a ruckus. It was a terrible scene, and on a Saturday in July, too, at the height of the tourist season. She scared away four of my customers. They wouldn't come down the street because they didn't want to get near her. Abel finally went out and asked her to leave."

This surprised me. Abel was Esther's older brother. From what I could tell, he mostly loafed about and let Esther do all the work around their family shop. He seemed to think that because he was the man of the family, he had the right to boss his sister around and do little work.

"What did he say to her?" I asked.

"He told her to leave. I already told you that."

I had a feeling that Abel's delivery had been less than polite. "And she left?"

"She stumbled down to Apple Street. Not long after that, I saw you. You were covered in frosting." She wrinkled her nose. "It was a disgraceful sight, but something I have unfortunately become accustomed to seeing since you came to live in our village."

"Jethro knocked over the wedding cake," I said, and then wondered why I felt I had to explain myself to Esther. It seemed there was nothing I could do to change her opinion of me.

She pressed her lips together.

"Was there something else, Esther?"

A strange look crossed her face, and I thought she wasn't going to answer me. After a long pause, she said, "The woman in the dress, I thought I had seen her before . . ."

"On Saturday?" I asked.

She shook her head. "*Nee*, she looked like someone I used to know a long time ago." She shook her head. "It is of no matter. I must get home. It is Sunday and the day of rest."

"Who did she look like?"

She ignored my question and went into the pretzel shop. I wasn't going to follow her inside. It would only make her dislike me more, and I wanted to make amends with Esther, if not for my sake, for Emily's.

I had intended to go straight home, but after running into Esther and having her say that she thought she recognized Leeza, I decided to step into the candy shop to see if my grandmother was there. Before I unlocked the door to the shop, I sent a text to Cass, telling her that I had to stop by the shop. She wouldn't find that alarming. The murder, she would, so I'd wait until we were face-to-face to share that news.

Nutmeg ran to the door as soon as I was inside. His thin-striped orange tail whipped back and forth in anticipation. When he saw that it was me with no Puff or Jethro in sight, his tail dipped down.

I bent over and scratched the little cat behind the ears. "Be patient. I swear, the three of you have become quite the trio. You will see your friends soon enough."

The tail came up just a hair at my promise.

"Where's *Maami*?" I asked the cat.

As if he understood my question, he spun around and galloped through the doorway that led to the staircase to the second floor. By the time I made it to the foot of the steps, he was already at the top, looking down at me.

"Show-off," I said with a smile. I didn't usually pop into the shop unannouced on Sundays, so I called out. "*Maami?*"

A faint voice called back, "I'm in the sitting room."

I walked up the stairs and down the narrow hallway that always reminded me of the servants' quarters in an old Victorian home. Doorways lined either side of the hallway. They led into the bathroom, tiny kitchen, two bedrooms, and, at the very end of the hallway, the sitting room. From the top of the stairs, I could see my grandmother on the sofa, surrounded by her knitting.

She set her knitting aside when Nutmeg and I stepped into the room. Nutmeg jumped onto the arm of the sofa and eyed *Maami's* pink ball of yarn. His whiskers pointed at the ceiling as he zeroed in on his mark. *Maami* noticed his behavior, too. She wiggled her finger at the little orange cat and said, "*Nee*, don't you dare."

Nutmeg sat back on the sofa's arm and began cleaning his face with his paw as if he had no idea was she was talking about.

"Where's Charlotte?" I asked.

Maami smiled. "The young people from the district are having a Bible study and picnic together outside of the district schoolhouse. I convinced her to go."

"She didn't want to?" I asked. This surprised me. Charlotte was a bit of a social butterfly who had come out of her cocoon ever since she'd left behind her home district and joined my grandmother's. She always seemed to be up for a new adventure.

My grandmother pressed her lips together. "She has grown more and more distant with the youth in the district. It worries me."

"You think she's not going to choose the Amish way," I said.

She pressed her lips together. "It's not my choice to make for her. My opinion is of no value. Every Amish man or woman has to make this choice for him or herself. No one else can make it."

I bit my lip to hold back some suspicions I had about Charlotte. I believed that she had a crush on a young man who decidedly was not Amish. However, until Charlotte told me that herself, I wasn't putting the idea out into the world, not even to my grandmother, who I trusted implicitly.

"You look troubled, child. What is it?" my grandmother asked.

I sat across from her on an old rocking chair that my grandfather had made as a wedding present for my grandmother. The chair was over fifty years old and worked as if it was brand new. I rubbed my eyes. "I don't even know where to begin."

She picked up her knitting, and soon her needles were clicking together again.

I smiled to myself. My grandmother was always the best person to go to when I was in need of advice, but she was Amish to her very core. That meant when she was chatting with a neighbor or listening to her granddaughter, her hands had to be busy all the time. Even if it was only her hands that moved. I told her about my discovery at the church that morning.

Her needles froze in place as I spoke. "Oh, my dear child. What a frightful thing to find!"

It was.

"I just wish I had been more insistent about finding out what was going on before she got into that car. If I had, she might still be alive."

My grandmother leaned forward and patted my knee. "You said the woman was rude to you and didn't want your help. You tried. My granddaughter, the sad truth is, you can't help those who refuse your help. You can only try your best and keep them in your prayers."

I wished I could say that her words soothed me, but it was difficult to allow myself to be comforted when Leeza was dead.

"If you won't believe me, you can do something," *Maami* said.

I looked up. "What do you mean?"

"Find out who killed this young woman." She met my gaze with clear blue eyes that were the same color as mine.

I blinked. "You *want* me to investigate?"

She nodded. "I have come to realize that you are very *gut* at finding information that will lead Aiden to the culprits he seeks. Do I want you to put yourself in danger as you do many times?" She shook her head. "*Nee.* But I think there are times when your help is necessary for those who have been hurt."

I blinked back tears. "Thank you, *Maami.*"

She straightened up and began knitting again.

"I actually wanted to ask you about Leeza. When you saw her at the wedding, did you recognize her?"

She frowned at her stitches. "Recognize her?"

I went on to tell her what Esther had said to me about Leeza looking familiar to her. "I thought if Esther had seen her before, perhaps you had, too."

She shook her head. "I don't think so."

"Oh."

She smiled. "But you are asking because you have already decided to help Aiden to find her killer."

I nodded. "I have."

She smiled. "*Gut.* I can help you."

I blinked. "Help me?"

"If you think she was in the village before or even in Holmes County, I can ask around the district to see if anyone knew her."

"Really?"

She chuckled. "I can tell you think that this is unusal for me, but remember, my child, you had to get your insatiable curiousity from somewhere." She winked.

I laughed. "Okay, that would be a great help. I really do want to find justice for Leeza. Even if I did nothing wrong, I can't run from the guilty feeling that is gnawing at my heart."

She reached across her lap and grabbed my hand. "I understand how you can feel that way, but please remember my dear, *Gott* is the only one who can help you with that feeling."

I swallowed hard.

At that moment, Nutmeg pounced at the ball of yarn next to my grandmother. He gripped it with all four sets of claws and did a somersault off the sofa onto the hardwood floor. The cat and the ball of pink yarn rolled across the floor in a puff of orange fur until they bounced off the wall.

Nutmeg lay upside down next to the wall and blinked at us. His front claws were still in the ball of yarn.

Maami laughed and shook her head. "Cats."

CHAPTER TWELVE

After leaving Swissmen Sweets, I felt much better about my intention to help Aiden solve the murder, even if Aiden didn't know about it yet . . .

Ten minutes later, I walked into my small rental house and found Cass and Puff in the kitchen. Cass was drinking coffee, and Puff munched on her morning carrot. They both appeared to be pleased with how their calm morning had gone so far.

Cass cocked her head. "You were gone a lot longer than I expected you to be. Until you texted to say you were stopping by the candy shop, I figured Juliet had roped you into something at the church, and I was just about to head that way to rescue you."

I winced.

She set her coffee mug on the table. "What is it? I know that face; something's happened. Is Juliet okay?"

"She's fine. Why would you assume she wasn't okay?"

She folded her arms and leaned back in the chair. "The wedding didn't exactly go off without a hitch."

That was one way to put it. "It's sort of related to the wedding, but Juliet is fine." I took a breath. "I found—"

"A dead body," Cass interjected. "Do *not* tell me that you found a dead body."

I grimaced.

Cass hopped out of her chair. "Holy cow, Bai, you found another dead guy? How is that even possible? This must be some kind of record. Do you go out looking for trouble?"

"No!" I cried.

Puff hopped across the kitchen, the remains of her carrot carefully held in her teeth. Maybe she was searching for peace and quiet to finish her breakfast.

Cass pointed at her. "Look at the bunny's face— she doesn't believe you either, and don't even get me started on the fact that you have a bunny to begin with. Honestly, I think you have moved to Ohio and completely lost your mind. It's all the country air."

"It's not Ohio's fault, and not all of Ohio is country."

"The parts I've seen are, and you are trying to change the subject." Cass looked at me sternly. "What are you going to do now? You have decided to find the killer, which I'm sure you have, so what are the next steps?

I shook my head. "I wish I knew." I gave her a brief narrative of the morning's events.

"You have the worst luck." She brushed her purple bangs out of her eyes. "And this is bad news for Juliet, too. Everyone will assume that Reverend Brook had something to do with Leeza's death."

I knew she was right. Poor Juliet. I felt sorry for Reverend Brook, too, but more for Juliet.

Cass went to the coffee maker, poured a second cup of coffee, added cream and sugar to it, and set it in front of the seat opposite hers. "Sit and tell me everything. I want to know more about the moonshining."

I sat and held the mug in my hand. "I don't know much about it. Leeza was involved with or dating a moonshiner; at least that's what Reverend Brook said. I don't know if she actually participated in the business."

"A still in Amish country. I can't imagine there was much business with the Amish. They don't drink, do they?"

"Some do. It depends on what the bishop allows in each district, but many Amish drink alcohol. They don't all view it as wrong, as long as the drinking stops before the person is inebriated. They also wouldn't buy moonshine from an illegal still."

"Maybe the Amish are looser than I thought," Cass said.

I shrugged. I was too deep in thought to reply.

Cass stood up and rinsed her mug in the sink. "So, I'm guessing that our sightseeing day around Holmes County is off."

My face fell. "I'm sorry, Cass."

"Don't be. It's Sunday. Isn't everything closed anyway?"

I nodded.

"It's much more important that we get to work on finding out who killed this Leeza person."

"We?" I asked.

"Well, you're going to try to find out, aren't you? You might as well have backup. I can't think of any backup better than me."

I couldn't either.

"Is there anything else I should know before we start?"

Kayla's face came to my mind, but that had nothing to do with the murder. I shook my head. "Nope, that's it."

Twenty minutes later, Cass rode shotgun in my car with Puff in her lap. "Tell me again why we're taking the rabbit."

The large, white bunny snoozed peacefully across her thighs.

"She likes to spend the day with Nutmeg at the shop," I said, as if it made perfect sense to shuttle my rabbit back and forth from my little rental house. I knew if I left her alone in the house all day, it would only lead to trouble. Puff was more like a dog than a rabbit. When she was bored, she tended to destroy my possessions. So far, she had shredded a throw pillow and two pairs of flip-flops, and she had gnawed on the leg of my dining room table. Thankfully, the table was secondhand, but the flip-flops were a great loss.

"You do realize that she is getting white fur all over my black jeans," Cass said.

"I didn't say you had to hold her. She would have sat in the back seat."

Cass shook her head. "Back there, she wouldn't be able to see what was going on."

I suppressed a smile. Cass might not admit it, but she had a soft spot when it came to the white rabbit.

Out of habit, I parked on Apple Street. I could have parked in front of the candy shop because it was Sunday, and there was no traffic.

Cass and I walked to the front of the shop, and she

carried Puff. She made no further complaint about Puff's white fur. I knew she would be covered in white fluff when she set the rabbit down. I let us in the candy shop and wasn't surprised to find neither my grandmother nor Charlotte there now. Even though they didn't have church that Sunday, it wasn't unusual for them to go call on their Amish friends on Sunday afternoon. Sunday was all they had. Both of them worked in the candy shop six days a week, and as much as I tried to convince them to take another day of the week off, their Amish work ethic wouldn't allow it. Not that I was much better; I was a workaholic, too.

As soon as Cass set Puff on the pine-plank floor, Nutmeg ran down the stairs from my grandmother's apartment to the front room of the shop and touched noses with the rabbit. I wondered if Nutmeg would tell the rabbit about his somersault off the sofa earlier. I shook my head. My life had changed a lot since I'd left New York if I now believed that a rabbit and a cat could communicate. I kept that little realization to myself.

Cass looked down at them. "Aren't cats supposed to eat rabbits?"

"Not these two, and besides, Puff is twice the size of Nutmeg."

It was true. The large, white bunny dwarfed the small cat.

Cass shook her head, and I was about to say something else about the animal odd couple when my cell phone rang. When I removed it from my pocket, a picture of Juliet holding Jethro was on my screen.

"Juliet?"

"Oh, Bailey, I'm so glad you answered. Could you come over to the church?" Juliet said breathlessly in my ear.

"Is something wrong? Did something else happen?"

"There are no more dead bodies."

That was a relief, though it was telling that she felt she had to reassure me.

"Then what's wrong?" I asked.

"There is a man here at the church, and he's looking for Leeza. He's quite upset. Can you come and calm him down?"

"What about Aiden or another deputy? If this man knows Leeza, Aiden will want to talk to him."

Cass put her ear next to mine so she could hear the conversation, too. I put the call on speaker.

"Aiden left. Deputy Little is here and talking to the man. It doesn't appear that he's having much luck. I thought you might do better."

"Why?"

"Because the man is Amish."

And there was the Amish connection I had been looking for.

Cass and I left Puff and Nutmeg in the shop. We walked briskly across the street and square. Cass, who was several inches shorter than I, had to jog to catch up.

"Are you going to call Aiden?" Cass asked.

I glanced over my shoulder. "I'm sure Little has already told him."

"Then what's the hurry?" she asked.

"I want to get to the Amish man before Aiden does. Many Amish refuse to talk to the police. This guy Juliet called me about isn't going to talk to Little. I want to question him before he clams up even more."

On the other side of the square, I crossed Church Street and stepped onto the church's front lawn. Yellow crime scene tape stretched across the front steps of the church, marring the usually tranquil country scene.

There was only one police vehicle left in the parking lot, and I assumed it was Deputy Little's. I spotted the deputy and an Amish man, who was about forty, with a neat, brown beard, standing at the edge of church property near the village playground.

Juliet stood a few feet away from them, holding Jethro's leash. The pig snuffled in the grass as if he were looking for food. He was the only one of them who didn't appear to be concerned about this turn of events.

The Amish man glared at Deputy Little. "I tell you, I need to see her. I have heard that she is at the church. Now, tell her to come out to speak to me. I'd rather not do this on my Lord's Day, but she has left me no choice."

The young deputy pulled at his collar. "I must first have your name."

"My name is no matter. I want to see the woman who calls herself Leeza. I heard she would not leave this church yesterday. When I have my say with her, I will leave." He folded her arms.

I glanced at Deputy Little. Hadn't he told this man that Leeza was dead? It was clear to me he had not. Why withhold the information? Was it to keep the man here until Aiden appeared?

Juliet walked over to me, tugging Jethro along on

his leash. The pig was reluctant to follow her lead, but that wasn't anything new. "Oh, Bailey," she said in hushed tones. "I'm so glad you came so quickly. Deputy Little is having a terrible time."

"We can see that," Cass said.

"What do you want me to do?" I asked.

Juliet wrapped the end of Jethro's leash more tightly around her palm. "I don't know, but you have to get them away from here. There are only a few minutes left in the service. Any moment, parishioners will come spilling out of the church." She grabbed my arm. "Bailey, we can't have any more scandal at the church. The reverend had a terrible time sharing his message today. There were so many people whispering about the dead woman."

"She *was* found on the church steps," Cass said. "I would be more concerned if they weren't talking about it."

Juliet brushed a tear from her cheek. "Please, Bailey. I can't take much more. I've only been married a day and it already feels like everything is ruined. The reverend said he's being punished for what he's done."

"Punished? That sounds a little extreme," Cass said.

"More than a little," I said.

To our right, Deputy Little set his hand on his duty belt. "Sir, please calm down. Just as soon as my supervisor comes back, we will talk all about it."

The Amish man glared back at the young deputy. "I don't want to speak to you or your supervisor. I want to talk to Leeza."

"Oh," Juliet cried. "You poor man, you don't know."

The Amish man turned around and glared at Juliet. "Know what?"

"Leeza," Juliet said. "She's dead."

All the blood drained from Deputy Little's face. I had a suspicion that Aiden's mother had just told this suspect exactly what the young deputy was instructed not to say.

"Dead?" The Amish man turned. "How can that be? How can she be dead and rob me so?"

"Rob you of what?" Cass asked.

The Amish man looked at Juliet, Cass, and me standing there. Jethro, too. The little pig was unconcernedly snuffling the grass at his mistress's feet.

"She has no right to be dead before giving me what she owes me. Her selfishness robs me of my due." He turned and stomped toward the village playground.

"Stop," Deputy Little said. "I have a few questions to ask you."

Instead of stopping, the man broke into a run, heading away from the church and through the playground. From there, he disappeared around the side of the bright yellow Sunbeam Café, the closest building to the church.

Deputy Little yelped. "Stop!" He took off after him.

We watched as the deputy disappeared around the side of the café, too. Just then, the church's great bell rang, and members began streaming out of the back door. Usually they would exit from the front door, but the area was blocked off due to the murder.

Juliet clapped her hands. "Thank goodness. I don't think any of the church members saw this latest disturbance."

"Don't you want to know who that guy was?" Cass asked.

Juliet shook her head. "No, I don't want to know anything else. I just want this nightmare to be over. It's killing Reverend Brook." She grabbed my arm again. "I have to go greet the church members. Bailey, you will help make this go away, won't you?"

"I don't know if I can make it go away," I said quietly.

But Juliet wasn't listening. "Good. Thank you. I knew I could count on you. Please know, dear, that you are better for Aiden than Kayla ever was or ever could be."

"Who's Kayla?" Cass asked.

I was saved from answering that question by the arrival of Aiden's departmental SUV. Deputy Little came around the Sunbeam Café and across the playground with his head down. Dirt covered him from head to toe.

CHAPTER THIRTEEN

"You were supposed to keep the suspect here," Aiden said in a strained voice.

The younger deputy's Adam's apple bobbed up and down. "I tried, Deputy Brody. He just took off. Someone let it slip that Leeza was dead. I was following your instructions and keeping it quiet."

Aiden glanced at Cass and me. "Who did that?"

"Not us," Cass said.

Aiden turned back to Deputy Little. "Who, Little?"

His Adam's apple worked overtime. "Your mother, sir."

Aiden closed his eyes for a moment and looked at the church. Juliet and Reverend Brook stood on the sidewalk near the back door, saying goodbye to the church members. Many of those members made a point of walking over to the crime scene tape in the front of the building. They pointed and whispered to one another. If the reverend wanted to downplay Leeza's death, he was going to have a hard time of it. Even from where I stood on the other side of the parking lot, I could tell her demise was the topic of conversation, not Reverend Brook's sermon, as he might have liked it to be.

"Okay," Aiden said, seeming to have gathered his thoughts. "I suppose it was a long shot that we'd be able to keep that fact from him. At least tell me his name."

"I can't." Deputy Little looked as if he might cry. "He refused to answer me. I suppose I could have arrested him to make him talk, but I didn't want to tip him off that Leeza was dead."

"All right. What did he look like?"

"He was Amish," Deputy Little said.

Aiden sighed. "Do you have any more than that?"

The other deputy cleared his throat. "Age around forty, brown hair and average build, tan from working outside. He wore a white shirt, black trousers, suspenders, black running shoes. No hat."

Aiden nodded, but he knew as well as we all did that that description could have fit half the Amish men in the village. "Did you see where he went?"

Deputy Little shook his head. "I came around the other side of the Sunbeam Café and he was gone. It was like he disappeared. I checked with the people in the café, but no one else saw him either."

Aiden sighed. "Go ask them again. Lois will let you take a look around, at least. Check and make sure he's not hiding in the kitchen."

Deputy Little nodded and took off. It was clear he was happy to have an assignment. Looking for clues was much better than standing there under Aiden's judgment.

"Cass," I whispered. "Can you go check with Juliet to see if she needs anything else?" I asked.

She eyed me. "You want to talk to Hot Cop about the case. I get it."

I rolled my eyes. "I wish you would stop calling him that."

"Why? It's an accurate description, isn't it?" She smiled.

I had to admit it was.

"Go on, have a chat with him, but remember, you have to tell me everything later." She narrowed her eyes. "And I still want to know who Kayla is."

I'd hoped she would have forgotten about that. I should have known better.

After Cass left me alone with Aiden, I cleared my throat.

He rubbed the back of his neck. "This is a disaster. I should have just let Little interview that man, or at the very least told him to get the basics, like his name or where he lived. I was so concerned that he would mess it up; I wanted to do it myself. It backfired."

"I thought you liked Deputy Little. You've always said he was a good cop."

"He is, but I can't have screwups on this case. There are complications."

"Your mother?" I asked.

"She's one of them, but not even the biggest one."

"What's the biggest one?"

Aiden studied my face but said nothing.

"Aiden, I can help you. Now that we know that Leeza's death has some tie to the Amish in Harvest, I can help."

He removed his departmental baseball cap and ran his hands through his hair. "It's dangerous. This is one of the most dangerous cases I've ever worked, and if something happened to you, I would never forgive myself. An illegal still is nothing to trifle with."

"Nothing is going to happen to me." I put what I hoped was a reassuring hand on his arm. "Just tell me why you are extra worried about this case."

"It's the way she died," he said finally.

"She was hit with something on the back of the head. Even I could tell that."

"It's how she was hit."

I raised my brow and waited.

He slapped his ball cap on his knee.

"The coroner found metal lodged in her skull. It was some sort of sheet metal. We think it flew from something with a great deal of force. Her hair was singed, which makes the coroner believe she was hit by an explosion of some sort."

I gasped. "Like a bomb?"

Aiden pressed his lips together. "I wouldn't go so far as to say that."

"How far would you go?" I shaded my eyes against the sun for a better look at his expression. It was unreadable. I knew that was on purpose.

He studied the hat in his hand, as if looking to it for guidance to tell him how to answer this question. "I would go so far to say that she was close to some sort of blast."

"Okay, say there was an explosion. Wouldn't you or someone in law enforcement know about it?" I asked.

"She didn't die here at the church. There would be more fragments of whatever it was that hit her around the body. Besides, the coroner believes that if a blast like that had happened nearby, there would be evidence around the church. Damage to the building, shrapnel, that sort of thing."

"So she died in an explosion and someone, probably the killer, dumped the body." I glanced back at Juliet and Reverend Brook. "I can't help but believe whoever did that was intentionally trying to send the reverend a message."

Aiden swallowed. "That's what I think, too. It gives me even more motivation to clear the reverend's name of the crime and send the newlyweds away on their honeymoon. I want my mother away from this situation. If Leeza did die in an explosion, it won't take long to prove the reverend wasn't involved."

"Where could it have been?" I asked.

"There was a big storm last night. It was possible that something blew up in the middle of the storm and wasn't heard. The rain would have doused any fire, too. Or it's possible it happened way out in the country or the woods, and the only ones who might have heard it were Amish and were reluctant to report anything."

"You think it's related to the still," I said.

He nodded. "It's my best guess. Making moonshine is a delicate process. There are many chances to make mistakes that would cause a blast. The 'shiners aren't working under the best conditions. A simple mistake can lead to disaster. That is one of the many reasons such stills are outlawed. They are just too dangerous."

"Will the coroner know if there is alcohol on her body or other ingredients from a still?"

"I hope so. He believes he will be able to pick something up, but it might take a few days to know for sure. We have to send over whatever he is able to collect to Ohio's BCI for tests. We don't have that kind of equipment in the county." He pressed his lips together. "And if this murder does involve an illegal still, the state, and even the FBI, might want to get involved. These are complications that the sheriff won't want. He likes to run the county with very little interference from the outside."

"But if they can help . . ."

"I know." Aiden set his ball cap back on his head. "This is another situation where the sheriff and I differ. In a big case like this, I will take all the help we can get. I always advocate for cooperation among members of law enforcement."

"If you think an Amish person might have heard or seen something, you do need my help. There will be rumors that will go around the community. I have better access to those rumors than you ever will."

"Please don't remind me of that." He rubbed the back of his neck. "I wish the department had a better relationship with the Amish, so that they trusted us. Unfortunately, as long as Sheriff Jackson is in charge, that's not to be."

I knew what he meant. Sheriff Marshall Jackson had been in his post as sheriff of the county for decades, and he detested the Amish. He did whatever he could to blame them for all the misdeeds in the county. He needed to be voted out, but, as of yet, there had been no luck in doing so. There were more Amish than English in the county, so the Amish could easily remove him in an election. However, the Amish didn't vote. They didn't participate in any form of the English government if they could avoid it. Until they decided to change that practice and start to vote, I was afraid they were stuck with the cur-

rent sheriff. In the last two elections, he'd run un-
contested.

Aiden needed me for this case, and I had to convince him of that. I needed this case, too. I was afraid
it was my only way to make amends for not stopping
Leeza from getting into that car.

"Just let me talk to some people in the district," I
said. "Maybe I can find out more about who that man
was and why he was looking for Leeza." I paused.
"Something tells me that she has a stronger tie to the
Amish than we realize."

"What do you mean?" Aiden asked.

I had an idea, but I didn't want to voice it yet. Instead, I said, "The man who was here today was Amish.
He seemed to know her, and know her well. If we can
find him, this whole mystery might unravel."

"How can we find him with no name and Little's
very broad description of him?"

"I can find him," I said with all the confidence in
the world.

"Bailey," he began. "I don't want you doing this.
You don't know what you're getting in to, and I can't
always be there to back you up."

"Cass will be with me at least for the next couple of
days. She's my backup."

"Believe me when I say that doesn't make me feel
any better." He sighed. "But I could use the help, especially if Sheriff Jackson is going to stonewall BCI
and the feds."

That's all I needed to hear.

CHAPTER FOURTEEN

After we left Aiden, Cass and I walked around the village for a little while, but there wasn't much more sleuthing we could do. It was Sunday in Amish country. The village was buttoned up. Aiden had to work, but I ended up taking Cass for a drive around the county, so she could see more of it.

"There is no shortage of cows around here," was her summary.

I wished Aiden could have come with us, but he was tied up with the murder investigation, and he had a battle in front of him if he was going to ask for help from another department. The sheriff would fight that. Sheriff Jackson didn't handle many investigations in the county any longer. He was an administrator more than a cop, but he made sure he got all the glory for anything that went right and someone else took the blame for everything that went wrong. Because he was second-in-command in the department, Aiden was the one who was typically the scapegoat. Thankfully, he was well-liked and respected in

the county, so he could absorb most of the criticism.
However, with the increasing number of murders in
Holmes County, I wondered how long the public's
goodwill could last.

The next morning, Cass and I walked from my little rental house to Swissmen Sweets. I had left my car
parked on Apple Street the night before. This time, I
was the one to carry the rabbit. I had tried to train
Puff to walk on a leash, but walking a giant, white
rabbit was like trying to drag a bag of sugar across the
ground. We never got very far.

I let us in through the front door of the shop a little after six. Cass had no trouble getting up in the
morning, for which I was grateful. In New York, she
had to be at work at four a.m. to make fresh chocolate creations and supervise her team. Getting to the
shop after six was a luxury for her.

Just like Cass, my grandmother and Charlotte
started their workday at four in the morning. I set
Puff on the floor next to Nutmeg, who seemed to
have been waiting since last night to say hello to his
friend. "You two stay here," I said, although I really
didn't have to. The bunny and the cat knew they
weren't permitted inside the kitchen.

Cass led the way into the kitchen. "What are we
making today?" she asked. She couldn't help but
take charge. As the head chocolatier of JP Chocolates in New York, she was used to bossing around a
staff of thirty to make sure that everything was done
perfectly and on time. Cass expected nothing less
than perfection from her sous chefs.

Charlotte looked up from the bowl of marshmallow fluff she was whisking with a hand mixer. "Bailey,
we have *gut* news."

"After the last two days, I will take any good news I can get."

"Yesterday, at the district summer picnic, Becca Stout came up to Cousin Clara and me." She took a breath. "She wants to sell our candies in her gift shop in Berlin!"

I blinked. This was one of the last things I'd expected. "Wow," I said. I had been talking to Becca and other shopkeepers in the popular Amish towns of Berlin, Sugarcreek, and Charm for months, trying to convince them to carry some of our candies.

Charlotte nodded. "I knew you'd be excited. She was at Juliet's wedding and loved the marshmallow frosting you made for the wedding cake." She paused. "At least how it looked, even if no one got to taste it."

I made a face at the memory. "Jethro got a taste."

"Becca ordered thirty marshmallow sticks to sell at her counter. I'm making up more marshmallows right now."

"We are making enough for fifty," my grandmother said. "I think it would be *gut* to have some for sale in our store as well."

I clapped my hands. "Excellent. Maybe that wedding cake wasn't a disaster after all, if it led to all this."

"It wasn't a disaster. Everyone loved it. It was beautiful." Charlotte cleaned off her whisk with a spoon. "Everyone said so."

"That was until Jethro took a bite out of it," I said.

My grandmother shook her head. "That pig."

"That pig" just about summed it up. Cass and I joined in the work to get the marshmallow sticks ready for Becca's shop and make the rest of the candies for that day. It was Monday, and the Fourth of July was just two days away. It promised to be a profitable week at the shop. While we worked, my mind wandered from murder to business and back again.

If the marshmallow sticks at Becca's shop did well, perhaps our candies could be sold in grocery stores someday. There were other Amish businesses that had made the leap. I bit my lip. But was that what my *maami* wanted to happen to the business? It seemed to me I was at a crossroads when it came to Swissmen Sweets. I needed to decide if I was going to keep it small or go big. In either case, I needed my grandmother's blessing. I couldn't do this without her.

The former New Yorker in me wanted to go big, so big that I would never be able to stop, but even I knew that wasn't the Amish way of thinking.

I needed to have a conversation with my grandmother about that, but it could wait until after this latest murder was solved.

"Cousin Clara told me what happened to that woman who ran into Juliet's wedding." Charlotte covered her mouth. "I can't imagine. How awful! The poor woman. How did she die?"

Maami nodded. "*Ya,* I forgot to ask you this when we chatted yesterday."

"She was hit in the back of the head with something," I said, not giving them any more of the details Aiden had shared with me. Until he could find the source of the explosion, I didn't think he wanted news of it out there, even to Charlotte and my grandmother. "Aiden doesn't think she was killed at the church. Instead, someone dumped the body there."

"Could it be to send Reverend Brook a message?" Charlotte asked.

Cass raised her brow at the young Amish woman. "You have been spending way too much time with Bailey."

I nodded my head because I was afraid that was true—both that Charlotte was spending too much time with me and that someone was trying to send the reverend a message. "She might have a connection to the Amish after all. An Amish man came to the church looking for her."

"Oh?" *Maami* poured warm chocolate into a bowl. "What was his name?"

"That's the problem. He ran away before Deputy Little could find out."

"I'm sure Deputy Little did the best he could," Charlotte said, coming to his defense.

The rest of us turned and stared at her.

She blushed and looked down at the marshmallows in front of her. "I'm only saying he does try his best."

"That he does." *Maami* frowned. "But the Amish man's arrival is very strange." She skewered three marshmallows on a wooden stick and dipped them into the chocolate. With a spoon, she scooped chocolate on all sides of the marshmallows to make sure they were perfectly covered. "I wouldn't think an Amish man would know a woman like that, if she drank too much alcohol, I mean."

"He seemed to know her, and he was angry at her. Maybe she has a tie to the Amish."

"Bailey said that some Amish do drink alcohol," Cass said.

Maami pressed her lips together. "*Ya,* that is true, if their bishop allows it. It's usually only the men, and drinking in excess is never permitted." She looked down at her marshmallows. "At least, it's not supposed to be in excess, but there are those in our community who struggle with the same demons as the *Englisch*. Alcohol can be a burden for many, and it ends with terrible results. There have been many accidents because of it."

"You mean drunk drivers hitting buggies?" Cass said.

Maami nodded. "*Ya,* but there are also those who drive buggies after drinking too much. Not that long ago, an Amish man ran his buggy into a tree. He was killed."

"That's awful," I said.

"Too much of anything *gut* or bad can lead to sin or worse." *Maami* returned to her task.

"Do you think Leeza's former Amish?" Charlotte asked me.

"I–I don't know," I said. "I just wondered what the connection was. He was mad enough about something to come to the church looking for her."

"Then you know he's not the one responsible for her death. Had he been, he wouldn't want to make a scene like that," *Maami* said logically.

Cass stared at her. "Bai, I think some of your detecting skills are rubbing off on your grandmother."

Maami chuckled.

I shook my head. "Before we do any more sleuthing, let's get these candies out. I think between the four of us, we can make short work of it."

"I know we can," *Maami* said. "Charlotte and I would be grateful for your help." She stepped back, and her foot bumped into the fire extinguisher box. Cass caught her arm before she tipped over.

"I'm so sorry, *Maami*. I should have hung that up by now. The old extinguisher was about to expire, and I bought a replacement." I grabbed a knife from one of the drawers to open the box.

"Do not worry, Granddaughter. There was no harm. As you can see, I'm perfectly fine," my grandmother said.

"Still, it needs to go up before the fire inspector pops into the shop on one of his surprise visits." I sliced through the tape on the top of the box and pulled back the flaps. "You all get to work on the candies and I will take care of this. I know what to do. I used to replace the extinguishers all the time at JP Chocolates."

Cass nodded as she walked around the island to one of the industrial refrigerators. She opened the fridge door and removed cream, butter, and two dozen eggs. "It's true. Bailey is crazy about having up-to-date fire extinguishers."

I pulled the red extinguisher out of the box. It was a lot heavier than it looked. "Fire safety is important."

"Bailey is such a rule follower," Cass said. "Must be the Amish genes."

Charlotte and my grandmother chuckled at her joke.

I glanced at the clock on the wall above the newly installed fire extinguisher. We had been working steadily for the last several hours, and it was already eight thirty. It was time to open the shop door. I excused myself and went to the front of the shop to do just that.

Puff and Nutmeg sat at my feet as I unlocked the door. They looked up at me expectantly.

"No," I said. "We have no time to go to the square today. You two will just have to stay inside the shop." I set the candy shop's chalkboard placard on the sidewalk. It wouldn't be long before the first bus tour rolled into Harvest, and I wanted Swissmen Sweets to be ready for them.

"I heard you are looking for moonshine," a gravelly, male voice said.

I knew who it was before I saw him. Abel Esh slunk over the sidewalk that separated my shop from Esh Family Pretzel.

"Do you have some drinking to do?" he asked.

"No," I said.

"Shame. I was going to tell you where to get it."

"How do you know?"

He took another step toward me, and it took all my strength not to recoil from his closeness.

"You think you know everything that happens in this county, but you don't. Aiden Brody doesn't either. There are secrets in Harvest that would make your hair stand on end."

I frowned. "If you are going to talk in riddles, I have no interest in continuing this conversation."

"You need hidden places to sell moonshine. That's all I will say about it." He stepped back and smiled.

I stared at him. "What does that even mean?"

He shrugged. "You're the one who solves all the little mysteries in this village. I would have thought it would be easy for you to figure that out."

I was about to ask him what he meant by that when

his sister Esther poked her head out the front door of the pretzel shop.

"Abel," Esther said. "I need help moving a large pot. I can't lift it." She spotted me standing a few feet away from her brother. "Bailey King, what are you doing? Pestering my brother, I see."

I frowned. Abel had spoken to me first, but I wasn't about to bother telling her that. It would make no difference to Esther.

Abel glowered at me and said in a low voice, so that his sister would not overhear, "It would serve you well, Bailey King, if you stopped meddling in our community. You only run the risk of getting hurt or hurting those you love." With that, he walked away from me toward his family's shop.

It seemed to be me that Abel Esh had just threatened me. It wouldn't be the first time, and I doubted it would be the last.

CHAPTER FIFTEEN

After the shop was open, Emily came in to work and Cass and I left to drop off the marshmallow sticks at Becca Stout's gift shop. This was what I told the ladies at Swissmen Sweets, but they all knew I wanted to find out more about Leeza as well.

A Simple Gift Shop was right on the main road in Berlin. There couldn't be a better place for me to promote my candies. This was the heart of Amish country, or at least it was the heart of the tourist's version of Amish country. There was every kind of Amish business on the street, from an elderly Amish man making kettle corn to a buggy ride stand where Amish men took tourists for five-dollar tours of the countryside.

Becca's store, A Simple Gift Shop, was in the middle of the street and in the perfect position to get the most foot traffic. At first I envied her this location. It was clear to me that she did much more business than I. When Cass and I entered the store, we could barely move through the crush of shorts-clad tourists.

I had second thoughts about expanding Swissmen Sweets. Maybe it wasn't a completely bad thing that my family candy shop was off the beaten path.

Becca stood at the cash register and waved to me when we walked in. She said something in Pennsylvania Dutch to the young woman standing next to her. The girl nodded and took Becca's post at the cash register.

Becca, who was as stout as her surname suggested, was close to my age and had beautiful brown eyes, walked over to us. She and I had met each other at shopkeeper events in the county. It seemed any time there was a gathering of that nature, Becca was there. "Bailey, it is *gut* to see you. Did you bring the candies?"

I held up the box of cellophane-wrapped marshmallow sticks. "I have thirty ready to go. We weren't sure how many you would need. We can always make more."

She took the box from me and wove around a group of customers murmuring over an Amish quilt that cost as much as the monthly payment on my car. Not that the quilt wasn't worth that price. It was handmade. Nary a stitch was out of place.

She set the candies on a cleared place by the cash register and smiled. "I wouldn't be the least bit surprised if they're gone by the end of the day." Just as she said this, a middle-aged tourist plucked three marshmallow sticks from the box and popped them in her shopping basket.

The woman smiled at us. "This will be just the thing for my grandchildren." She grabbed one more and tucked it into her basket. "And for me, too." She winked at us.

After the woman walked away, Becca turned to me. "Let's go to the back and discuss consignment for these." As she said this, I noticed for the first time her eyes were red-rimmed. Maybe it was allergies, but it looked to me as if she had been crying, and recently, too.

She walked to the back of the shop and stopped outside the wide, oak door. Removing a key from her apron pocket, she put it in the lock.

She glanced at Cass. My friend got the hint. "I think I will do a little shopping. This kind of stuff is what Jean Pierre loves most about Amish country. He will get a kick out of any little trinket I bring him. I thought I saw a bottle opener in the shape of a buggy. That will be just the thing." She strode away.

I followed Becca into a large stockroom that was full from floor to ceiling with merchandise. Most of it was handmade Amish goods, from quilts to tools to wooden toys.

There was one window in the room and a small desk under it. The desk was pristine. There was a green ledger in the middle and a calculator in the corner next to a cup of sharpened pencils. A small desk chair was tucked under the desk.

"Please," Becca said. "Have a seat on the chair."

"Where are you going to sit?" I scanned the room for another chair.

She pointed at two blue milk crates stacked on one another. She perched on top of them. "This will do well for me, and I need to fold these tea towels so we can stock them." She pointed at the bushel basket at her feet, which was full of white towels. "They were just laundered, so I need to fold them before they wrinkle. *Englischers* don't buy wrinkled tea towels."

She grabbed a stack of the towels and set them on her lap. I wasn't the least bit surprised that she wanted to do something with her hands while we chatted. It was the Amish way to continually be busy. I would have been much more surprised if she said that she just wanted to sit idly by while we spoke.

Becca folded four towels before she glanced at me again. She took a breath. "The consignment offer that you have suggested is fine. It's fair, and I believe it will be a good partnership between our businesses. I will put your brochures out, too, and those flyers that you gave me about your upcoming television show. We have been telling visitors about it, and they all seem very curious."

"I'm happy to put your brochures out at our shop as well." I sat across from her on the desk chair, wondering why she'd called me back to chat with her in the storage room if my proposal was fine. She could have told me that at the front door.

She nodded. "*Gut.* That's very kind of you." She folded four more towels in silence.

"Was there anything else you wanted to talk to me about?" I asked.

She folded two more towels, staring at her hands all the while. "I was at the wedding Saturday."

I blinked at her. I didn't remember seeing her, but there were a lot of people at the wedding. Even so, wouldn't I have seen her at the reception?

As if she could read my thoughts, she said, "Juliet is a good customer of mine. She stops in the shop every week or so. She invited me to the wedding at the last minute, but I didn't stay for the reception. I had to get back to the shop."

I nodded, knowing what it was like. When you have

a small business, as we did, keeping it open was constantly on your mind. In the case of Swissmen Sweets, we had closed the candy shop during the wedding and the reception—even on a very busy Saturday. All the ladies in the shop were close to Juliet, and it didn't seem fair to make any of them work. As the maid of honor, I couldn't.

"I'm sure Juliet appreciated your being there," I said.

She nodded. "She said she did. She is such a kind woman. Even toting that pig all about the county, there can be no fault found in Juliet."

I couldn't agree with her more. If Juliet's one fault was being the owner of a mischievous potbellied pig, I would say she was further ahead than most of us.

"Did you want to talk to me about the wedding?"

She shook her head. "*Nee.* At least, not exactly." She stopped folding towels. "I wanted to talk to you about Elizabeth."

"Who?" I searched my brain for an Elizabeth who I might know in the county. There could be several. It was a popular name among the Amish.

"I believe," Becca said with watery eyes, "she chose the *Englisch* name Leeza."

I gaped at her.

CHAPTER SIXTEEN

"Are you telling me that Leeza is Amish?"

"She was Amish. She's not any longer."

I wasn't completely surprised. It was something I'd suspected the moment I saw that Amish man arguing with Deputy Little outside the church. The truth was, nearly 70 percent of the people living in Holmes County could trace their lineage back to Amish roots. I was the perfect example. In some cases, the person's parents or grandparents had left the faith. Or, like Leeza, the person herself left the faith. It wasn't uncommon to see an *Englisch* person speaking to an Amish person in Holmes County in Pennsylvania Dutch.

"Did you suggest selling my candies here just so you could talk to me about Leeza?" I asked.

"Not completely. I do want to sell your candies in the shop. Juliet said they would do very well for us."

Juliet was always in my corner.

"But I did have to find a way to speak to you about Elizabeth without my husband hearing."

"Why's that?" I asked.

"She was not welcome in our community. Ten years ago, when we were nothing more than girls, she was shunned by our district." Tear sprang to her eyes. "It was terrible. She was my closest friend and I was told never to speak to her again. Do you have any idea how difficult that was?"

"How awful," I whispered, imagining being ordered never to speak to Cass again. I know I would disobey the rule.

"My husband believed I broke off all contact with her many years ago. I know that I should have. She was shunned by the community because of her drinking." She took a shuddering breath. "I stayed in touch with her because I knew it was my fault that she was shunned."

"Why do you say that?" I asked.

She folded another crocheted tea towel and set it on the shelf with the others. The stockroom was packed with Amish gifts. I made a mental note to keep Cass out of there or she would buy everything in the room, not that I knew what she could possibly do with so many tea towels embroidered with Amish buggies.

"When the bishop was trying to decide what to do about her behavior, he asked me if I thought she would repent and stop drinking." She folded yet another towel and then crinkled it in her hands. "I told him that I didn't think so. Drink was what kept Leeza going. She wasn't going to be able to stop even if she was ordered to by the district. Based on what I said, the bishop made the decision to cast her out of the community." A tear rolled down her cheek. "She never knew I was the reason she was cast out."

"You answered honestly," I said. "He asked for your opinion."

"Even so, I live with the guilt over what I said about her to the bishop. I should have said nothing instead of speaking the truth."

I could understand the guilt she felt. In my case, it was for the opposite reason. I should have spoken up more and told Leeza not to get in that car the evening of the wedding. I should've fought harder to reason with her.

"Tell me about Leeza. No one seems to know who she was or even her last name."

"I recognized her the moment she ran into that church. I have seen her off and on over the years since she left the faith. She had come to me asking for help." She started folding towels again. "And asking for money. I gave money to her when I could spare it. I only gave her money that I had set aside here at the store for emergencies. My husband doesn't know about that."

"I won't tell him," I promised.

She nodded. "Whenever she would come see me, it was always here at the store. My husband rarely comes here. We also have a thirty-acre farm, and he has to work the land most days. Leeza knew enough not to come to the farm. My husband would chase her away and tell the bishop that she was back."

"What was her Amish name?" I asked.

She folded more quickly now, her fingers moving in practiced motions. "Elizabeth Chupp. She was a member of my Old Order district. Even though my shop is here in Berlin, my district and farm are in Harvest."

"Whereabouts in Harvest?" I asked.

"Not far from Harvest Woods," she said.

Harvest Woods piqued my interest. It was the second time the woods had been mentioned in connection to this case. I had never been there myself, but it seemed to me that I would need to check out the woods if the name kept coming up in relation to Leeza—or should I say Elizabeth Chupp.

"Did she keep the last name Chupp?" I asked.

Becca shook her head. "I don't know. She only asked me to call her Leeza. I could never quite bring myself to do that, so I called her nothing at all."

"Had you seen her recently? I mean, other than at the wedding."

"*Nee*. In fact, that was the first time I'd seen her in a couple of months. It was a shock, because she clearly had been drinking again. She told me the last time she came to the store that she had made up her mind to stop." A shuddering breath escaped her. "She was excited and seemed more like herself than I had seen her in years. She said she'd stopped drinking. She said she'd found a good-paying job, too. She wanted to get herself sorted so she could come back to the community."

That fit with the timeline Reverend Brook had shared about Leeza coming to seek counseling from him. Because of privacy laws, I knew I would not have much luck getting any further information out of the counseling center.

The last thing Becca had said struck me. "Did she plan to return to the Amish?" I asked.

"I don't know that, but I know that she at least wanted to make amends with those she'd hurt with her behavior." She set the towel she'd just folded onto her lap.

"Her family, you mean?"

"Yes. Her parents are gone, but her older brother and his family still live in the farmhouse she grew up in. I know she wanted to make things right with RJ."

"RJ? Her brother?"

She nodded. "That's why I was so shocked to see her at the wedding, and in that condition. The last time I had seen her, she had been so determined to turn her life around." She looked up at me from her tea towels. "It broke my heart to see her like that again. It made me lose hope that she could make things right." She dropped her eyes again. "And now I know she will never be able to because she's dead. That is the worst part of all. When she was alive, there was always hope. Now, there is none." She took a breath. "My faith teaches me that I will not see her again because of the life she lived and the choices she made."

I knew this was the Amish belief. Disobedience to God resulted in punishment after death. As a non-Amish person, it was hard for me to wrap my head around that.

"But I believe that *Gott* looks at all cases individually. Elizabeth was sick. Maybe she caused her own sickness by taking that first sip of alcohol, but many cause their own problems by falling in love with the wrong person, straying from *Gott*, or even eating too many sweets. It is my belief that everyone will get a fair chance after death, no matter what wrong we have done."

"I think you're right," I whispered.

"That belief doesn't make me a very *gut* Amish woman, now does it? I disobeyed my bishop by being

Elizabeth's friend after she was shunned. I have done things that don't make me a very *gut* Amish woman."

"Maybe not," I conceded. "But it does make you a good human being. A true friend. Maybe that's enough."

She looked up at me with shining eyes. "I hope so, because I do not regret it."

I swallowed hard, and Becca dropped her eyes again to her task. In the time we had been talking, she had folded all the tea towels in the basket. There had to have been at least a hundred. She might disagree with me, but I took that as proof she was a very good Amish woman indeed.

She stood up. "I will leave this information with you. I know that you will want to talk to her brother, RJ, but I will not speak of this again."

"The police will want to talk to you." I stood, too.

"I won't. If you send the police to talk to me about it, I will deny everything, and my husband will, too. My husband hates scandal of any kind, and my entire family could be reprimanded by the bishop because I disobeyed the district rules by speaking to a shunned member."

I bit my lip. I knew that Aiden wouldn't like this impediment to his investigation, but I also knew that she told the truth. If an Amish person said she wasn't going to say something, I'd learned that it was best to take her at her word. They were experts in not saying too much. Several times, the Amish had iced me out or not backed up something they had previously said to me. "Thank you for telling me. I will do my very best to keep your name out of all this."

"*Danki*," she said quietly.

"Do you know if Leeza—Elizabeth—had contact with any other Amish?"

"*Nee*, as far as I know she only spoke to me." She patted her neatly folded stack of towels. If we sat here much longer, I suspected she would start refolding them just to have something to do with her hands.

"I ask because there was an angry Amish man who came to the church yesterday looking for Leeza. He clearly didn't know that she was dead." I described the man the best I could. I mentioned his dark hair, his beard, and his grumpy demeanor.

Becca turned pale and then shook her head. "I don't know him, but many men in the county look like that."

Beads of sweat appeared on her brow, and I surmised that Becca was lying to me. She did know who the man was. I decided to press her a little more. "You don't know who he is? Does the description fit her brother, RJ?"

She stood up. "*Nee*, RJ is much larger than you described, and he's blond." Holding a small stack of the tea towels to her chest, she walked to the door. "I need to put these out for sale. I thank you for wanting to partner with my shop."

I stood, too. I wasn't so dense that I didn't know when I was being dismissed.

CHAPTER SEVENTEEN

Outside the storage closet, Becca hurried away from me as if we had never met. I had a feeling she and I wouldn't be talking about much other than candy in the future. I found Cass at the cash register. The Amish teenager behind the counter was wide-eyed while she rang up Cass's purchases. Towels, dolls, clothes, napkins, and wooden spoons covered the countertop.

I raised my eyebrow at her. "Did you leave anything in the store for the other tourists?"

"Hey," Cass said. "I have done my Christmas and Hanukkah shopping for ten years here. Don't knock it."

I smiled.

"That will be two hundred thirteen dollars," the Amish teen said.

Cass swiped her credit card without batting an eye. I knew in NYC it was possible to spend that much on one meal out: It might seem like a large amount of money to the Amish girl, but it wasn't to Cass.

Cass signed her receipt and collected her giant bags of gifts. "I love a successful shopping spree even in the middle of Amish country." She took her bags to the door. "While you were chatting with Becca, four more people took marshmallow sticks. I think we might have to make more. Perhaps we should decorate them for the Fourth of July."

"That's a great idea," I said. "Actually, with the fireworks on the square tomorrow night, it's not a bad idea to have all sorts of patriotic candies. I will tell my grandmother and Emily and Charlotte as soon as we get back to the shop."

"I'm full of good ideas." Cass held out two of her bags to me. "These are getting heavy."

I took the bags.

"You were with Becca an awful long time," Cass said. "I can tell by the amount of stuff I bought. Was she giving you a hard time about the consignment agreement?"

"Actually, she was helpful." As we made our way out of the store and onto the street, I told Cass about Leeza's relationship to RJ of the Harvest district, and the way she'd been shunned by the Amish community but had been trying to make amends.

Cass gaped at me.

"And Leeza is not her name, or at least not the name she was born with. Her name is Elizabeth Chupp."

"Whoa," Cass said. "Did Becca know the Amish guy who came to the church yesterday?"

"I asked, and I would bet my candy shop that she knew exactly who I was talking about, but she wasn't saying."

"You were right to think Leeza was former Amish. You must have some kind of Amish radar."

"But I didn't guess that the Amish shunned her for her drinking problem," I mused.

"Alcoholism is a heartbreaking disease."

I filled in Cass on Leeza's bout of sobriety, and how Reverend Brook's counseling might have been helpful in steering her onto the road to recovery. "I wonder what happened that she started drinking again after being sober for so long."

"Unfortunately, it can be anything. Heartbreak, trouble at work, boredom. I've had friends struggle with alcoholism. It's terrible to watch and feel that you can't do much for the person until they ask for help."

I nodded. "At the very least, we have the name of her brother."

"Are we on our way to the Chupp farm?" Cass asked with a knowing smile.

"We will be just as soon as I find out where it is." I removed my phone from my pocket and made a call.

Charlotte answered the phone at the candy shop on the first ring. "Swissmen Sweets. Can I help you?"

I was relieved that Charlotte was the one who'd answered the phone. My grandmother would understand why I needed to speak with RJ Chupp, but she wouldn't like that Leeza's death now involved the Amish.

"Hey, it's me. I'm trying to find an Amish farm. Do you know where the Chupp farm would be?"

"Chupp? That's not a very common Amish name, but I do know at least three families in the county. Can you tell me anything else about them?"

"The farmer's name is RJ."

"Oh! Yes, I know where that is. They have a volleyball court on their property. That's where the young Amish go to play sometimes. It's not far from Harvest Woods."

And now the woods had come up for a third time. She paused. "I never did like going to those woods."

"Why's that?" I asked.

"They are so dense and dark. I'd much rather be out in the open, where I can see everything."

I silently agreed with her. It seemed to me that Harvest Woods was becoming a bigger and bigger part of this case. Aiden would be furious if he found out I'd gone into those woods alone. If I took Cass with me, he wouldn't think that was much better.

"Why do you ask?" Before I could answer, she went on to say, "It has something to do with the murder, doesn't it? Do you think RJ Chupp is involved?"

"I have no idea, but please don't say anything about him, or that Cass and I plan to go there."

"Oh, I won't," she said sincerely. "But I do have an idea for the perfect professional reason for you to go. It would be for the shop."

"What's that?" I asked.

"Strawberry picking. The strawberry patch is open for the season now."

"Strawberries?"

"The Chupps are fruit farmers. They have a pick-your-own strawberry patch. You can go there and pick strawberries and ask a few questions. It's the perfect cover."

"I don't know if I'm happy or sad that you know what the perfect cover is," I said into the phone as I watched the snarled traffic of cars, buses, and buggies on the main road through Berlin. Traffic was another reason I was glad Harvest wasn't nearly as popular to tourists as Berlin. "But this is an excellent plan, and chocolate-covered strawberries can be one of the sweet treats that we sell at the Fourth of July celebration on the square."

"Marshmallow sticks, too," Charlotte said.

"Can you tell me how to get to the strawberry patch?" I asked, knowing that my GPS wasn't always reliable in finding Amish farms off the beaten path.

Charlotte rattled off the directions so fast, there was no way I could have caught them, but she said the Chupps' farm was the second driveway south of Harvest Woods. I knew where the woods were, so I didn't think it would be impossible to find.

"Don't let on to Deputy Brody that I was the one who told you where it is," Charlotte said.

"I won't," I promised.

Cass raised her eyebrows at me.

I ended the call and looked at her. "Are you ready to pick some strawberries?"

"That sounds awful on a July afternoon in Ohio," Cass said. "Don't they have machines to do that?"

"Not in Amish country."

She sighed. "Why does everything have to be harder in Amish country?"

It was a fair question.

On the way to the Chupp farm, I filled Cass in about my conversation with Charlotte.

"That was a good idea Charlotte had about the strawberry picking," Cass said. "I see potential in that girl."

I arched my brow. "Potential for what?"

"For anything other than being an Amish wife and mother." She held up her hand before I could protest.

"There's nothing wrong with being an Amish wife and mother. Emily is on that path and clearly happy with it, but Charlotte . . . I'm just not buying that that's the life she wants to lead. She might do it, and she might be miserable because of it."

I nodded. I had the same worries about Charlotte, but I had learned months ago, when she first came to live with *Maami* above the candy shop, that Charlotte was the only one who could make the decision about what was right for her.

I turned onto the county road that held the entrance to Harvest Woods.

"Geez," Cass said. "That looks like a forest right out of a horror movie. Have you ever been inside it?"

I shook my head. "Never."

"Let's keep up that streak."

I didn't reply. I passed the first driveway, which led to an English farm. I knew it was English because of the electrical wires that traveled from the telephone pole on the road to the house.

"We are in real Amish country now," Cass said. "We haven't seen another car for miles."

And it was true. All we had passed for the last five miles was an Amish pony cart. There was a young couple in the cart, out for a Sunday ride. The young woman, who didn't look more than sixteen, sat so far away from the young man, she was at risk of falling out if they hit a rut in the road.

The next driveway didn't have an electrical pole or wires. I was at the Chupp farm.

The large strawberry patch was to the left of a two-story, pale yellow farmhouse with black shutters and a black front door. Near the field of strawberries, pickup trucks and minivans were parked along the side of the road. I parked my car behind a blue mini-van with a dent in the fender. Through the windshield, I watched as *Englischers* filled their berry baskets to the breaking point.

There was a hand-painted wooden board on the side of the road with a giant strawberry painted on the side of it.

"This must be the place," I said.

Cass looked at me out of the corner of her eye. "What was your first clue?"

I climbed out. In front of us, the strawberry patch went on for miles. Even from the road, I could see the bright red berries peeking through the leaves and vines, waiting to be picked.

Cass got out of the car. She wore her high-heeled boots, black jeans, and a black, silk tank top. The tank top was her only concession to the Midwestern July heat. "Don't think I'm in the right outfit for this."

"Probably not. In fact, you're not in the right out-fit for any activity in Holmes County."

She made a face. "Had I known that we would be farming today, I would have borrowed some of your clothes." She waved her hand. "You have the whole country vibe going over there."

I wasn't offended by her comment. I wore jeans, sneakers, and a T-shirt. The jeans were designer, left-over from my life in New York, but other than that, I fully embraced the casual country style.

Cass stood beside me and clapped her hands. "We're going to have a real country experience right here." Despite her poor outfit choice, she seemed ex-cited by the idea of picking strawberries. When the sun began to beat on her back, I wondered if that enthusiasm would continue.

"Have you ever picked your own fruit?" I asked her.

She put her hands on her hips. "I'm from New York City, born and raised. When would I have had a chance to do that? Not all of us spent our childhood visiting the Amish."

"I haven't picked fruit in Ohio before, but back in Connecticut, I grew up apple picking. It was a big deal in the fall in New England. And I always went to the fields to pick my own pumpkin to carve."

"Seems to me you grew up more like your Amish roots than you first thought."

"Maybe," I mused.

A wooden box that looked like a mailbox turned on its side stood atop a metal post at the edge of the road. On the post below the box was a small wooden sign that said, "$10 an eight-quart basket." Beneath the wooden box were three stacks of berry baskets ready for use.

"Ten dollars for all those berries," Cass said. "That's a steal. I pay triple that back in the city when a bride asks for chocolate-covered strawberries."

I smiled. "Well, you didn't pick them, and then there's the shipping cost."

We weren't the only *Englischers* who'd had the idea that it would be a nice afternoon for strawberry picking. Out in the field, there were three English families with baskets collecting all the fruit they could carry. Beyond the field, the large, yellow farmhouse loomed.

"That must be the Chupp home," I said.

Cass nodded. "The best clue to that is the car out front."

"What car?" But then I saw it. Aiden's department SUV was outside the farmhouse. Aiden already knew about Leeza's connection to the Chupp family? And here I thought I'd made a huge break in the case.

Cass grabbed two baskets and handed them to me, then grabbed two more for herself. "Hot Cop is here," Cass said.

"That complicates things. We can't talk to RJ now," I said.

"Then we might as well collect berries," Cass said. "We will wait until he leaves to talk to RJ."

I put eighty dollars in the wooden box to pay for our berries. That would be enough for us to fill eight eight-quart baskets. We'd have strawberries coming out of our ears by the end of the day. The berries might be very cheap by NYC standards, but to have enough for the holiday party and tourist season, we'd need hundreds on hand for chocolate-dipping.

We walked out onto the field.

"Pick good ones," Cass advised.

We set to work. I don't know how long I picked strawberries under the hot sun. But after a while, the repetitive activity was therapeutic. It gave me time to think. While I put strawberry after strawberry into my basket, I tried to remember the man Leeza had left with after the wedding. He wasn't Amish. I knew that. At least, he wasn't dressed Amish. He had been wearing a T-shirt and basketball shorts. I didn't think I had ever seen an Amish adult in shorts.

In no time, I'd filled both of my baskets with so many strawberries; they were tumbling over the sides. I put one of the bright red berries in my mouth. It tasted like summer. I straightened up from my stooped posture, bending backward. Berry picking was hard work.

An Amish girl no more than eight played on the grassy field next to the berry patch. It was the first I had noticed her, so I had no idea how long she had been there. She had a kite and giggled as it swooped through the air. Her prayer cap strings and the skirt of her lavender dress flew behind her as she ran. I watched the little girl for a while. Was she related to Leeza? Did she know that Leeza was dead? Did she even know who Leeza was?

I glanced at the house. Aiden's departmental SUV was still parked in front of the porch. I itched to speak with RJ, but it seemed less and less likely I would get a chance before I had to return to Swissmen Sweets.

I was contemplating getting a new basket to pick even more berries when there was a bloodcurdling scream from the next row of berries. The scream chilled me to the core.

Chapter Eighteen

"Ow!" Cass cried as she held her right hand in the air. "I got stung by a bee! I might die!"

I dropped my basket of berries. "Are you allergic?" I ran over to her.

She looked up from her swollen wrist. "No, I don't think so. I've never been stung before, so I don't know. It hurts like heck."

I studied her. "Your wrist is swollen, but I think you'd be having a more serious reaction if you were deathly allergic."

"Like what?" she whimpered.

"You'd stop breathing, for one." I studied her wrist and saw the stinger still in her skin. I grimaced. "I'm going to have to pull the stinger out."

"What? It's still there?"

"Just hold still," I said. As delicately as I could, I grabbed the stinger and pulled straight out. I tossed it into the strawberries. Cass let out a string of cursing that would impress any New York City subway employee.

"You're okay," I assured her.

She held her wrist. "How long before we know if I'm going to stop breathing?"

"I think you would have had trouble by now. Let's get some ice on it to help with the swelling. You'll be okay, but if you start acting strangely, we'll go straight to urgent care."

"Urgent care? What about the hospital?"

"The closest hospital—real hospital—is thirty minutes away."

"I hope I don't lose a limb out here," Cass mumbled. "They won't amputate my hand, will they?"

I gave her a look. "Even Ohio has advanced beyond Civil War–era medicine."

"That's a relief," she said. "I don't want to die in Amish country. It's not how I imagined my end."

"I don't think you are having a serious reaction. You're still able to complain."

"Oh," Cass said with a smile. "That has nothing to do with it. I will be able to complain on my death bed."

That's when I realized all the other English people who had been picking berries had left. It was just Cass and me, and the Amish girl with the kite. Her kite was now on the ground as she stared at us. Her brown eyes were huge, and I couldn't help but wonder if she had heard some of Cass's more colorful speech. I hoped not.

I smiled at the girl. "My friend got stung by a bee. Do you have any ice we can put on her wrist?"

"*Ya*," the Amish girl said. "My home is just over there." She pointed at the yellow farmhouse. "We have ice. I will tell my *daed*, and he can help you."

Cass was jumping in place, waving her wrist around.

"Is your friend having some kind of fit?" the girl asked nervously.

I smiled again. "She's from the city. This is the first time she's been stung by a bee."

"Oh." The girl's pink mouth made a little "o" shape. "I have been stung many times. There are a lot of bees around our home because of the berries. They are *gut* for the farm. *Daed* says you can never have too many bees."

"I know they are," I said.

"They are good until they sting you," Cass complained.

"I will take you to my *daed*," the girl said and glanced at the house. "He told me to take my kite and go play by the strawberries." She lowered her voice. "There is a policeman at the house."

"How long has the policeman been there?" I asked.

The girl shrugged. "A long time. It seems to me that I have been playing with my kite for a very long time."

"What's your name?" Cass asked.

"I'm Essie Chupp. I am so sorry that you were stung. You are not going to sue us, are you? My friend at school, Belinda, says that's what the *Englisch* spend most of their time doing, suing each other and the Amish when they can."

"We aren't going to sue you," I said. "We picked berries at our own risk."

She nodded solemnly. "Come to the house, and I will fetch your ice."

I glanced at Cass, and she shrugged. Perhaps she was thinking what I was thinking. Aiden had been in the Chupp home for a very long time. We couldn't wait all day, and Cass's beesting was a bit of cover to explain why we were there. Who was I kidding, though? Aiden would see right through our story.

"Lead the way," Cass said to the girl. "I really don't want to have to go to a clinic in the middle of nowhere."

I rolled my eyes. "The clinic is just fine for minor illnesses or scrapes."

Cass snorted, as if she didn't quite believe me.

Essie picked up her kite and ran ahead of us. Cass and I moved at a much slower pace. I eyed her. "You got stung in the wrist, not in the leg. Why are you walking so slowly?"

"I'm giving the girl some time to find her dad." There was a slight twinkle in her eyes.

"Please don't tell me that you got stung so we could talk to RJ."

She shook her head. "No way. This hurts worse than a tetanus shot, and now it itches. If it itches, does that mean I'm going to stop breathing?"

"I don't think so. I was told that means it's healing. At least, that's true with other wounds. I don't know about beestings."

She snorted. "You'd make a terrible nurse."

"Then it's a good thing I'm a chocolatier, right?"

She sighed. "I'll never pick strawberries again," she said forlornly. "But I guess that was a safe bet anyway. It's hard work, and I think the back of my neck is sunburned. I'm going to go back to New York looking like I just trekked through the Amazon." She turned her head so I could see the back of her neck. "Do I have a burn?"

I stepped behind her to look at her neck. "Maybe a little."

She touched the back of her neck and winced. "I'm not built for country life. Give me a high-rise and recycled air any day of the week over this."

I thought it was best not to comment on that. We were just a few yards away from the house now. The girl had run through the open front door. A moment later, a tall Amish man with a long, blond beard, wearing a denim work shirt and trousers, came out of the house. Aiden was just a few steps behind him. Aiden's eyes widened when he saw Cass and me standing in the middle of the Chupps' yard.

Above their heads, another much smaller girl stood in an upstairs window and watched us.

Essie popped out of the house behind Aiden and ran to the blond man.

"Essie, what is going on here?" the Amish man said, and then added something in their language.

Essie replied in Pennsylvania Dutch and pointed at Cass as she spoke.

The Amish man stared at Cass, as if sizing her up, and then settled his dark glare onto me.

"I feel like I'm on trial," Cass whispered. "You know, the Salem witch variety."

I felt the exact same way.

The Amish man, who I assumed was RJ Chupp, spoke again to his daughter. I didn't catch all the words, but one of them was "go." It was clear he was telling her to go inside the house. She disappeared from the doorway, and the little girl's face in the upstairs window also disappeared.

RJ folded his arms. "Which one of you got stung?"

Cass waved with her good hand. "It was me. I was just squatting in the strawberry patch, picking away, and the bee bit me. I didn't do a thing to him."

RJ walked over to her. "Bees don't bite. They sting."

"It hurts, whatever it was," Cass said.

"May I see your wrist?" RJ asked.

Cass hesitated at first and then held up her wrist for him to see. I wasn't surprised when he didn't touch her as he examined the sting. Amish men rarely touched women they weren't related to. At times, they were even uncomfortable shaking hands with a woman they didn't know.

"It is just a minor sting. The swelling is not much. The ice should help. I am very sorry that this happened to you on our property. We are happy to give you your money back for the strawberries you've picked today."

Cass lowered her hand.

"That's not necessary," I said. "But thank you for the offer."

The front door opened again, and Essie ran out a second time with a hand wrapped around a plastic bag of ice. She handed the bag to her father and ran back inside the house without a word.

RJ handed the bag of ice to Cass. "Hold this ice on it. It will fix you right up."

"Hey," Cass said. "If you're Amish, how do you have ice?"

"We have a propane refrigerator and freezer." RJ scowled.

"Oh," Cass replied.

"I didn't know the two of you were in the market for strawberries." Aiden spoke for the first time. His arms were folded across his chest and his gaze was squarely on me.

RJ looked at the deputy. "Do you know these ladies?"

"I do," Aiden said, and didn't elaborate on how well he knew us, especially how well he knew me.

Cass looked up from the ice bag, which she was holding against her wrist as if her life depended on it. I think she was still a little worried that she might be allergic to bees. I shouldn't have scared her by mentioning the no-breathing thing.

"What brings you two here?" Aiden asked.

I raised my eyebrows at Cass. This was where she was supposed to jump in and give me an out.

"I asked Bailey to come out with me," Cass said, and winced at she touched the ice to her sting again. "It was completely my idea. Charlotte mentioned this strawberry patch, and I thought chocolate-dipped strawberries would be just the thing to sell at the Fourth of July celebration on the square. I mean, what's more summertime than that? Besides, I just wanted a real country farm experience before I left."

Aiden eyed her. "And how long are you here?"

"I won't be going back until Wednesday. I'm staying through the Fourth of July, tomorrow. I took a few vacation days. Jean Pierre was itching to be in charge of the shop again. He's the worst retired person ever."

Aiden pressed his lips together. I didn't think it was because he disliked Cass. The two of them got along quite well, but I knew he was thinking I always got into much more trouble when she was around. I wasn't sure that was fair or true. I seemed to find plenty of trouble on my own and always had.

Cass turned to RJ. "Thank you for the ice, Mr . . ."

"Chupp," he said. "I'm RJ Chupp, and this is my farm."

"Thank you, Mr. Chupp. My wrist is feeling much

better already." Cass showed him, as if he needed proof.

He tugged on his beard. "I'm glad to hear it. I appreciate that you came out to pick. I hope there are no hard feelings about the beesting. You do pick at your own risk. A beesting is better than a snakebite. That's what I always say, but I can give you your money back."

"No need," I said.

"Wait, what?" Cass asked. "I could have gotten bitten by a snake? There are snakes in Ohio?"

"There are snakes all over the country," RJ said.

"Where's St. Patrick when you need him?" Cass muttered. "I never have to deal with bees or snakes back home. There are advantages to living in the city. We killed all those creatures with pavement."

"I suggest that you take your strawberries and go back to Swissmen Sweets," Aiden said. "I think staying indoors will be best for you." He eyed me. "For both of you."

"We are happy to," I said evenly. "RJ, the strawberries look lovely. I know they will do very well in my family's candy shop."

Cass's eyes went wide. I knew I'd surprised her by agreeing to leave. However, I sensed that I wouldn't have any luck trying to have a frank conversation with RJ as long as Aiden was there. I would have to come back another time, or find another way to question RJ.

That was much more easily said than done.

CHAPTER NINETEEN

"RJ, thank you so much for your time." Aiden shook his hand. "I know this is hard on your family."

"It's not as hard as you think."

Aiden's brow went up.

RJ made fists at his sides. "We lost my sister a long time ago. We already cried any tears we could spare over her. She's facing her judgment now. My only regret is that she didn't return to the straight path before she met her end. I suppose I always expected this day to come. Expected the police to knock on my door and tell me that she'd come to a sad end. I steeled myself for this moment and am relieved that I have been able to rise to the challenge of it. In our family, I was the one who faced the life *Gott* planned for me. Elizabeth did not."

"Harsh," Cass whispered in my ear.

RJ's reaction was so much different from Becca's. Becca had hoped that God would take mercy on her childhood friend. RJ expected judgment for his sister. I could only wish that of the two, Becca's hopes stood closer to the truth.

On the bright side, I wouldn't have to bring Becca into the conversation at all; Aiden already knew that Leeza was RJ's sister. I was happy to be able to keep my promise to Becca.

RJ nodded and marched back to the house. A petite Amish woman met him at the door. She wore a navy dress and appeared to have been crying. Her thick glasses magnified the tears in her eyes. My heart constricted when I saw her. It seemed to me that some of the Chupp family still had tears to shed over Leeza.

RJ ushered the woman into the house. They both disappeared as he closed the door. Above, two faces reappeared in the upper window. I recognized Essie and the smaller girl.

Aiden turned to Cass and me. "Where are you parked?"

"We're up by the strawberry patch because we really did pick strawberries. It wasn't like I got stung by a bee on purpose." Cass smiled sweetly up at him.

I rolled my eyes, and Aiden studied her as if he wasn't quite sure if that was the truth.

"How did you know the Chupps were related to Leeza?" Aiden asked as we walked back across the field to the strawberry patch.

"I heard it through the Amish grapevine," I said, thinking of Becca Stout.

"Was it Emily?" he pressed.

I shook my head.

"Was it Charlotte?"

I shook my head again.

"Are you going to tell me?" Aiden stopped in the middle of the Chupps' yard.

I shook my head for a third time. Aiden groaned and started walking again.

"Fine," he said. "For now. I will find out eventually."

"How did you find out her relationship to the Amish?" I asked.

He frowned. "She went by the name Leeza Chupp. We followed the trail from there. It's much harder to hide your past from the authorities than people think."

I guessed that was true.

Aiden hooked his thumb through his utility belt the way I had seen him do it a thousand times before when he was frustrated, usually frustrated with me, if I was being completely honest. "Is there anything else you learned that I should know, Bailey?"

I closed the back door. "I assume RJ told you that Leeza—or Elizabeth Chupp—was shunned by her community for her drinking."

He nodded. "Her brother said she was removed from the community eight years ago. According to him, her drinking was out of control, and the district bishop believed that she was leading other young people in the church astray."

I frowned. "How old was she?" I paused. "It was difficult to tell because she had led such a hard life. It clearly had taken a toll on her appearance."

"Twenty-seven," Aiden said.

"She was only nineteen when she was kicked out of her church and home," Cass said. "That seems cruel."

Aiden nodded. "It is the age when young Amish people are supposed to choose their own path, Amish or English."

"It sounds to me," I said, looking down at my shoes in the bright green grass, "as if alcohol chose her path, not Leeza herself."

"She chose alcohol," Aiden said, and there was a twitch in his jaw.

I bit my lip. I knew about his own father's history with alcohol; drinking was something Aiden did not tolerate well. "Recently, she was sober," I said. "She didn't drink for six months. She was trying to get her life back."

"How do you know that?" Aiden's voice was sharp.

"I can't tell you, but until very recently, she was sober. That's why she was getting counseling from Reverend Brook. She knew she needed help this time to stop. She knew enough to get help outside herself. It's not the Amish way to ask for help from anyone other than their own church elders or family."

"She didn't have any church elders," Cass said. "Not after she was kicked out of the community."

I nodded. "That's a good point."

"Do you have any theories about what might have happened to cause her to start drinking again?" Aiden asked.

"Not a single one," I said, feeling as if I'd failed some sort of pop quiz. "But I think if we can figure that out, we just might find the person who killed her."

"What if it was nothing?" Cass said. "What if it was boredom?"

I glanced at her. "That wasn't the impression I got. She wanted to put her life back together so she could see her family again."

"She wanted to rejoin the Amish?" Aiden asked.

I touched my cheek. It was hot. I guessed I had gotten a bit of sunburn, too, while picking strawberries. "I don't know that."

Aiden seemed to consider this.

"Any luck tracking down the car or driver who gave her a ride Saturday?"

"No, the car description you gave us was very vague, and without a license plate number, it will prove difficult. We don't have traffic cameras or technology for monitoring cars as they enter and leave the village." He shrugged. "We depend on those plate numbers to make a positive ID."

I bit the inside of my lip.

Aiden squinted at me. "Don't feel bad about missing the number. Even trained officers can miss them, and most of the time they aren't covered in marshmallow and cake." There was humor in his voice.

I wrinkled my nose. "At least now we know why that Amish man came to the church. He must have known Leeza when she was Amish, but it definitely wasn't RJ Chupp. The Amish man outside the church was a bit younger and had dark hair."

Aiden took his department-issued ball cap out of the back pocket of his uniform and put it on his head. "It stands to reason, but we can't be clear about his motivation until we find him. I hope Reverend Brook can shine some light on who he is."

"Did you ask him?" I asked.

Aiden nodded. "And he avoided the question. I'll press him a bit more about it when my mother's not around." He nodded to the car. "You should get those strawberries home. It can't be good for them to be in the heat after they're picked."

This was true, but I was dying to ask Aiden about his conversation with RJ. I had a feeling I knew how he would answer, but I had to try. "So, RJ has had no contact with his sister since she left the community?"

Aiden rocked back on his heels. He didn't say anything for a moment, and I knew he was weighing just how much information he could share. I knew most of it would be off-limits. As an officer of the law, he took his job very seriously. He would not do anything to jeopardize the integrity of the case.

"I'm not asking about forensics, Aiden. Only if an Amish man had seen his sister in a while."

"No," he said after a few seconds. "He said no one in his home has seen, spoken to, or even spoken *of* her since she left."

"That's worse than if she were dead," Cass exclaimed.

"And you believe him?" I asked.

"Unfortunately, I have no choice but to believe him. He's in a very conservative Amish district, so his word is law in that house. I don't think his wife or any of the children would disobey him."

I frowned as I remembered the woman in the doorway with tears in her eyes. I could only assume she was RJ's wife. I guessed that she had thought about Leeza since she'd left the district. I realized I had missed an opportunity to talk to Essie about her shunned aunt. Leeza had been out of the community for so long, it was possible that Essie hadn't been born when her aunt was pushed out of the district. Also, it probably wasn't ethical to pester a child about that sort of thing. Still, a small part of me couldn't help but wish I had asked.

Aiden looked from me to Cass and back again. "I want the two of you to be careful. The coroner has confirmed that Leeza's injuries were the result of an explosion. The sheriff's department is actively trying to find out where that explosion occurred. This is not your run-of-the-mill case. Someone willing to blow something up to kill someone has no concern for who else might get hurt or killed in the process. It is not a means of murder that can be well contained."

"Do you think the explosion was meant to kill her?" I asked. "Could it be she was at the wrong place at the wrong time?"

"Maybe. But then why did someone go to the trouble of dumping her on the church steps?" Aiden countered.

I didn't have an answer for that.

Not long after saying goodbye to Aiden, Cass and I drove back to Swissmen Sweets in silence. In the quiet, I wondered what choices Leeza had made in her life to come to such a sad and terrible end.

I parked on Apple Street and paused to look around. Sometimes I would leave it on the street for days because I preferred to walk back and forth to work. In New York, I would've amassed quite the collection of parking tickets. Then again, in Manhattan, I hadn't even kept a car. Here in Ohio, no one seemed to notice or mind.

Cass stared at me. "What are you looking at?"

I glanced at her. "This was the spot where the man picked up Leeza." I took a breath. "I'm still kicking myself that I didn't stop her from leaving with him or get the plate number."

She shaded her eyes. "How could you have known what was going to happen?"

"I didn't, but I did have a bad feeling when the car drove away. That's why I reported it to Aiden."

"Look at this," Cass said. "I found something." Cass bent down and picked up something that was stuck to the curb

She held up what looked like a piece of purple cardboard. On taking a closer look, I saw that it was a matchbook. She dropped it into my hand. "Stardust Winery" was emblazoned on the cover in silver cursive.

I opened the matchbook and found the matches inside water-logged. "It could have been there from Saturday or it could have been there for a month. In any case, we haven't had any rain since that storm on Saturday night. This has to have been here at least that long."

"Good detective work, Sherlock," Cass said.

I rolled my eyes. "I don't know if this means anything at all. The matchbook could have been dropped by anyone. The wineries in Holmes County are a popular stop for tourists. It could have fallen out of a tourist's pocket."

"Or it could have fallen out of Leeza's pocket," Cass countered.

She had a point.

"Did Aiden or his deputies come to look at this street as a possible crime scene?"

"Not that I know of, but I can ask him," I said.

Cass held up her hand. "Don't ask him just yet. We

have to look into this lead. You don't want Aiden running all over the county on a wild-goose chase. We can save him some time by checking this one out." She took the matchbook from my hand. "Because, Bai, my friend, this is what they call a clue."

It was indeed.

CHAPTER TWENTY

B efore Cass and I could follow the maybe clue she'd found, we went to Swissmen Sweets to check on my grandmother and Charlotte. When I walked into the shop, I almost turned around and walked back out again. I would have made it without being seen if Cass hadn't been right behind me, causing me to run into her.

"Ouch, where are you going?" she asked.

I didn't have time to answer her because the person I wanted to avoid clapped her hands. "Bailey, thank heavens you are here," Margot Rawlings said. Margot was a box-shaped woman in her sixties with short, curly hair she constantly fluffed when she was agitated, and Margot was agitated a lot.

"Margot, I didn't expect to see you here." My voice went up an octave as I spoke.

Charlotte, who stood behind Margot on the other side of the counter, covered her mouth to stifle a laugh. She knew how I felt about Margot. It wasn't that I didn't like the woman. She had a lot of good ideas, and under her leadership, tourism in Harvest had grown tenfold. However, she'd been able to do that because she had a special gift for convincing people to do things they didn't want to do. I was a prime victim. It was almost impossible to say no to her, I had a feeling that that would be the case again today.

"As you know, the Fourth of July celebration is tomorrow on the square. I want all participants to be on point."

God forbid someone not be on point.

Cass held up the baskets of berries we'd bought. "Chocolate-covered patriotic strawberries are added to the menu."

"How lovely!" Margot said. "I knew Swissmen Sweets would come through."

"I had another idea because it's so hot out," Charlotte said. "What about chocolate-covered frozen bananas, too?"

"That's a great idea," I said. "Good thinking, Charlotte."

Margot beamed. "I'm glad to see that you have everything well in hand. I'm checking with each of the businesses that will be on the square for the celebration to make sure we are good to go. I leave nothing to chance."

I knew that was true.

"I'm especially happy that you don't seem to be distracted by the murder, Bailey." Margot studied me as if assessing the truth of her own statement. "I know it can be very tempting to get involved, but the Fourth of July celebration must come first."

I made a face, but Margot went on without noticing. "I was very sad to hear about Leeza's death and to think that Reverend Brook was associated with that poor woman as well. It must have come as quite a shock to Juliet."

"Juliet doesn't believe her husband is involved in Leeza's death," I said.

"Nor should she." Margot nodded. "They've only been married for forty-eight hours, give or take. It's too soon for her to lose faith in her husband."

"Is she implying it will be okay for Juliet to lose faith in him later?" Cass asked out of the side of her mouth.

"I knew of Leeza," Margot went on, clearly not having heard Cass's comment. "I didn't know her name, but I had seen her before around the village. I had my eye on her."

"You kept an eye on her?" Cass asked.

Margot nodded. "And I wasn't the least bit surprised that Leeza ended up the way she did. Every time I saw her she was drunk and could barely walk."

I frowned. Everyone seemed to think Leeza was drunk all the time, but that didn't fit with what Becca had told me about her friend.

Margot clapped her hands. "In any case, I'm glad to see you concentrate on the shop instead of this unseemly murder. Also, I have a surprise for you at the celebration."

I didn't like the sound of that. "What kind of surprise?"

Margot smiled. "I can't tell you that. It will lose the 'wow' factor if I do."

I was more afraid that Margot's surprise would have a "yikes" factor. "I don't mind knowing about the surprise early," I said. "Maybe that would be better in case I have a big reaction. I don't want to overreact in front of the tourists."

"A big reaction in front of the tourists would be perfect. Now." She adjusted her shoulder bag on her arm. "The festivities tomorrow start at five sharp. I would like to have all the booths in place by four. I hate it when vendors set up after the event has already begun. It looks so amateurish." She wrinkled her nose. "This will be our first fireworks display in the village and it needs to go off with a bang. Excuse the pun, but it's true. This year, the display will be funded by donations from members of the village. However, I can't always count on that. We must make sure that Independence Day in Harvest is the premiere Fourth of July celebration in the county, so the village council will budget for it in the future should donations dry up."

I had to hand it to Margot; she always thought ahead and planned for the worst.

"The celebration will be a hit," I said.

"I know it will be," Margot said. "I won't allow anything less." With that, she patted her curls and bustled out the door.

After Margot left, Cass and I carried the strawberries into the kitchen. "You know, Margot scares me just a little," Cass said.

"Me too," I admitted.

"Everyone is scared of her," Charlotte said as she held the swinging kitchen door open for us. "Except maybe Ruth Yoder. The bishop's wife fears nothing."

That was accurate.

Maami was in the kitchen making more marshmallow sticks. "What are all these?" she asked, pointing to the strawberries.

Cass told her our idea for the Fourth of July celebration.

"That sounds lovely, and it will be a quick and easy treat, too. We can use the same chocolate we have already melted for the marshmallow sticks. Charlotte, would you whip up some white chocolate for decoration? We can dye some of it red and some of it blue for a patriotic theme. I think the visitors will love it."

As much as I wanted to get to the winery and follow up on the matchbook Cass had found, I didn't feel I could leave my grandmother and Charlotte alone with this oversize job. I glanced at Cass and she gave a slight nodded. We'd help out at the shop and then get back to sleuthing.

Maami spooned chocolate over another marshmallow stick. "Did you ever find out who that man was at the church?"

I shook my head as I stirred white chocolate over a double boiler. "No, no one seems to know who he was. However, we did find out who Leeza was." I went on to tell them about the Chupp family.

"Oh my," *Maami* said. "I've bought berries from them in the past. They aren't members of our district. I didn't even know RJ had a sister."

"I think that's how he likes it," I said.

An hour later, the strawberries were cooling in the fridge next to dozens of marshmallow sticks. Be-

tween the two, we would have plenty of treats to satisfy the residents and visitors coming to Harvest for
fireworks the next evening.

Cass raised her eyebrows at me.

I nodded. It was time to follow up on her clue.

CHAPTER TWENTY-ONE

When some visitors find out that there are wineries in Holmes County, they are surprised. Alcohol of any kind doesn't fit with their understanding of Amish beliefs. Some think because the Amish are ruled by their faith, they must also abstain from liquor, but that just isn't the case. Many Amish make beer at home and other forms of spirits.

The wineries in the county, however, are run by English families. They chose Holmes County because the soil is rich and there were already tourists in the county visiting the Amish businesses. It made sense to open a winery in a location with guaranteed traffic.

As I drove to Stardust Winery, which was on Route 62, Cass flipped the small purple matchbook in her hand. "When we get there, let me do the talking."

I took my eyes off the road for a second to look at her. "Excuse me?"

"Just this once. I know wine much better than you

do. You hardly drink anything more than a rosé."
She shook her head. "The winemakers aren't going
to answer your questions or take you seriously if you
can't speak their language."

"We really aren't there to ask them about the
wine."

She shook her head as if I'd just proved her point.
"You can't go into a winery and not ask about the
wine. That's like going into a library and not asking
about books. It's just not done."

I shrugged. "Fine. If you are so confident about it,
we can try it your way."

"There is no try." She grinned. "Don't worry; it'll
work. Just let me take the lead to warm them up and
then you can ask them all the Amish stuff."

We came to a consensus just as I turned off the
road into a gravel lot beside a purple, one-story
building. The winery was small, but the vineyard behind it seemed to roll over the hillside for miles.

Cass wrinkled her nose. "They must make their
wine at a different location. This building is way too
small for production."

The building didn't look much bigger than your
average dentist's office.

She turned back to me. "Okay, again, let me take
the lead."

"Got it." I held up my hands. "Let you take the
lead and no one gets hurt."

She rolled her eyes.

Despite the size of the building, the winery's parking lot was packed with cars and one senior tour bus.
Cass nodded at the bus. "Don't get between that crew

and their wine." She said this as though she spoke from experience.

Shaking my head, I followed her inside the purple building.

"This is just our tasting room," a woman dressed in black linen said from behind the black marble counter as she poured white wine into the waiting glasses in front of her. "The production building is at the very back of the vineyard."

"Can we see it?" an elderly woman asked as she swirled and sniffed her glass.

"I'm afraid you can't," the woman in black said. "It's closed for renovations." She smiled over the older woman's head at Cass and me. "Welcome to Stardust Winery. Can I interest you in a sample?"

"You most certainly can," Cass said and stepped around the other women to the counter. Cass was so tiny, she could bob and weave around others. I, on the other hand, had to say "excuse me" half a dozen times.

By the time I made it to the counter, Cass had a glass of merlot in front of her and was chatting up the server. The server had wrapped her black hair in a tight bun on top of her head and she wore long, dangly, mismatched earrings. One was in the shape of a wineglass. The other was a wine bottle.

"Oh," the woman said. "We make all our own vintage, but as I said, it's not made here. It's in a building at the back of the vineyard."

"Where is it made?" Cass asked. "Is it somewhere that we can tour?"

She shook her head, and her earrings swayed back

and forth. "I'm afraid not. The building is under construction. It's still in operation, but it's not safe for visitors."

"You have been so helpful," Cass said and held up her half-empty glass. "I think I have found a new favorite."

"If you like that, let me pour another that's just a touch heavier. This vintage will really tell you how red you like your wine."

"The redder the better," Cass said.

The server placed a new glass on the counter, opened a new bottle, and poured the wine into a decanter. She left it on the counter for a little while to let it breathe, or I assumed that's what she was doing. I knew much more about candy and chocolate than I did about wine.

While the decanter sat, Cass waved her away. "Please help the others while we wait."

The server thanked Cass and moved down the bar. She chatted with the other women and poured the wines of their choice, not once missing a beat.

Cass sipped her original glass and said out of the side of her mouth, "I think she will be just the ticket to learn about what Leeza's connection to this place is."

"If there is a connection," I said.

"There is. I can feel it in my bones."

I rolled my eyes and was about to make a smart remark about Cass's bones when the woman with the earrings circled back.

She beamed at Cass. "That should have rested for long enough. Let me pour you a glass. Now, hold it under your nose for a moment and register the notes it gives off."

"Oh, it smells earthy," Cass said as she held the wineglass just below her nose. "I can already tell that this one will be my favorite."

"Swirl and sip," the woman said.

Cass did as instructed. "Wow, that's wonderful." She held the glass out to me. "You try, Bai."

I took the glass from her hand, and swirled and sipped as well. The wine had a very bitter taste and reminded me of the darkest form of chocolate, one that I had used for some recipes at JP Chocolates in New York. It had been 98 percent cacao and cost a small fortune. However, it was the exact chocolate that a well-to-do bride had wanted for her wedding truffles. If she was willing to pay the price, who was I to argue?

"It has a cacao flavor," I said.

The server beamed at me. "Right! Not many people pick that up. They think of chocolate as being sweet. They don't know that it's the sugar that makes it sweet. Cacao itself is quite bitter."

"We are chocolatiers visiting from New York," Cass said, including me in that statement. It was true that I had been a NYC chocolatier, but I wasn't anymore. I wasn't going to argue the point in front of a possible source, though.

"How lovely! I love New York. I go there as often as I can." She leaned across the counter. "My big dream is to be a wine critic in the city. I'm doing all I can to save up and study so that I can make the move."

"If you do," Cass said, "look me up when you make it to the city. I'm Cass Calbera. I'm the head chocolatier at JP Chocolates."

"I heard that there's a candy shop here in Holmes

County that has a former chocolatier from JP Chocolates working there."

"That would be me," I said, and glanced at Cass. "I used to be at JP Chocolates, but now I'm working here at my family's candy shop in Harvest."

Something flashed in her eyes for a moment. I don't know if it was recognition or possibly even fear. "I'm looking forward to moving to New York. This place is way too small. If the fire marshal happened by and saw how many people were in here right now, he'd shut us down," she said with a laugh.

I examined the crammed space. Other than Cass's server, I spotted three other staffers in black filling the tourists' waiting wineglasses.

"What was your name?" Cass asked. "You have given us such great service, I want to mention you in my review. I love writing reviews of places when I travel. And if you stop by JP Chocolates and I'm not there, you can leave your name with one of my staffers. I'll be sure to add you to our friends and family list, for a special treat."

She hesitated for moment. "Aubrey."

"How long have you worked here, Aubrey?" Cass asked.

Aubrey touched her wine bottle earring and it swung back and forth.

Cass smiled. "You are so knowledgeable about the wines. You must have a lot of experience."

Aubrey blushed and her nerves seemed to melt away. "Why, thank you. I just had my fifth anniversary with the winery. Working for this company has been a great decision for me, especially with my plan to move to New York."

"Yes," Cass said. "By the time you arrive in the city, you will have made a great start on your career."

Blushing again, Aubrey asked, "Is there anything else I can get either of you?"

"Just a bottle of that last wine," Cass said.

"Very good," Aubrey said. She hesitated for a moment. "That is one of our more expensive wines." She handed Cass a price sheet. "It's a ninety-five point wine . . ."

"It's delicious and worth every penny." Cass smiled. "Besides, I have a credit card."

Aubrey nodded. "Just let me go grab it for you." She stepped around a coworker who was pouring wine for an elderly couple and into the next room, marked "employees only."

"You don't have to buy it just for information," I said.

"I want to. It's actually very good. I was thinking of giving JP a bottle and suggesting we work on a wine truffle series. This just might be the wine for it. I've never tasted anything like it before."

"That's not a bad idea. I wish I could do something like that as Swissmen Sweets, but I don't think I could get away with a wine truffle series in my grandmother's Amish candy shop. It took a long time to convince her to sell lavender blueberry fudge, and that was alcohol-free."

"Who knew solving a murder could lead to a new truffle?" Cass asked.

"I think when you're a chocolatier, just about any experience leads to a new truffle."

Aubrey returned with the bottle of wine wrapped

carefully in a canvas bag. When she said the total cost of the wine, I stifled a gasp. Cass, however, didn't even flinch as she handed over her credit card. Had I been in New York, I would have expected the price Aubrey quoted, but I realized that I had lived in Ohio long enough now that I had a serious case of sticker shock.

Aubrey rang up the sale and handed Cass the bag and her card.

"Thank you. I had one more question you might be able to help me with," Cass began.

"Of course," Aubrey said. Now that she had made a sale, her guard appeared to be all the way down.

"Is there someone by the name of Leeza here?" Cass said. "A friend of mine suggested that I come to this winery and look her up. That was several months ago, so I wonder if Leeza even works here any longer."

Aubrey looked pale. "I don't know anyone by that name."

"That's strange. My friend seemed quite sure that she worked here at Stardust." Cass looked over at me. "Bailey, don't you remember our friend Susan saying that?"

I simply nodded. I didn't like the idea of lying— and Cass and I didn't have a friend named Susan.

"I don't know anyone by that name." Her expression closed off. "If that's all you need, I should move on to the next customer."

"Of course," Cass stepped back. "I'm sorry for keeping you so long."

The rapport between the two of them had fizzled out. Aubrey stepped away from us and, instead of going to the next customer, went into the back room where she had retrieved the wine bottle.

Cass and I shared a look and, after a beat, trailed Aubrey through the doorway. I loved that we didn't even have to say "follow her" to know that's what we both had in mind.

CHAPTER TWENTY-TWO

To my surprise, none of the other staffers tried to stop us when we went into the room marked "employees only."

Wine racks lined the walls of the second room, and it was at least fifteen degrees cooler than the tasting room. I shivered and rubbed my bare arms.

"Who knew a little winery in the middle of Amish country would make so many different kinds of wines?" Cass asked. "There must be fifteen varieties in here."

"I can see that, but where did Aubrey go? She came into this room and disappeared. There's nowhere to hide among the rows of bottles," I said.

"She had to go somewhere. People don't evaporate."

"Maybe there is a door behind one of the wine racks."

"Like a secret door?" Cass asked. "This case gets weirder by the second."

I agreed as Cass and I moved around the room in

search of such a door, but it was quickly evident that there was nothing like that in the room.

The floor beneath my feet shifted. I stumbled away from the spot as a three-by-three-foot square of floorboard lifted.

"Ahh!" Cass and I screamed at the same time.

The person coming up from the trapdoor screamed, too. He looked like a head without a body. We could only see him from the neck up.

When we all caught our breath, a young man with a pencil-thin mustache climbed the rest of the way out of the floor. "This room is for staff only. What are you doing here?"

"We're waiting for Aubrey," Cass said. "She was going to talk us through the wines that you have in this rack." Cass held up the cloth bag Aubrey had sold her. "We are buyers."

The young man smoothed down his minuscule mustache. "You don't have to wait for Aubrey. I'll be happy to talk to you about what's in this room just as soon as I deliver this bottle to another customer. Come out to the tasting room and we can chat."

"If it's all the same to you," Cass said, "we'd like to stay in here. It's so much cooler. Bailey doesn't do well in the heat, and I'm afraid that she suffered a bit of heat stroke out in the sun today. I told her to stay hydrated and keep drinking water, but she rarely listens to me."

Cass elbowed me, and I put a hand to my forehead. "I'm so hot. I need a cool place to collect myself. This room is just what I need."

He glanced over his shoulder at the other room. "I don't want anyone getting sick. Stay here and I'll be back in a minute." He went into the tasting room.

When the door closed behind him, Cass bent down to look at the trapdoor. "That's very well concealed. I wouldn't have known there was even a door there."

There was a small hole in the floor just big enough for two fingers. I put my fingers into it, and the door opened easily to reveal a narrow staircase. It was dark inside, and we couldn't see much farther than the first five steps.

"Whoa," Cass said.

"We don't have much time," I said. "If we want to go through the trapdoor, we have to do it now, before he comes back. He'll be back soon. He didn't want to leave us in here alone. I'm sure it's not allowed."

Cass nodded and went down the stairs. "It smells musty down here. I can't see a thing."

"Use the flashlight on your cell phone."

"Oh, right." Her voice was muffled.

I heard shuffling from down below, and then the weakest pinprick of light appeared.

"Come on down. This is cool."

I looked back at the closed door that led into the tasting room and then went down the stairs.

If the wine room was fifteen degrees cooler than the tasting room, the cellar beneath it was thirty. I started to shiver the moment my sneakers hit the floor. A T-shirt and shorts were not the proper clothing for a place as cold as this. "It's freezing down here."

"Not quite freezing but cold. It's for the wine."

Around the cellar there were dozens of wine barrels. The names of the wines and the years were written on them in black block letters.

"They should give tours of this place," Cass said. "This is what someone would imagine a wine barrel room in France looks like. I bet they would sell a lot more wine if they highlighted this space."

I rubbed my arms. "It is neat." Then I spotted another set of stairs leading up to a door that looked like it was right out of the pages of *The Wizard of Oz.* Bright light slipped through the cracks around the door. I pointed at it. "Now we know where Aubrey went."

Cass nodded.

Above our heads, the hatch opened. "Are you down there?" a squeaky male voice asked. "Hello? This area is off-limits to the public."

"That's our cue," I whispered.

Cass and I hurried up the second set of stairs and out into the sunshine.

We found ourselves on the other side of the building, away from the parking lot. There were rows of grapes in front of us, and two picnic tables. Aubrey sat at one of those tables with a man. They held hands across the table and appeared to be in the middle of an earnest conversation.

"It looks like a where-is-this-relationship-going talk," Cass whispered.

I agreed, but what caught me off guard about the pair was that I had seen the man before. He was of medium height with spiky brown hair.

I tugged on my friend's arm. "Cass, that's the guy who picked Leeza up on Apple Street."

Cass stared openmouthed at me. "Are you sure?"

"I'm pretty sure." I shook my head. "No, I'm almost certain."

"You might want to be more than certain when

this guy could very well be the one who tried to blow Leeza up."

The man made eye contact with me, dropped Aubrey's hand, and jumped from his seat. He tried to leap away from the picnic table, but his left foot got caught on the seat and he toppled to the ground with one leg still under the table.

"Graceful," Cass quipped.

Aubrey got up and peered down at him. "Gabe, are you all right?"

Gabe pushed her away. "I twisted my leg."

Aubrey tried to untangle him from the picnic table.

"Get away from me. You're making it worse!" Gabe shouted.

Aubrey shrank back from him.

"Doesn't look broken," Cass said.

Gabe untangled his leg and struggled to his feet. He winced as he put weight on his left foot.

"Gabe, maybe we should go to the clinic," Aubrey said. "I can drive you."

He glared at her. "We aren't going to the clinic." He scowled at Cass and me. "Were these the women asking about Leeza?"

"You bet we were," Cass said. "What do you know about her murder?"

Aubrey gasped, and I groaned. I hope that I would have put it a bit more delicately than that, but Cass's tactic seemed to do just the trick with Gabe. "I didn't kill her." Tears gathered in the corners of his eyes. "I cared about her a lot. This has been very hard."

Aubrey took another step back. I didn't know what her relationship with Gabe was or what she wanted it to be, but I was willing to bet all the chocolate in my shop that she didn't like hearing that he cared about another woman.

"Why don't you have a seat, Gabe, and tell us about it?" Cass said.

"I don't have to tell you anything," he snapped.

"Would you rather talk to a sheriff's deputy?" I asked. "I can arrange that."

He glared at me. "You're not covered in cake now, but I remember you. You were staring at Leeza and me when I picked her up on Saturday. You looked ridiculous, by the way."

I put my hands on my hips. "What did you do with her?"

"What do you mean, what did I do with her? I took her home. She was drunk, and I wanted to stop her before she made a giant scene."

"You were a little late for that," Cass said.

Gabe stared at her openmouthed. "What do you mean?"

"She'd just crashed a wedding before you picked her up," Cass said. "She ran into the church and yelled at the groom."

He frowned. "She didn't tell me that. That's not normal for her. She was sober for months. She promised she'd given up drinking. I don't know what happened in the last couple of weeks that changed that."

Gabe was the second person to tell me that Leeza had given up drinking. Her friend Becca had been the first.

"This is all her counselor's fault. I told her to stop going there, that she didn't need that place. Sometimes she'd come home from those meetings all upset. And then she started drinking again. She said there was no point in being sober."

I winced, knowing the counselor he was talking about was Reverend Brook. I wasn't going to mention his name, though. I didn't know what Gabe was capable of.

Gabe bent and rubbed the side of his knee. "That counselor was a terrible idea. All he did was bring up bad memories for her. The best way to deal with a bad past is to bury it. That's what I've always done."

And he was the picture of mental health, I was sure.

"And now she's dead. I blame him." Gabe curled his hands into fists. "She died because she was drunk and careless. When I find out who her counselor was, and I will, I will make him pay for what he did."

I didn't for a moment doubt it.

He marched away, jumped in the red car I had seen Leeza climb into the day of the wedding, and drove away. This time I got the plate number.

CHAPTER TWENTY-THREE

"See! See!" Cass said as we walked back to my car. "I knew this winery was connected to the murder." Cass was this close to jumping up and down over it.

I removed my phone from my pocket. "You were right, and now I have to tell Aiden. He's not going to be happy we spoke to Gabe without him."

"He wouldn't have even found Gabe if it weren't for us."

"We didn't do a great job of finding him. Neither of us got his last name," I said.

"How many Gabes could be working at this winery? Besides, the license plate number will tell Aiden his last name."

"At least we got that," I said and looked back at the purple building, where Aubrey was watching us through one of the windows. There was a love triangle there, I thought. That made both Gabe and Aubrey suspects.

"Do you think he killed Leeza?" I asked.

"He seems like he could get angry enough," Cass said, and then she lowered her voice. "I think he would like to take Reverend Brook out if he knew his connection to Leeza."

I thought so, too. I leaned against my car and made the call I had been dreading since I'd followed Cass down into the wine cellar.

"Bailey," Aiden answered on the first ring. "Where are you? I was just at the candy shop looking for you."

"Something up?" I asked.

"Yes, something is up. A woman was killed in an explosion in my county." He took a breath. "I'm sorry. I shouldn't have snapped at you like that. This case is increasingly frustrating. Leeza's Amish family and bishop won't talk to me, and Reverend Brook is being decidedly unhelpful, too."

"Do you think he's hiding something?" I asked.

There was a pause, but it was a long enough pause that it was all the answer I needed.

"So where are you? I just stopped by Swissmen Sweets to see you. I've had a terrible day. BCI is coming in on this case because it involves a bomb, and the sheriff is blaming me for tipping them off."

"Did you?" I asked.

"No, but the coroner has to file a report with BCI when explosives are used. It wasn't like we could keep it a secret."

"I'm sorry, Aiden," I said, feeling worse and worse that I had more bad news for him. Maybe he wouldn't take it as bad news. Maybe he would just accept the new information.

"I think you should talk to Aubrey and Gabe at the Stardust Winery on Route Sixty-Two."

There was a long pause. "Why?"

"Because they know Leeza. Aiden, Gabe is the guy who picked Leeza up Saturday night."

"What! Where is he? Where are you?"

"Cass and I are at the winery right now—in the parking lot, actually. Gabe left, and he was driving the same car I saw Saturday."

"Did you get the plate number?"

"I did," I said with relief. I rattled the number off to him.

"Okay, I will check on this number. Where is the other person? Aubrey, you said?"

"Right. She's still inside the winery."

"And you are still there in the parking lot?" he asked.

"Yes," I said. "Cass and I were just about to leave."

"Are you safe?" Aiden asked.

"Yes, we are fine. Cass even bought a bottle of wine."

He sighed. "Stay there, then. I'm jumping into my car now and can be there in twenty minutes. Tell me everything you know about that place and Aubrey and Gabe while I drive."

Twenty minutes later, Aiden pulled into the Stardust Winery parking lot with all the backstory on the winery I could give him. I'd got an earful for not reporting the matchbook to him the moment we found it.

Aiden parked his departmental SUV next to my car and climbed out.

"Were you able to run the plates?" I asked.

He nodded. "Yes, the car belongs to Gabriel Johnson. My deputies are out looking for him. They should have him in custody shortly, and then maybe this nightmare of a case will be over." He held the door open, and Jethro hopped out, too.

I stared at the pig. "Wait, what is Jethro doing with you?" I asked.

Aiden looked down at the pig. "Ummm, I didn't mention that he was with me?"

I put my hands on my hips. "No, you didn't." Then, my eyes narrowed. "That's why you went to Swissmen Sweets looking for me. It wasn't to make sure I was okay. It was to dump the pig on me."

"Oh," Aiden said. "Look at him. You hurt his feelings when you speak like he's a burden."

Jethro had his nose buried in a cluster of daylilies edging the parking lot. "He doesn't look sad at all to me. Why do you have him?"

Aiden sighed. "My mother asked me to take him."

I should have suspected as much.

"Honestly, I think she wanted to ask you," Aiden said. "But she couldn't find you. I was her backup plan."

Cass eyed him. "Must be tough being a pig babysitter backup plan."

"It's better than being a pig first sitter."

"Point taken," Cass said.

"Can you just take him for now?" Aiden gave me puppy-dog eyes.

"I know your mother was going to leave him with me for the honeymoon. Does that mean it's back on?"

Aiden nodded. "I was able to clear Reverend Brook. The sheriff said they could go. I think he's so upset about BCI pushing its way into this case that he wants to remove as many of the suspects as possible."

"Can they go without BCI's permission?" I asked.

"I don't know if they want to thumb their noses at the state like that."

"I wondered the same, so I had the reverend talk to the investigator from BCI today. BCI gave its blessing. They don't believe the bombing was related to Reverend Brook, and I tend to agree with them." He looked down at Jethro, who had moved from smelling the daylilies to eating them. "Can you take him? I've got my hands full with this case."

"Why didn't you just leave him at Swissmen Sweets?" Cass asked. It was a fair question. My grandmother and Charlotte had become accustomed to caring for pets while in the shop. I took Puff the bunny in every day, and Jethro was also a frequent visitor. As long as the animals stayed out of my grandmother's kitchen, she was fine with it.

Aiden blushed. "I tried to leave him at the candy shop, but Emily was working and she doesn't like it when Jethro is there."

I knew this, too, but it made me smile that a young Amish woman could intimidate Aiden enough to convince him to take a pig on patrol with him.

"I don't know why Emily has an issue with Jethro," Aiden complained. "He's a perfectly clean pig. My mother makes sure that he has all the best soaps and beauty products. I think she spends more time and money on caring for him than she ever did on me when I was a child."

There was probably some truth to that.

"Fine, I'll take Jethro," I said, not that there was ever much chance of my giving him any other answer. It was always going to be fine.

Aiden beamed.

Behind us, there was chatter as the side door of

the winery opened and the black-clothed servers came out in a line. Aubrey was among them.

I pointed at Aubrey, who walked to a compact car. "That's her, the one with the black bun. She was the one who we spoke to about Leeza."

"Miss," Aiden called as he walked over to Aubrey. Her coworkers jumped in their cars and scattered as Aiden approached. It didn't look to me as though she had many friends at the winery.

She clutched her right earring, as if it had some special power to protect her from Aiden. He reached her and showed her his badge, but they were too far away from Cass and me for us to overhear their conversation.

"Do you think it would be bad form if we just walked over there and eavesdropped?"

I scooped up Jethro before he could completely decimate the winery's daylilies. Also, I didn't know what plants might be poisonous to pigs. The little bacon bundle wasn't getting sick on my watch. Juliet had enough anxiety about him as it was.

"I think it would be very bad form," I said.

"Darn. I was hoping it would be fine."

Aubrey waved her hand and shook her head, and then she burst into tears. Aiden looked over his shoulder with pleading eyes.

"It looks like he wants your help," Cass said.

It certainly did. I walked over to Aiden just to have Aubrey thrust herself into my arms. "It's my fault she's dead," she sobbed.

I widened my eyes at Aiden over her head. "Shh, shh." I patted her back. "I think you need to tell Deputy Brody what's going on here."

"I can't. It's just too horrible."

I glanced at Aiden. "You're going to have to," I said. "This isn't about you. It's about Leeza, who was murdered. Don't you want to find out who is responsible?"

She straightened up but still held onto my arm as if she needed support to stay upright. "I know who is responsible. It's me. Leeza would still be alive if it weren't for me. I can't believe I did this to my friend."

CHAPTER TWENTY-FOUR

"You and Leeza were friends?" I asked as gently as I could.

Aiden looked as if he wanted to arrest Aubrey that very moment, and he even made a move for the cuffs on his belt. I shook my head.

"How long had you known her?" I asked.

"Not very long, just as long as she worked here. A few months maybe? However, we were together every day. Both of us needed extra money for bills and things. We both were willing to pick up extra shifts if someone called off."

I nodded.

"We had a lot in common. We worked hard and had big dreams." She glanced at Cass. "I have already told you mine about wanting to move to New York, but Leeza had dreams of owning a business of her own, too. She said once that she wanted to show her family she'd turned out all right."

I thought about RJ and wondered if he would

even care if Leeza hit it big. I had a feeling as long as she continued to live the English life, he wouldn't see much value in what she was doing.

"We became friends fast, and probably told each other things too soon. Things that you shouldn't tell someone about yourself maybe ever. I didn't know that she had a drinking problem for the first couple of months. She was fun, and she loved to teach people about wine. Unlike the rest of us, she never took any of the samples home. Most of us thought it was strange, because who wouldn't want to take home a two-hundred-dollar bottle of wine if the boss gave it to you? Leeza always turned it down. I asked once why she never went drinking after work or took any of the extra wine that the bosses offered us. She told me that she was a recovering alcoholic then. It was the first of her secrets."

"Why would an alcoholic work at a winery?" Cass asked. "I mean, that's like a diabetic working at a cookie shop. Sounds like a recipe for disaster."

"It was intentional," Aubrey said. "She said that she worked at the winery to test herself. She believed that she wasn't truly sober unless she could be around alcohol and have the strength to say 'no' to it."

"And you had a problem with her being an alcoholic?" I asked.

"No, of course not. She was sober, and I had seen her willpower and the choices she made every day to resist drinking. She was so strong." Tears came to her eyes. "Much stronger than me. My problem with her was that I told her my secret, too, and she didn't care."

"What do you mean?" I asked.

She looked at her hands. "She knew how I felt about Gabe, but it didn't matter to her. She started seeing him."

"You told her and she immediately started dating him?"

"No." Aubrey shook her head. "It wasn't like that. I told her how I felt about him, and the moment Gabe saw her, he zeroed in on her. Leeza was beautiful and friendly and was always the person the male customers gravitated to. She was also the person Gabe wanted. I had worked with him for the last five years, and he always talked to me. We talked about everything. But it was all at work. He never showed any signs of caring for me the way I cared for him. Still, I thought it was just a matter of time. Someday, he would see what was right in front of him. He would see what he had been missing all this time and ask me out."

Internally, I winced, thinking of my ex-boyfriend, whom I had left behind in New York. Even though my relationship with Eric had been different, I had been a lot like Aubrey. I thought—wrongly—that I could change him. That he could be the man I needed him to be if I just had the strength to wait for him to sow his wild oats. How stupid I had been, and how much time I had wasted in that relationship. The best—and worst—thing that had happened to me was finding out Eric was cheating on me. It was the wakeup call I needed to teach me I wasn't going to change him. In fact, it taught me that I couldn't and wouldn't change anyone. I glanced at Aiden. Aiden was as close to perfect as I could imagine.

"What does Gabe do here?"

She shook her head. "He doesn't work here. Not

officially. The owners hire him from time to time to help with various tasks around the vineyard. He knows a lot about making wine. He's here at least once a week doing one odd job or another."

"Did Leeza initiate their relationship?" I asked.

Aubrey shook her head. "He told me how he felt about her, and that he was going to ask her on a date. I was crushed. I felt like my life was over. Before I could stop myself, I told him about her drinking. I said he might want to rethink how he felt because she was an alcoholic. She could fall off the wagon at any time. He didn't want that kind of baggage." She licked her lips. "I told Gabe she was a recovering alcoholic, but it backfired on me." She shook her head. "He thought it was brave of her to work here, and he was impressed that she was able to stay sober in this environment." She rubbed her forehead as if even thinking about it gave her a headache. "He said it made him want to get to know her even more."

"Then what happened?" asked Cass, who was clearly enthralled by Aubrey's story.

Aubrey crossed her arms. "I went to Leeza and told her about my conversation with Gabe. I didn't tell her that I'd told him she was an alcoholic. I only said that he had a crush on her and wanted to ask her out. She knew how I felt about him and promised me up and down that she wouldn't date him." Her face darkened. "But then, weeks later, I learned she'd gone behind my back and was seeing him. I caught them together in the vineyard . . ."

Cass winced, and I felt I had the same face.

Aubrey let go of my arm and balled her fists at her sides. "She apologized, but she said that she and Gabe were meant to be together. She said they had a connection I couldn't understand. Whatever happened to girl code? She was supposed to be *my* friend. Whatever connection she had with him should not have mattered as much as my friendship." She stretched out her hands as if she realized that she had been squeezing them too tightly. "After that, I swore I would make her life miserable. I tried to make work hard for her. I gave her all the terrible customers, and when things went missing around the winery, I would tell the owners that she was the one who might have taken them." She shook her head. "But it didn't matter. She was still loved at the winery. She made the tough customers love her, and the owners never believed that Leeza was capable of stealing anything."

Wow, that wasn't very nice. Aubrey had revealed a level of spitefulness that I hadn't anticipated. "Okay," I said carefully, wanting to keep her talking. "But why do you feel responsible for her death?"

"Because I divulged another secret she told me." She covered her face with her hands. "Of all the things I'd done to her, this was the one that was the very worst. I was blinded by jealousy. I have no other excuse for what I did."

"What was it?" Aiden asked.

She shook her head back and forth and began crying in earnest.

I frowned. What could be worse than telling everyone that Leeza was a recovering alcoholic? Then, it hit me. "Did you tell someone that she grew up Amish?"

Aubrey looked up at me with tears in her eyes. "How did you know that?"

Before I could think of an answer, she said, "Leeza told me that she was kicked out of her Amish community because of her drinking, and she wanted to clean up her act so she could see her family again."

"So you told Gabe?" Cass asked.

She shook her head. "No, I found her Amish family and told them she worked at a winery. Her brother was furious and told me never to come to his farm again or speak of her. He told me that he didn't have a sister. I had hoped that he would come to the winery and make a scene that the owners couldn't ignore. He didn't. The next day, I told Leeza I'd gone to visit her family and told them where she worked. She said her brother hated alcohol in all forms and would not approve of her job. She was very upset and said I'd ruined her chances of making amends with them." Aubrey shivered. "I told her that she'd ruined my chances of being with Gabe, so now we were even."

I grimaced at her rationale.

"How did that lead to her death?" Aiden asked.

"She said that she would have to talk to her family to make things right."

"She made contact with her family?" I asked. This was news—if it was true. And, given how forthright Aubrey had been about her ugly behavior, I was inclined to think she wasn't straying from the truth now. Yet RJ had been adamant that no one, including himself, had seen or even thought about Leeza since she'd left the district eight years before.

"Did she go?" Aiden asked.

"I think so. She never told me. At that point, we were no longer close."

That was an understatement.

"But a few days later, I caught her drinking in the cellar. She broke into one of the most expensive cases of wine and drank the whole bottle. She was fired on the spot." She licked her lips. "She acted like she didn't even care. She said that she had no reason to make anything of her life now."

"What did she mean by that?" I asked.

Aubrey rubbed at her eyes and smeared black eyeliner and mascara across her cheeks. With her makeup smeared, she looked much younger than she had. When I'd first met her I'd thought she was my age or older, but now I saw that she was likely no more than twenty-two.

"She said that her family didn't want her back, so there was no reason for her to stay sober." She took a breath. "I was starting to feel bad at that point. I mean, before she and Gabe got together, we were good friends; best friends really. I was the one who'd told her about the counseling service at the community center when we first met." She looked up at the three of us in turn. "So you see, I *am* responsible for her death. Gabe said her counselor was the one who killed her. I was the one who sent her to him." She covered her face with her hands.

CHAPTER TWENTY-FIVE

"**H**er counselor wasn't the one who killed her," Aiden said, leaving no room for argument.

Aubrey blinked at him. "But that's what Gabe said."

"He's wrong. The counselor has an airtight alibi for the time of the murder."

"Then who could have done it?" She blinked, and her eyelashes stuck together for a second before we could see her eyes again.

"That's what I would like to know," Aiden said. "At the very least, you've told us why she took up drinking again. That's helpful."

It was also helpful, I thought, to know that Leeza had had contact with her family shortly before she died, and RJ had lied about it.

"Do you know where I can find Gabe Johnson?" Aiden asked.

Aubrey shook her head. "He never told me where he lived . . ."

I winced. I would have taken that as a hint that he

wasn't romantically interested. Apparently, Aubrey missed that message.

"We have his address from his car registration. He's not home right now. Where else might he have gone?" Aiden asked.

She shook her head. "I don't know."

"What's your boss's number?" Aiden asked.

Aubrey pulled her phone out of her pocket and rattled off a number. Aiden made a note on his minuscule notepad.

"Aubrey, I'm likely going to need to talk to you again. Please give me your contact information."

She told him her address and phone number.

Tears were in her eyes. "Can I go now?"

Aiden nodded.

She jumped into her car and pulled away as fast as possible. I stepped back to escape the dust and gravel coming off the back of her tires as she peeled out.

When her car disappeared from sight I set Jethro back down on the gravel parking lot.

Cass folded her arms. "Aubrey spoke about girl code, but it seems to me that she broke it way worse than Leeza did. How could she go to Leeza's family like that? That's cold."

"Jealousy is a powerful motivator," Aiden said.

"Bull," Cass said. "It was plain cruel, and I think that we are going to learn that Aubrey's action was the catalyst for Leeza's murder."

I thought that was true, too. Jethro bumped his snout against my bare leg.

"I'm not happy that the two of you came here alone, but you did open up a whole new avenue for the investigation, and I'm grateful for that," Aiden said. "It shouldn't be long before we have Gabe Johnson in custody."

Cass swung an arm over his shoulder. "Just admit it, Deputy Brody. We make a great team."

Aiden made a face.

I picked up Jethro again. "We'd better get back to Swissmen Sweets. We're pretty well set up for the Fourth of July celebration, but I want to double-check everything. Margot seems to think this will be the biggest event the village has ever seen."

"Margot thinks every event on the square is the biggest," Aiden said.

I nodded.

"I need to get back, too. Not only is the department investigating this murder, but we have to monitor firework use across the county. You would not believe the number of injuries that will go to the clinic over the next forty-eight hours."

"I thought personal use of fireworks was illegal in Ohio," I said.

"It is, but you can sell them."

"So stores can sell them, but the people who buy them can't shoot them off?" Cass asked.

Aiden nodded.

"That's stupid."

"It's Ohio law," he said in a resigned way.

We walked back to our cars. Cass opened the back door for me, and I tucked Jethro inside. On the back bench seat, he circled three times before settling down in the middle. He really was more like a hairless cat than a pig.

"Thanks for taking Jethro," Aiden said.

"I didn't have much of a choice," I replied with a smile.

Aiden laughed. "Maybe not, but I still appreciate it."

We climbed in our cars, and I noted that Aiden didn't pull out of the parking lot until I pointed my compact car in the direction of Harvest. There might be some trust issues there, not that I didn't deserve them. I should have told him about the matchbook as soon as Cass found it.

Cass turned to me. "Are we really going back to Swissmen Sweets?"

I nodded. "We really are. I think we need to take some time to make candy and think over what we should do next."

Cass looked behind her. "And Hot Cop seems bound and determined to follow us all the way to the candy shop."

Jethro put his front hooves on the back seat for a peek at Aiden, too.

"I think if Aiden had his way, he wouldn't let us out of his sight for a second," I said.

"Smart guy," Cass said with a chuckle.

When I parked in my usual spot on Apple Street, Aiden accelerated and passed by with a toot of his horn.

"If he wasn't such a great guy otherwise, I would find his following us super annoying," Cass said.

"Me too." I opened my car door.

As we walked back to the candy shop, I got a text message. I pulled my phone from my pocket, expecting it to be Aiden. Instead, I found that it was a message from his mother.

"Bailey, Aiden told me that you have Jethro. I'm so glad! You take such good care of him. You are just the sweetest almost-daughter-in-law. Aiden wouldn't take

Jethro's things. Can you stop by the church and pick up his bag? I just packed a few things for him to make his stay with you more comfortable. I will meet you at the church in a few minutes. Love, Juliet."

I showed the text to Cass. "She does know that she doesn't have to sign her text messages, right? Your phone will tell you who the message is from."

"I don't know what Juliet knows when it comes to technology. Do you want to come with me to the church?"

"I think I'll pass. If I go along, you will just end up being there longer because Juliet will ask me a hundred questions after asking you a hundred questions."

I laughed.

"You should take the pig with you," Cass said. "If she's really leaving for her honeymoon soon, she will want to say goodbye to him."

I sighed and scooped up Jethro, who had been toddling along after me on the sidewalk.

Cass stopped me. "Before you go, I think someone is here who wants to talk to you."

"Who would . . . ?" I asked, but the rest of the question died on my lips when I saw Becca Stout standing outside Esh Family Pretzels, her hands clasped in front of her apron. She glanced at Cass nervously.

"I can take a hint," Cass said. "Tell me everything later." She went inside Swissmen Sweets then, leaving me on the sidewalk with Becca.

I walked over to her. "Becca, can I help you?"

She looked up and down the street. "I'm so sorry to bother you like this, and if my husband knew that I was here, he would be furious with me. I really should not have come."

"Do you want to sit down?" I pointed to the park bench in front of Swissmen Sweets.

"*Nee, nee,* I can't stay long. I have to get back to the gift shop. It's a busy day, and I left two of the young girls in charge. It does not take much for them to become frazzled."

"Then how can I help you?"

"I've been thinking about Elizabeth—Leeza. It's just horrible what has happened." She was on the verge of tears. "I can't even bear to think of it. Have the police had any luck finding the person responsible?"

"They are still looking," I said.

"And you are helping them?" she asked.

"I'm doing what I can. Because I have a good relationship with the Amish community, it is easier for me than it might be for sheriff's deputies to get information."

She frowned. "I can't believe that an Amish person would have done this. Elizabeth left the faith so long ago. I know that she wanted to make amends with her family, but I can't see them hurting her. I wouldn't pester them if I were you. I know this is very painful for them."

No matter how much RJ denied it, I guessed that she was right. Even so, I said, "The police have to talk to them."

"Have you told the police about me?" she asked in a panicked voice.

I shook my head. "No, I haven't needed to yet."

"And you won't," she assured me. "I'm so sorry that I have lost my dear friend, but I can't be involved. My husband wouldn't like it," she said in a low voice.

I bit the inside of my lip and wondered how strict Becca's husband actually was. If she had been in my grandmother's district, I just would have asked *Maami* if she knew, but she wasn't.

"I'll do my best not to tell them," I said.

"*Danki.* You don't know what that means to me." She licked her lips. "Please, if you learn who is behind this terrible thing, will you tell me? I'm not sure I will hear the whole story otherwise, and it would bring my spirit peace to know that justice has been served."

"I will."

"I should go."

I glanced up and down the street, but I didn't see a horse and buggy anywhere. That was unusual in Harvest. "Did you come with an *Englisch* driver? I have to run an errand at the church." I nodded to Jethro. "I need to take him to say goodbye to Juliet. She and Reverend Brook will be leaving soon, but after I am done with that I would be happy to drive you over to your shop in Berlin."

"*Nee,* I will be fine. I left my horse and buggy at the Harvest market. It was a short walk between the market and your candy shop. It is a warm but fine day for a walk, and it gave me time to gather my thoughts."

"Do you want any more marshmallow sticks for your shop?" I asked. "I can run inside and get you more to stock up."

"*Nee,* they sold very well, but let's wait until after the holiday."

"Okay," I said.

She nodded at me one more time and then made her way down the sidewalk in the direction of the small village market. My heart went out to her. It

must be awful to know her close friend had died and
she couldn't grieve as she wanted to because her
community had shunned Leeza. It sounded to me as
if her husband was controlling, which wasn't unusual
in the Amish world. I frowned. I wished there was
some way I could help her.

Jethro tugged on his leash, heading toward the village square. I thought that he must be eager to see
Juliet. I knew Juliet would have a tough time away
from Jethro, and the reverse would be true, too. The
little pig was used to being treated like a king by his
mistress, and he wouldn't be getting that kind of
treatment in my house, not by a long shot.

Several Amish men were already on the square setting up for the Fourth of July celebration the next
day. Uriah Schrock, who was the temporary caretaker
of the square, wrapped red, white, and blue twinkle
lights around the trunk of a tree. He smiled at me.
"*Guder owed* to you, Bailey King." His face broke into a
wide smile as he said good afternoon to me.

"*Guder owed*, Uriah."

He nodded at Jethro. "I see you have the troublemaker *sau* with you."

"Troublemaker pig?"

"Oh yes, that little rascal was on the square earlier
today with Juliet, and when no one was looking he
pulled a string of lights from the gazebo." Uriah
wiped at his brow with a blue bandanna. "He's lucky
they weren't plugged in or he would have gotten
quite a shock indeed."

I looked down at Jethro. He cocked his head as if
to ask me *What?*

"Despite Jethro's behavior, the square has always
looked nice since you've taken over its care. Visitors

to the village have noticed, too. Many who come
back year after year have commented to me about
how nice it all looks."

"I do enjoy the work and give it my best. It gives
me something to do while I'm in this time of waiting."

I wanted to ask Uriah what he was waiting for but
thought it was best not to pry. I was dealing with
enough problems at the moment.

"Margot runs a tight ship," he went on, shoving
the bandanna into the pocket of his trousers. "I knew
when she hired me that she would expect the very
best. That's why I'm here just about every day, working." He put a finger to his lips. "Don't tell my bishop
that I'm out here on Sundays. That's a no-no for my
community."

"Are you really working on Sundays?" I knew every
Amish district considered it bad form to work on the
Sabbath.

"Not too much. I pull a weed here and there. Mostly,
I'm just checking on the place. I want the green to always look its best."

"And it does," I said with a smile.

I had every intention of leaving then when he
cleared his throat. "I heard about what happened
over at the church. Terrible business."

I nodded, but I wasn't the least bit surprised that
he had heard. The Amish grapevine was widespread,
and now that it was known Leeza was former Amish,
there would be even more tongues wagging.

"You found the body?" he asked.

I nodded.

"I hate to hear about something like that happening to Elizabeth."

I blinked when he said her Amish name. "Elizabeth?"

"Elizabeth Chupp. That was the woman they found on the church steps. I happened to be walking by on my way to the square and had the misfortune to see her face. I recognized her right away. She was a member of my district here in Ohio."

"You knew Leeza?" I asked.

"I didn't know her very well," he said. "But her grandfather was a great friend of mine, and he told me all about the choices she made."

"What kinds of choices?"

"Choices that could have gotten her killed," he said quietly.

CHAPTER TWENTY-SIX

"**I**'m glad that my *gut* friend Abram has passed, so that he isn't here to see what a sad end his granddaughter came to." Uriah shook his head. "You called her Leeza?"

I nodded. "That was the English name she was using."

He clicked his tongue. "It's all very sad. I know from what Abram told me that Leeza had many struggles. When she was in *rumspringa* she got a taste of alcohol, and as much as the family tried, they couldn't break her away from it. It was as if a demon had taken hold of her. I was already in Shipshewana when all this was happening, but Abram told me in letters. He wrote me one letter a week until he died five years ago. I treasured those letters so. Even among the Amish, the art of writing letters seems to be fading away," he said forlornly.

"When did Elizabeth leave the church?" I asked.

"The way Abram told it, she didn't want to leave. She asked the bishop if there was someone who could help her deal with her drinking while she was still a member of the community." He shook his head. "The bishop wouldn't have it. The Amish aren't ones to air their dirty laundry, and the bishop, who was a much older man, didn't want anyone outside of his district to know that they were harboring a drunk. The Amish look down on pride, but at the heart of it, we are a very proud culture. Our pride doesn't come from material things. We take pride in how *gut* we are. Maybe at times to our own detriment." He spoke as if he had some experience of this himself.

I thought about what he'd said. "So the bishop kicked her out instead of letting her find help?"

He nodded and removed the bandanna from his pocket again. "That's the short version of it." He folded it neatly this time before putting it back into the pocket. "Abram never told me exactly what happened. He only said in a short letter that Elizabeth had to choose the English life, and he could no longer talk about her in our letters." He paused. "He kept his word when it came to that. He never mentioned her again. Neither did I, because I knew he was a sensitive soul, and it must have pained him to know he had a granddaughter out there that he couldn't help."

I watched Jethro for a moment as I thought this over. The little pig had his snout under one of the bushes near the gazebo.

"What about the rest of the Chupp family? How did they feel about her leaving the community?" I asked.

He finished wrapping the lights around the tree and then walked over to the large storage bin that was full of twinkle lights. He pulled out another red, white, and blue strand. The lights were in a perfect coil. I knew that it must have been an Amish person who'd left them that way last year. If I put Christmas lights away, they were always in a jumbled mess and I swore I would never put lights up again. When Christmas came, though, I always changed my mind.

"I don't think they took it well. She has scores of extended family, including aunts, uncles, and cousins. The Chupps are one of the largest families in my district."

"I know she has a brother." I paused. "I met him."

"Ah yes, RJ. He's a sour fellow. Nothing like his *grossdaddi* was. Abram had a very amiable disposition. RJ still works the family berry farm not too far from here."

"I've been to it," I said. "I was there picking strawberries."

He nodded. "The Chupps have the best berries around." He untangled the next string of lights. "My friend Abram was the one who started the farm. He would be happy to see his grandson carrying on the tradition. That's something to be thankful for. Other than Elizabeth, the rest of the family has been faithful to the Amish way." Uriah shrugged. "Every Amish family has a child or two who strays from the faith."

I thought of Charlotte when he said that. I thought of my father as well.

There was a sound at our feet, and I looked down to see Jethro gnawing on the coils of twinkle lights. "Jethro!" I cried.

The pig turned up his head with a red string hanging from his mouth.

I took it from him and handed it to Uriah, trying not to worry about the pig slobber I was getting all over myself. "I'm so sorry about that."

With two fingers, Uriah took the cord. "It's quite all right."

"I should get him to the church. I'll be watching him while Reverend Brook and Juliet are on their honeymoon. I think he has some chew toys in his overnight bag."

"Overnight bag. He is more like a toddler than a pig."

"No kidding," I said, giving the little bacon bundle a look. It was going to be a very long week caring for him while solving a murder at the same time.

"It would be *gut* if he found something else to chew on." Uriah frowned at the chewed string of lights.

I said goodbye to Uriah and continued on my way to the church. I had Jethro tucked under my arm like a football as I went. I wasn't taking any more chances that he would get into trouble.

I reached the church without incident and let out a great sigh of relief. That sigh was short-lived, though, when the church doors opened and Christine came down the steps. She was wearing strappy espadrilles and looked as if a stiff wind would topple her right over. Just in case she fell down the stairs, I waited at the bottom for fear I might have to break her fall.

I smiled.

She looked down her long nose at me. "What are you doing here?"

I blinked. That wasn't typically the greeting one expected at a church door. I held up the pig. "I came to talk to Juliet about Jethro before she leaves on her trip."

She reached the pavement in front of the church where I stood. "I'm sorry if my question came off as rude," she said in a way that made me think she wasn't sorry in the least. "I should have known you were here to see Juliet. I know the two of you must be very close. I was surprised when she picked someone she hasn't known for very long as her maid of honor."

"The Brody family has been friends with my family for years. I know she would have picked my grandmother if she could, but since *Maami* is Amish, that was not to be," I said and stepped around her. I was about to walk up the steps when she spoke again.

"Kayla told me that she had a nice talk with Aiden yesterday. They cleared up some things."

"That's nice," I said. I was dying to ask her what those things were, but I refused to give her the satisfaction.

She wasn't going to let me avoid the question, though. "It's clear they both still care for each other. Kayla says she doesn't want to put any pressure on him right now, but she isn't worried about Aiden coming through. He has always been a man of his word."

I bit down hard on the inside of my cheek to stop the smart remarks that were on the tip of my tongue.

I couldn't believe what I was hearing. Was this woman from outer space? Aiden was dating me and everyone in the village knew it. Everyone in the village had tried to push us together for months, which was why we'd taken so long to finally realize we cared about each other in that way. Where was Kayla in all this? Why was she just showing up now?

I swore the woman could read my mind. "I suppose you are wondering why you haven't met Kayla before. She was working as a journalist overseas and just came back at the beginning of the summer. She's looking for work here now, and I'm very happy to have her home."

"Where is she going to work as a journalist around here?" I asked, and then winced at my blunt question. I could only think of a couple of newspapers in the area, and competition was fierce for those. One of them was the Amish *Budget*, and I certainly didn't think that was the beat a globe-trotting journalist would want.

"She's looking for a change. I think after all those years abroad she was just ready to come home and make a new start. She left Holmes County right after high school. That's when she and Aiden went their separate ways. I'm sure if she had stayed, they'd be married with children now." She shook her head. "But my girl went in search of adventure. Aiden, on the other hand, never considered living anywhere else. They really did—excuse me, really do—love each other. It was such a joy for me to see them together again, dancing at the wedding."

I did my best not to make a face. I wished Kayla all the luck in the world finding a new job. If a person didn't want to work in tourism, farming, or for a factory, work was scarce in Holmes County. I was lucky; I'd had a ready-made job waiting for me when I moved here, but I couldn't imagine moving to the county without something in place. I didn't get the impression that a service job would be right for Kayla, but maybe I was wrong. I had only met her briefly.

I held up Jethro again. "I should go find Juliet. I have her pig after all." It was one of those rare times that I was happy to have Jethro at my side. He was my excuse to get as far away from Christine as possible.

She nodded. "Just know that Kayla will give Aiden time, but she is very determined to hold him to his word that they will marry if neither is attached by the end of the year."

I refused to take the bait—even if Christine's words did leave a pit of concern growing in my stomach.

She smiled at me. "Tick tock."

She strolled away. I should have let Cass come with me to the church. She would have knocked the woman in the teeth. It wasn't something I was capable of doing.

"Well, I won't keep you," I said. "I'm sure you have a lot to do . . ."

She smiled, as if she knew what I was up to. "I'm sure we will be seeing each other again."

I hoped not, but because she was a member of the church, I didn't know how I could avoid her.

And now I worried about the conversation Aiden had had with Kayla. I closed my eyes for a moment. I was being ridiculous. I trusted Aiden. I loved Aiden. Yes, things had been tense since the wedding and the murder, but it was just a momentary lapse. He was the best man I knew. He was the best man I had ever known, and I wasn't going to let some boyhood crush with a fancy degree steal him away from me.

I stomped up the church steps feeling more determined than ever to solve this murder. Maybe when I did, Aiden and I could have the heart-to-heart talk I knew we needed to have. We were dating and we had been for a while now, but neither of us had spoken of our intentions.

I didn't want to get married now. My television show would air soon, and I was beginning to really get some traction with the candy shop outside of the county. I was busy. I had a lot of work to do, just as he did. But like any red-blooded woman in a relationship, I wanted to know where this was headed. If it was headed nowhere, nowhere wasn't a place that I could go. It was too emotionally taxing. I had been in a relationship like that before, and what it taught me was exactly what I didn't want. That lesson was the best thing to come out of a year of heartbreak and secrets. I couldn't go back to that place. And even though I didn't think Aiden would send me there, I had to know. I had to hear him promise. I needed his word. I frowned. Wasn't that what he'd given Kayla when they were young? Did Aiden's word from ten years ago mean as much as it would today?

When I stepped into the church, I set Jethro on the floor. "Please don't chew on anything that's not food."

He cocked his head as if he were seriously considering my odd request. I had a feeling that Jethro thought whatever he could fit in his mouth would be considered food.

The church was empty, and I could hear our steps echo through the building as we made our way to Reverend Brook's office near the front of the sanctuary. It was the most likely place for us to find Juliet. Jethro and I walked down the center aisle just as we had on the day of the wedding. How much had changed since that time. I glanced down at the little pig. "You haven't changed, though. You are ever the constant in Harvest."

Jethro smiled up at me as if he was glad to have this title.

There is something eerie about an empty church. A church needs people to make it come alive. My grandmother had told me that church was made up of the people, not the building; that was the Amish belief and the reason the Amish didn't have church buildings of their own. Instead, they met biweekly in members' houses. Every family with enough space was asked to volunteer their home for Sunday mornings. My grandmother's district had never met at Swissmen Sweets because the shop was too small to host all her district members, but she was a regular, making a side dish or sweets to take for the meal after Sunday church wherever it was hosted.

A door creaked somewhere in the building and I spun around, half expecting to see Christine standing in the aisle behind me.

But there was no one there. I told myself it was just the old building settling that made the noise. I really didn't believe that, but I had to tell myself something.

CHAPTER TWENTY-SEVEN

Jethro and I walked up the steps in front of the altar, where there was a narrow door behind the pulpit. This was the door through which Reverend Brook entered the sanctuary each Sunday. The doorknob turned easily in my hand. I let Jethro through and then followed him. The little pig strode down the dark hallway with confidence. If Juliet was now the first lady of the church, I supposed that made Jethro the first pig. It was a title I knew he'd revel in.

I followed the pig down the narrow hallway. To my right was the choir room. The door was open, and navy-blue choir robes hung from metal racks. Two dozen folding chairs stood in a half circle around the room and just as many music stands were lined up in the corner by a large window.

Jethro passed the choir room without so much as a second glance. He was on his way to the reverend's office. Perhaps Jethro viewed it as his office now, too, with his new title as top pig.

I really didn't need Jethro as my guide. I had been to the reverend's office before. The last time I was there I'd caught him playing with Juliet's engagement ring as he contemplated popping the question. Now, they were married. I was happy for Juliet and I wanted her to have the honeymoon she'd always dreamed of—even if that meant pig sitting for the next week. I couldn't think of anyone who deserved a happy life more than Juliet. She was one of those people who was pure sunshine. She was rare in that way, especially considering everything that she had been through in her life.

When Jethro waltzed right in, I guessed that meant I could, too. The minister sat behind his desk, looking at his hands as if he had never seen anything like them before. I had found him in a very similar position before, when he had been playing with Juliet's engagement ring. The one word I would use for the quiet pastor was sad. There was always a melancholy air about the man. Juliet, in contrast, was joyful. That wasn't to say she was never sad, but overall she was a very positive person. She would have to be to put up with so many of Jethro's antics.

"Oh!" Reverend Brook said. "I see you have Jethro with you. Juliet will be very pleased."

"She asked me to meet her at the church to get Jethro's things. I'll be watching him while you two are on your honeymoon."

"She just texted me to ask you to wait. She left the house, then realized that she'd forgotten Jethro's teddy bear. She had to go back for it. He can't sleep without it." He said as if it made perfect sense that a potbellied pig would need a teddy bear to sleep at night.

"The honeymoon is on?" I asked.

"Very much so. The B and B has been very nice about changing our arrival date. The airline was not as helpful. It has been a burden to change the tickets to tomorrow morning, but it's worth the extra money to see a smile on my bride's face."

"Juliet has been looking forward to it." I stood awkwardly in the doorway. Reverend Brook wasn't a person I'd spent much time talking to. He was quiet and reserved, and everything I knew about him came from Juliet.

He nodded, and I saw the strain on his face. I knew he had to be in his fifties, but to me, this was the first time he looked every bit his age. He had always had a youthful appearance, but seeing him now, I would think that he was ten years older than his real age. Something weighed on him.

"I'm glad that you and I have a moment to speak before Juliet arrives. Why don't you have seat, so that we can chat for a moment." He gestured at an armchair in front of his desk.

I raised my eyebrows but did as he asked.

Jethro walked around the room and snuffled the floor. Seeming satisfied, he finally settled on top of my feet with a contented sigh. He could be cute when he wanted to be.

"I hope we aren't keeping you away from your candy shop."

"It's all right," I said. "My friend Cass is there. If they need more help, she is more than willing to jump in." I laughed. "In fact, I have to be careful, because she may have changed where I put everything by the time I get back to the shop. When we worked together at JP Chocolates we could never agree on how the utensils should be stored."

"Yes, well, that does sound problematic." He sighed, as if the weight of the world was on his shoulders.

"Does this have to do with Leeza? Is that why you want to talk to me while Juliet isn't here?"

"Yes." He nodded. "This does involve Leeza. I made a mistake with her, and now I feel terrible because of what happened."

"You mean making the anonymous call about the still?"

He nodded. "I should have handled it differently. At the very least, I should have secured her safety before involving the police."

"Then what made you do it?" I asked.

He put his elbows on the desktop and pressed his fingers together, making a steeple. "Leeza and I had a lot in common. I suppose that's why I wanted to help her when she came in for counseling. She was at rock bottom that very first session. I know what it looks like, and I know what it feels like, too."

I blinked at him. "What do you mean?"

He took a breath, as if he had to gather his strength. "I'm an alcoholic. I haven't taken a drop of alcohol in over thirty years, but I'm still an alcoholic. You're always one. Even if everything else in your life seems to be perfect, you are still an addict and have to fight the temptation. When you have a real addiction, you're always in recovery."

My mouth fell open. This was the last thing I had expected him to say.

He licked his lips. "I went to AA for years. The reason I wanted to sign up for Compassion for Crisis was because I know what it feels like to be without a home. I thought I could make a difference in the lives of people like Leeza."

"Did you tell them that you were a recovering alcoholic, too?"

He looked down at his hands folded on the desktop. "No. I've never told anyone in Holmes County before. It was something that I struggled with as a young adult growing up in Iowa. A local pastor helped me and encouraged me to attend the seminary. I haven't had a drop of alcohol since. I attended seminary in Indiana, where no one knew me." He took a breath. "That was intentional. I didn't want anyone to know about my past. I didn't want to give them a reason to doubt my decision to be a pastor, or watch me to see if I was drinking again." He swallowed and looked up at me. "By the time I finished seminary, I had completely changed who I was. I was a new man."

"But doesn't your family back in Iowa know about your history?"

"I was an only child and my parents passed away when I was a young man. I broke off contact with everyone else in Iowa. I suppose some of my old friends could have looked me up. I didn't change my name, but I have been careful to stay off social media. I don't want to be found, and for the last thirty some years, I haven't been."

I squeezed the armrests of my chair. "Why are you telling me all this now? You could have easily kept your secret."

"I'm not so sure of that." He sighed. "I am a suspect in this case, and I know that the sheriff's department is looking into my history. I never committed any crimes, but I fear that Aiden will find out and wonder why his mother doesn't know."

"You never told Juliet?" I asked, surprised. I knew that he'd said he had never told anyone in Holmes County, but I didn't count Juliet in that number. They were married after all. Maybe I was naïve in assuming that married couples told each other everything.

As I thought this, I remembered Aiden's past relationship with Kayla. We weren't married, but he had never mentioned her. I remembered having a conversation with him about my past relationship, but he'd also met Eric, who'd come to Holmes County with the hope of winning me back during the Christmas holidays. Would I have been so candid with Aiden about Eric if I hadn't been forced to?

I didn't have the answer to that.

"I didn't tell my congregation because I wanted the church to believe I was their mild-mannered minister and had always been that way. That wasn't my reason for keeping it from Juliet. When Juliet told me about her ex-husband . . ." He trailed off.

I immediately understood. Juliet's first husband, Aiden's father, had been an abusive alcoholic. She'd run away from everything and everyone she knew in South Carolina to escape him and to save her son from abuse. It was very likely Juliet would have shied away from Reverend Brook if she knew he was an alcoholic, too.

"Juliet believes that I don't drink because I am a man of the cloth. She doesn't know about my recovery. No one in Harvest does. It all happened before I came here to take over the church."

I shifted to the edge of my seat. It felt as if the armchair was trying to swallow me whole. "Then why are you telling me now? What bearing does this have on Leeza's death?"

He flattened his palms on his desk. "I suppose I want to explain my reason for calling the police."

I waited.

"It just made me so angry when I learned about the still. I knew it would hurt people like Leeza, those struggling with drink. I thought I did the right thing by telling the police."

"Anonymously." I let the word hang in the air.

"Maybe you're right and I should have admitted who I was, but I was too afraid it would get back to Aiden that I was the one who'd reported it. I was afraid somehow he would learn about my past because of it. Maybe this wasn't logical thinking, but there you have it." He leaned back in his chair, deflated.

"Why don't you want Aiden to know?" I asked. "He won't tell his mother if you ask him not to."

"I don't want him to worry. And he would worry if his mother married another alcoholic. I had my own fears about it, too. There are times I want a drink so badly I break out into a sweat. I have been able to resist that temptation the last thirty years. Aiden would look at me differently if he knew."

"I think you aren't giving Aiden enough credit, or Juliet either, for that matter. Everyone has demons they have to wrestle with. No one is perfect," I said.

"Maybe so, but whether it is fair or not, the church holds pastors to another standard. We may not be perfect, but we are supposed to be close to it. Please promise me that you won't tell Juliet or Aiden. It may be that I will have to tell them myself, but I need them to hear it from me. They deserve the whole story. Juliet most especially."

"If Aiden asks me outright, I won't lie to him," I said.

He nodded. "That's fair."

"Tell me more about Leeza."

He sighed. "When I first met her, she had just started drinking again. Not heavily, she said, but as any recovering alcoholic knows, it doesn't take more than a sip to fall back into the pit."

"Did she tell you why she'd started drinking again and how long she was sober?"

He shook his head. "She was sober for almost seven months. She refused to tell me why she began drinking again. However, she did tell me the business she was in."

"The still?"

"Yes, she admitted that she was a runner for the still. I suppose that was what really spurred me to tell the police. It made me so angry." He looked at his hands again. "I shouldn't have taken it personally. That is the first thing they teach you in pastoral counseling. What the other person is dealing with isn't about you. I was supposed to be a sounding board for her as she worked out her problems and decided what to do next, but I couldn't be just that. It's people like her that make it so easy for people like me to slip up. And moonshine is powerful drink. It wouldn't take much to fall off the wagon with a drink like that. It made me furious that she, who struggled with drinking, too, would tempt people away like that."

I bit the inside of my lip. "So what did you do?"

He looked up at me again. "I knew I had to do something to stop it. She couldn't continue to lead people astray. It wasn't right. The next time she came in, I talked to her more about the still. She was certainly under the influence of alcohol then. She was more forthcoming. She told me the still was in Harvest Woods. Not the exact location, but I thought it was enough." He frowned. "That's what I wanted to learn. After I left the community center that night I made an anonymous call to the sheriff's department and told them about the still. However, I didn't mention Leeza."

"Did the department act on your tip?"

"I believe they did. In church the next Sunday, my parishioners were chatting about a raid that took place in Harvest Woods."

I raised my eyebrows.

"I felt relieved when I heard. I felt I had done the right thing."

"This was why she called you a traitor at the wedding?"

He frowned. "I believe so. She must have surmised that I was the one who tipped off the sheriff's department." He paused. "But I don't even know how she knew who I was. We didn't talk about my church or what I did for a living. I certainly wouldn't have told any of the people who I counseled that I was about to get married."

"She must have found out who you were some way. It wouldn't be hard."

"I suppose not."

"Do you think this was why she was killed? Because of your tip?"

"It is my fear, yes." He folded his hands. "I'm afraid that moonshiners retaliated for losing their still and killed her. They left her body on my church steps to send a message."

It was a decent theory.

"The worst part is, I need to tell Juliet all this. Telling her about my past had been my greatest fear ever since I met her." He rubbed his forehead. "I suppose wrestling with whether or not I should share this secret was why it took me so long to tell her how I really felt. When I counsel engaged couples, I always tell them that honesty is the most important thing in a relationship. I know that's true, but I couldn't bring myself to be honest with Juliet. I thought I could keep the secret. And now that we are married, I will be forced to tell her anyway. What's worse, I *should* have told her before we ever took our vows!" He put his face in his hands. "I don't know if she will ever be able to forgive me."

"Juliet loves you," I said. "I knew that a year ago when I first moved here, even before she admitted it to anyone."

The minister lifted his head.

"Yes, it's very possible that she will be upset," I said. "But if it's real love, you will get through it."

He gave me a small smile. "Have you thought of being a counselor?"

I smiled. "No, I have too many jobs as it is." I leaned forward in my chair. "You have to tell her."

"Simon?" Juliet's voice called from the hallway. "Is Bailey here?"

I leaned back in my seat. "And now is your chance."

CHAPTER TWENTY-EIGHT

Juliet thanked me up and down for taking care of Jethro while she and Reverend Brook went on their trip, and then she showered Jethro with hugs and kisses before putting him back on the floor. "The reverend and I are on a flight early tomorrow morning to Halifax, Nova Scotia. From there, we will rent a car and drive to Prince Edward Island." She clasped her hands in front of her chest. "I cannot wait! This has been a place I've wanted to go since I was a young girl. It's made even more special because I will be sharing the experience with my love." She sighed. "Because we will be crossing an international border, there is no way to take Jethro with us. Not taking him is my only regret about this trip. Do you know the Canadians consider him livestock? I don't know when I have heard something so offensive."

I glanced down at the little pig, who by the definition of livestock was just that. I kept those thoughts to myself.

Juliet smiled at me. "I am sorry to be giving Jethro to you so early. I don't know if Aiden told you or not, but we have to leave for the airport at three in the morning. I thought it was best to give you Jethro now. He doesn't like to have his beauty rest disturbed."

Neither did I, and neither did Cass, who was staying at my house. I could imagine the choice words she would have said if she'd been woken up in the wee hours by Jethro.

"He will be well-taken care of," I promised.

"I know." Tears welled up in Juliet's eyes.

Reverend Brook put his arm around her. "My dear, let Bailey and Jethro go back to the candy shop. There are some things you and I need to discuss before we leave on our trip." The reverend nodded at me.

Inwardly, I gave a sigh of relief. He needed to tell Juliet about his past. I didn't think it was fair of him to ask me to keep that secret.

Juliet's eyes were wide, and she nodded. Juliet kissed Jethro's snout one more time, and then the pig and I were out the door. Jethro and I trotted back through the sanctuary. This time I had him on his pink-and-white, polka-dotted leash that only made me feel slightly more confident he wouldn't run away.

Over my opposite shoulder was his giant duffel bag of pig supplies. When I went back and forth to New York, I traveled lighter than Jethro did to stay in his home village. It was true that he would be living with me for a week, but how many toys did a pig need?

"What are you doing with that pig?" a deep voice

asked. I was just about at the sanctuary door. I turned and saw Sal walking down the aisle carrying a spray bottle and a rag.

I frowned at him. "I'm taking care of Jethro while Reverend Brook and Juliet go on their honeymoon."

"No one ever asks me to take care of the pig. I'm just as capable as you are."

And with such a sunny disposition, too.

"I saw your friend outside the church again."

"Cass?" I asked.

"Who?"

"My friend from New York?" I asked.

He sprayed the cloth, and there was a sharp scent of lemon in the air. He began polishing the back of a pew with a cloth. "Not the purple-haired woman. What's gotten into people's heads that they want to color their hair all these unnatural colors? It's shameful, if you ask me. Just a bunch of young folks who want to get attention. At least that's what they are in my book."

I was about to leave when he said, "It was one of your Amish friends. He came to the church the afternoon after you found that dead lady on the steps."

I frowned, trying to remember what Amish man he could be talking about. Then it hit me. "Do you mean the man who was talking to Deputy Little?"

He nodded. "Deputy Little, you, and Juliet. He seemed mighty angry. He was just here and wanted to see the minister, but I told him Reverend Brook wasn't here. He left."

I stared at him. One of the prime murder suspects was right here at the church while I spoke to Reverend Brook, and Sal had chased him away? Not that I wanted the Amish man to find Reverend Brook. I didn't think that would end well.

"Where did he go?"

"Don't know. He left in a buggy."

I bit the inside of my lip before I headed out of the church. Since the Amish man had had a head start, it was unlikely I'd be able to catch him even if I ran out of the church that very moment and jumped in my car. "Why are you telling me this when he's gone?"

He shrugged. "No particular reason. I just thought you would like to know, seeing how nosy you can be."

I did like to know.

Jethro and I left the church and I was even more confused than I had been. We walked toward the gazebo. It was close to six now, but because it was the middle of the summer, the sun hung high in the sky. Even so, Uriah and the other Amish men who were setting up the square for the Fourth of July celebration had gone. In their wake, tables, booths, and twinkle lights dotted the square. I knew when the booths were full and the visitors arrived, everything would go perfectly. Margot wouldn't accept anything less.

As I drew closer to the gazebo, I noticed two people standing very close together in the middle of it. It was a man and a woman. The gazebo was a common spot in the county for proposal and wedding pictures. This was neither of those. It was Aiden and Kayla standing there. She held his hands in hers. "Do you remember when we stood here all those years ago and made our promise to marry each other?"

"Kayla . . ." Aiden said.

At the same time, I gasped. Aiden heard it, because his head swung in my direction, and I ducked below the bushes. Jethro stared at me with wide brown eyes, as if to ask what was going on.

I put a finger to my lips. This was not the time or the place for any piggy antics.

"Aiden, you need to pay attention. This is important."

"I think you misunderstood . . ." Aiden said.

"I didn't misunderstand anything." Her tone became huffy. "You said if neither of us were married by age thirty-three, we'd marry each other."

"You can't hold me to a promise I made when I was eighteen."

A sharp stick poked me in the back, and Jethro chewed on his leash. I wondered if I could slink away without being seen. I might have been able to do it if it had not been for the pig. Jethro didn't slink anywhere. He barreled, marched, and pranced. As far as he was concerned, people should be happy to see him.

"It was your idea," Kayla snapped in a nasal voice.

I made a face at the pig. It seemed to me Miss Perfect was a wee bit testy. I can't say I felt bad for her; she was in the process of trying to steal my boyfriend.

"It was my idea when I was eighteen." Aiden kept his voice level. It was the same tone I had heard him use many times with irate criminals. I thought that might be telling where this conversation was about to go.

"Now," Aiden went on, "I agreed to come here and meet you because you implied you knew something about the murder."

"That's what you have driven me to, Aiden. I just want your attention, and I have to lie about the murder to get it." She sounded as if she was about to cry.

"You shouldn't waste a law enforcement officer's time like this." His voice was colder than before.

I shifted my crouched stance to move away from

the pointy branch and nearly tipped over like the teapot in the children's song. Jethro gave me a little bump with his snout to keep me upright. "Thanks," I whispered. He wasn't always a bad pig.

"You shouldn't waste my time by making me believe that you are a man of your word," she snapped.

Aiden said something I couldn't hear.

I gave Jethro a look. I thought it was time to make our exit. It was clear to me that I didn't need to worry about Aiden running away with his high school sweetheart, and I very much did not want to be caught spying. There was a good chance I might be if I crouched there like this any longer. My thighs were already cramping from the awkward position.

However, the question was how to make my escape. I couldn't walk by the gazebo. They would surely see me. My best bet was staying in the bushes under their eye level. If I had been alone, I could have done it. Jethro, however, might blow my cover. As if to prove my point, he stuck his nose in the bushes and began to make a snuffling sound. I pulled him back from the branches, and he snorted. I covered his mouth to muffle the sound, and he licked my hand.

"Gross," I hissed.

There was a scuffling sound above us in the gazebo.

"There's still something between us and you have the nerve to deny it. I thought you were better than that, Aiden Brody. I'm sorry to see I was so very wrong," Kayla cried.

Jethro snorted again. I clamped my hand down on his snout.

Stomp, stomp, stomp sounded over the gazebo floor, and a second later, Aiden marched across the green and jumped into his car. Kayla ran after him. "Aiden, wait!"

He turned around. "Please, Kayla. It's over. Please leave me alone. I have to get back to work. This murder investigation might not be important to you, but it's very important to me and those who knew the victim. Go back to wherever it was you ran to when we were young and leave me be."

"This is about the candy maker, isn't it?" She sniffled.

"Her name is Bailey," he snapped.

Jethro and I shared a look. It was sort of like watching a soap opera in which you were a main character but not invited to the reading.

"Are you interested in her because she's from New York?" Kayla flipped her long red hair over her shoulder. "I've heard of her television show. Her rising fame must be very enticing, not that I've ever taken you for a guy who was into that sort of thing."

"It's not just about Bailey, although she's a big part of it. It's about me not being eighteen any longer. I've changed. I want different things than I did before. Now, if you would let me get on with it, I have a murder to solve."

"If you leave now, Aiden, you will never have another chance with me. This is it," Kayla said.

"Good, because that's what I want." He climbed into his departmental SUV and drove away.

Around the corner of the gazebo, I watched Kayla, who stood on the side a long while with her head down. I bit my lip. I didn't know why, but I felt bad for her. She must really have loved him, or thought she did. Either way, she was hurting.

After what seemed like forever, she walked to another car parked along the square, climbed in, and drove away. When her car was out of sight, I released the little pig and let myself fall on my backside. My legs were screaming from crouching so long. I lay on my back in the grass.

I let myself rest there for a bit. Jethro cocked his head.

"Hey, maybe I'm looking a little pathetic at the moment, but at least I don't have to worry about my boyfriend leaving me for his childhood sweetheart."

Jethro cocked his head in the other direction.

When I stood up, I picked up Jethro's huge travel bag. "And okay, I need to tell Aiden what I overheard. I know that, but that conversation can wait until after the murder investigation is settled."

"I'm really worried about going back home now that I know you lie in the middle of the village square and converse with a pig," Cass said.

I jumped. "How long have you been standing there?"

"Just long enough to witness your heart-to-heart with this little oinker."

I brushed grass off my backside. "You didn't see Aiden, then?"

"Aiden?" She looked around. "Is Hot Cop here?"

"He was, but never mind."

Cass looked as if she wasn't going to let it go, so I interrupted her. Before she could say anything more, I told her about my conversation with Reverend Brook. I left out his confession about alcoholism—it didn't feel right to tell her that when Aiden didn't even know—but shared what he had told me about Leeza and the still.

"I think we should go to Harvest Woods and take a look," I suggested.

"Haven't the police already done that?" she asked.

"Probably," I conceded.

"Wouldn't Aiden have told you if they'd found the still?"

"I'm not sure," I said.

She stared at me. "You mean go into the woods? There are bugs and it's stinking hot, too."

"We aren't going into the woods. I just want to see if there is any sign of what might be going on from the outside."

"Sure," Cass said and looked down at the pig. "That's what she said."

Her sarcasm wasn't lost on me.

CHAPTER TWENTY-NINE

We crossed Main Street in front of the candy shop, and I was about to turn in the direction of my car when Cass placed a hand on my arm. "Wait. Before we leave, you have to talk to your grandmother."

I shook my head. "You're right. I don't know where my head was at. Yes, we should tell her what we are up to and—"

Before I could finish speaking, she grabbed my arm and squeezed.

"Ouch. Why did—"

She pointed down the sidewalk. He was here. It was the man who'd ran away from Deputy Little. He had a heavy-looking knapsack slung over his left shoulder as he walked behind the far side of Esh Family Pretzels and disappeared.

I dropped Jethro's overnight bag outside the candy shop, scooped up Jethro, and Cass and I went into the alley between the pretzel shop and Swissmen Sweets.

Jethro kicked at me a bit, but I whispered in his ear that if he was good, I'd give him three marshmallows as a treat when we got inside the candy shop. He stopped wiggling then. Cass stopped at the back edge of the pretzel shop and peered around the corner. She waved at me to do the same. Jethro and I peeked around the side.

Cass was right. The man with the knapsack was the Amish man who'd run away from Deputy Little, and he wasn't alone. He stood across from Abel Esh. I stifled a gasp. Cass put a finger to her mouth.

I clamped my free hand over my mouth. I should have known Abel would somehow be involved with this. He'd hinted as much the last time I saw him.

"Do you have it?" Abel asked.

The other man patted his knapsack. "I have your order right here. Do you have the money?"

"I'll give you the money when I see the 'shine."

Cass tensed up when Abel said that. I was sure I did, too. We watched with fascination when the unknown Amish man set his knapsack on the dirty ground, opened it, and removed a liter glass bottle.

"There's two of them?" Abel asked.

The man zipped up the knapsack and straightened. He slung it over his shoulder again. "That's right. Do you have the money?"

Abel reached into his pocket and came out with a wad of bills.

Cass poked me in the ribs, as if to tell me to pay attention. I winced. I didn't know how I could miss that money. Just then, the back door of Swissmen Sweets opened and Emily came out holding a bag of trash. She threw it in the dumpster and froze when she saw her brother standing there with the other man.

"Abel, what are you doing?" Emily asked.

He said something back to her in Pennsylvania Dutch. I didn't know what it was, but it was clearly rude. Her face turned bright red and she took a step to go back in the shop. She froze a second time. "Bailey?"

"The jig is up!" Cass cried.

The Amish man took that as his cue to bolt. He didn't give Abel the moonshine, nor did he take the money. He ran back around the side of the building and Cass dashed after him. What on earth did she think she was going to do if she caught him? I prayed she wouldn't. I didn't want her to get hurt.

Abel glowered at me. "What are you doing there?" He paused. "With a pig?"

"You were with the man who was looking for Leeza. That could very well be her killer and you were buying moonshine from him. That's illegal!" I cried.

He laughed.

"I can call the sheriff's department and report you for buying illegal moonshine."

He laughed again and shook his head. "I'm not worried."

Cass came back around the side of the building, panting. "That Amish dude, whoever he is, really should consider being an Olympic sprinter. He can move." She looked at Abel, Emily, and me. "What's going on?"

"I was telling Abel it's illegal to buy moonshine and I'm going to report him."

"I didn't even get the 'shine," Abel complained. "What good will it do you to report that I almost bought moonshine? It's your word against mine."

Cass glared at him. "It's both of our words against you, and Emily's, too."

Emily turned pale when Cass said that.

Abel focused on his youngest sister. "Emily, you won't do anything more to cause pain for our family, will you?" He cocked his head condescendingly. "Don't you think you've done enough?"

"Leave her alone," I snapped. Then I turned back to Emily. "Emily, you don't have to be here for this. Go back into the candy shop."

"That's right, Emily," Abel said. "You're free to abandon your family at any time. It's what you're *gut* at."

Emily wrung the end of her apron. "Bailey, are you really going to the police about this?"

"I think I have to," I said. "Aiden is looking for a killer with ties to moonshine. It could be that very man who fled just a minute ago."

"*Ya*, but Abel had nothing to do with it," she replied. "Please, Bailey. My family has been through so much already. They don't need any more trouble."

Abel's lips curved into a Grinch-worthy grin. "That's right, Sister. Tell her everything we have been through."

Tears gathered in Emily's eyes.

The back door of Esh Family Pretzels slammed open. "What is going on out here?" Esther Esh wanted to know. Then she said to her sister, "Emily, I should have known. You have been the root of all the trouble in our family."

Emily's delicate face flushed.

"Fine!" I said. "I won't say anything about you to the police, but it's not for your sake. It's for Emily's."

Abel nodded. "I'm fine with that."

"But you have to tell me about the man who was just here."

Abel shrugged, as if it was of no consequence to him, and maybe that was true, because I'd promised to keep him out of it, at least as far as the police were concerned.

"That's Jonathan Troyer. He's from a district close to Berlin, and he just happens to be a moonshiner. He makes the best 'shine in the county."

"Amish moonshiners?" Cass asked. "Now I've heard everything."

"What's his connection to Leeza?" I asked Abel.

"They are from the same district," he said.

"Where can I find him?" I asked.

Abel shrugged. "I don't know that. When I want some 'shine, I leave a note in an old abandoned potting shed."

"Where's the shed?" I asked.

"It's near Harvest Woods. It's on the edge of the berry farm."

Cass and I shared a look. Did that mean Leeza's whole family was involved in the production of moonshine? I tried not to get ahead of myself with my questions. "Was he making moonshine in Harvest Woods?"

"That would be my guess." Abel shrugged. "But unlike some people, I don't ask a lot of questions."

"That's enough," Esther said. "No more questions."

"Esther—" Emily began.

Esther glared at her younger sister. "You made your choice about whose side you're on long ago, little sister." She added something in the Amish language that I didn't understand. However, by the sharpness of her tone, I knew it was cruel. That was confirmed when Emily ran back inside the candy shop.

"Are you satisfied, Bailey King?" Esther asked. "What makes you think that you can come into our world and ask all these questions and disturb our simple lives? Life was so much better in this village before you came along."

I jerked back at her words.

Cass took my hand in hers. "I do know one thing. I used to think all Amish people were sweet and kind. I'm sorry to say that you've proved me wrong." She tugged on my hand. "Let's go, Bai."

I stumbled after her with Jethro still in the crook of my other arm.

CHAPTER THIRTY

Cass and I hurried through the front door of Swiss-men Sweets. It was evening, and the shop had closed over an hour before. *Maami* came through the kitchen door. "What has happened? Emily ran into the kitchen crying, and she won't tell Charlotte or me what is wrong."

"Esther and Abel happened," I said.

Maami patted her white hair. "I was afraid it was something like that." Her face fell. "No one can cut you to the quick quite as well as someone you love."

"I don't know why she would love them after the way they have treated her," Cass said. "She should forget about them. She has Swissmen Sweets now, and her husband's family."

My grandmother shook her head. "It's not that easy, and even if you do have to say goodbye to someone, you will continue to think of them."

Cass pressed her lips together as if she wasn't sure about that, and I wondered if my grandmother was speaking from experience. Was she referring to the time when my father left the Amish, or was it something else? I thought she and my father had come to terms with his choice.

Emily and Charlotte came out of the kitchen. Emily's eyes were red, but she was no longer crying. "Clara, I'm sorry I came in like that."

My grandmother wrapped her in a hug. "My girl, there is no need to apologize. We all have tears under the surface."

Emily stepped back and swallowed hard. I thought that she might cry again, but she was able to keep it together.

A buggy pulled up in front of the candy shop, and Emily sighed with relief. "That is my husband. I will be here early tomorrow to help prepare for the Fourth of July celebration." She gave my grandmother another hug and then turned to me. "Bailey, I hope you intend to keep your promise."

I opened and closed my mouth. Whether I intended them or not, the words came out. "I will."

She hugged me, too, then. "*Danki.*" She then scooped Nutmeg off the floor and kissed the cat's cheek before she set him down again next to Jethro and Puff. I shook my head. Swissmen Sweets looked as much like a petting zoo as a candy shop with the menagerie we had in it.

Emily waved at all of us. "Tomorrow." She went out the door.

The bell attached to the front door clanged as it closed behind her.

"Yeesh," Charlotte said. "And I thought I had problems with my family."

My grandmother looked at her. "Everyone has burdens. It's the way you choose to face the burdens that is the measure of a person. When you can, you should deal with them prayerfully and look to *Gott* for guidance."

I bit my lip. I didn't know how God was going to mend the rift between Emily and her older siblings. I thought the only way that would happen was if Abel and Esther had a change of heart. I couldn't imagine that happening at this point.

"What led to Emily speaking with her siblings?" *Maami* asked. "I didn't know they were even saying hello to her."

As quickly as I could, I told Charlotte and *Maami* about Abel and the moonshiner. "Emily doesn't want me to tell Aiden that Abel tried to buy moonshine."

My grandmother nodded. "I can see why she would feel that way."

"What do you think I should do?" I asked.

"Let *Gott* lead you to what is right."

That was decidedly not helpful, and I started moving around the front room of the shop, flipping chairs over onto the tops of the tables for the night. Charlotte went back into the kitchen to finish cleaning up in there.

"*Maami*, do you know this Jonathan Troyer who was about to sell Abel moonshine?"

My grandmother pulled a spray bottle of vinegar and water out from under the counter and began cleaning the glass-domed counter. "*Ya.* Although Jonathan dresses like an Amish man, he no longer belongs to any one district. He wasn't baptized into the church. There have been rumors that he has been involved in crimes around the county, but those are only whispers."

"Any mention of moonshine?" I asked.

Maami shook her head. "People say Jonathan would do anything to make money."

"Anything?" I asked with a shiver.

"Wow, Clara," Cass said after she put the last chair on one of the tables. "You are quite a font of information. It must run in the family."

I looked at Cass out of the corner of my eye. "Please don't say that in front of Aiden. He will have an instant ulcer at the very idea."

Cass gave me a thumbs-up.

Maami finished cleaning the counter and tucked the spray bottle away. "What are you going to do now, Bailey?"

I rubbed the back of my neck. "I'll call Aiden and tell him what we know."

"And then we are going to check out Harvest Woods," Cass said.

I glanced at Cass. "On the way back to my house."

Cass eyed me. "That's so not on the way to your house, but I'll go with your story. That's what best friends do."

"What do you think we should do, *Maami*?"

She took a deep breath. "Calling Aiden is *gut*. He would not want you to visit Harvest Woods, but if I were you, I would go."

"You would?"

She nodded. "This man, Jonathan, has to be found. Whether he killed Leeza or not, he's still a danger to the Amish community. I have told you about the buggy accidents that have happened in the county because of alcohol."

I nodded.

"There was one a few weeks ago in which a young man died."

"The one with the tree."

She nodded. "One of the customers told me that moonshine was in the buggy with him."

As Cass and I walked to my car on Apple Street, I carried Puff and she walked Jethro on his leash. I was well aware of what an odd foursome we must have made.

With the animals tucked safely in the back of my car, I turned it on, cranked up the air conditioner, and called Aiden, but my call went directly to voice mail. I knew he was busy. He was juggling a murder investigation, the sheriff, and now BCI. This was one of the most high-pressure cases he had ever had. I left a message, telling him what I knew about Jonathan Troyer and omitting any mention of Abel as I'd promised Emily I would. I also told him that Cass and I were going to drive by Harvest Woods.

When I ended the call, Cass looked at me. "You do know that he's going to be upset about the Harvest Woods thing."

"I know, but I promised him once I would tell him where I'm going . . . most of the time."

She shrugged and buckled her seat belt. "It's your funeral."

"Let's hope it doesn't come to that," I said, worried that she just might be right.

CHAPTER THIRTY-ONE

Fifteen minutes later, I slowed my car to a roll as we went by the Chupps' strawberry patch on the way to Harvest Woods. Though it was late afternoon, there were two buggies parked by the strawberry sign, and I spotted Amish women and children in the patch picking berries. I recognized Essie Chupp running through the patch along with them. A woman was with her. I thought it might be the woman I'd seen at the Chupps' home, the woman I had assumed was RJ's wife and Essie's mother.

I glanced at Cass. "Should we stop?"

She shook her head. "Let's look at the woods first, and then we will come back. I really don't want to be anywhere close to those woods after dark."

It was a couple of hours before sunset, but I felt the same way, and I continued down the road. Harvest Woods was about a mile and a half from the Chupp berry farm. Between the farm and the wood was wide-open, overgrown pasture. The grass and weeds were so tall that if we got out of the car, they would come up to my hip. At the moment, there weren't any cattle or other livestock in the field.

"Just think of all the bugs that must be in there," Cass said with a shiver.

"There will be bugs in the woods, too. It's July after all."

"Yeah, but we aren't going into the woods."

"Right."

Jethro peered out the back window as if he wanted to have a better look. Puff sulked on the seat, probably because the little pig was paying attention to something other than her.

The pasture fell away and the woods came into view.

"Do you think we have enough strawberries for tomorrow?" Cass asked. "When we go back to the patch, maybe we should pick a few more."

"We picked four hundred and eleven. I know the exact number because Charlotte counted them when she dipped them in chocolate."

"That's probably enough." She grinned.

"If it's not, we have plenty of other candies to sell." Cass nodded.

I shifted the car into Park. There was no trail sign or real entrance into the woods. I stopped the car along the side of the road.

Cass and I stared into the woods through the car window. It was an impenetrable wall of trees. Before learning about moonshining in Harvest, all I had ever known about the woods was that it was a popular place for hunters. It was summer, so I believed it wasn't the season for hunting of any sort. I wasn't going to go inside the forest and risk it, though.

She glanced at me. "Are we going to get out?"

"I don't know. Maybe we shouldn't."

She cocked her head. "We can't sit here all day. What did we come all this way for if we never get out of the car?"

I arched my brow at her. "I guess I just wanted to see it. I'm trying to imagine why Leeza would have gone in there if I'm right in guessing that this is the place where she died."

She opened the car door and got out.

I sighed and followed her. "Stay here," I said to the pig and rabbit. I left the front window open for them.

Cass walked to the edge of the woods. "Looks like there is some semblance of a path here." She swatted the air and smacked her own arm. "And mosquitoes. I need bug spray."

"It is the Midwest and it is summer." I swatted one away from my face. "There's some on the floor in the back seat." I had learned last summer that I shouldn't go anywhere in Holmes County in the summer without bug spray. The horse flies and mosquitoes were fierce out in the country.

Cass opened the back door and reached under her seat. She pulled out the largest bottle of bug spray I had ever seen and doused herself with it. It wasn't like the small bottle I kept in the car.

"Where on earth did you get that?" I yelped and swatted at a mosquito that landed on my arm.

"I brought it from New York. I ordered it online from this outbacker trail website. See." She pointed to the bottle. "It promises right here 'no bites guaranteed.'" She held out the bottle to me. "Want some?"

Another mosquito landed on my shirt and I smacked

it away. I took the bottle from her and sprayed myself, not quite as liberally as Cass had. I wasn't a fan of the medicinal-herbal scent.

"Are you sure it's safe to shower with it like you are?" I asked when she took the bottle from me and doused herself with round two.

"No, but neither is West Nile virus."

She was about to put it under the seat when Jethro jumped out of the car and knocked her down onto the grass beside the country road.

"Jethro!" I leaped for the pig, landing on my stomach in the dead leaves along the side of the road. I missed. The little pig squealed and ran into the woods.

Cass and I just stood there for a moment in complete shock.

"That's not good," she said.

No, it wasn't.

"We have to get him out of there," I said.

Cass glanced back at the car. "Will Puff be okay?"

"She will be fine. Let's just open all the windows for her. She can't climb out." I ran around the car and lowered the power windows.

We did this as quickly as possible, and Puff looked at us with big, blue eyes. I could almost read the question on her bunny face. *Where did Jethro go?*

"I don't know," I whispered to her. It was taking all my willpower to fight back the panic that rose in my chest. I had to find Jethro. I couldn't lose him. Juliet would never recover.

Cass sprayed herself with more bug spray for good measure. "Let's move out."

I had an awful feeling about this.

Inside the woods, I called, "Jethro! Jethro!" There

was no answer. "How can we possibly know where he went?"

"No idea," Cass said and swatted at another mosquito. I didn't know how well her spray was working because I was sure I'd been bitten twice since we'd entered the woods.

"He's not the bravest pig in the bunch. He's probably hiding," I said. "That will make it even more difficult to find him. There are so many places to hide in the woods. Maybe we should call Aiden."

"And report a missing pig to the police? Do you really think the sheriff will contribute any extra manpower to that search?"

I chewed on the inside of my lower lip.

"You do know that this is how every horror movie starts, right? Two girls walking in a place they shouldn't be. It's very possible we will be chopped into bits."

There was a scuffling to my left and I thought I saw a flash of white and black. "Jethro!" I took off after what I thought was the pig. I heard Cass crash through the forest after me, cursing as she went. I kept running, following the white-and-black bullet of a pig. It was incredible how fast he could run.

"Bai! Stop!" Cass called behind me. "I'm going to die."

I slowed down. Jethro was nowhere to be seen. I'd lost him. I spun around and watched as Cass stumbled her way through the brush to reach me.

"Dear God, did you take up running after moving to Ohio?" she panted.

"The only running I do is after that pig, but it seems to happen with a certain amount of frequency." I bent at the waist to catch my breath. I didn't realize how much I had exerted myself until I stopped moving. My body was happy to remind me that I was not an athlete by any measure.

"Where the heck are we?" Cass asked.

I grimaced. "In Harvest Woods."

She gave me a look. "I know *that*."

I removed my phone from the back pocket of my jeans and turned on the GPS. From what I could see, we were in the middle of the great, green glob that was Harvest Woods. I zoomed in to see the road where we'd left the car. "I think we went a mile away from the road."

"No wonder I'm dying. I haven't run the mile since high school gym, and even then I cheated by running across the soccer field when the gym teacher wasn't looking. We should go back."

I frowned down at the light blue arrow that marked where we were. "Jethro was right here." I pointed at the screen, as if it was some sort of proof. "Let's give it ten more minutes, and then I will call Aiden. If we don't find Jethro in that time, we will need help."

She shook her head. "A pig search and rescue— only in Ohio."

"Maybe not a sanctioned one, but Aiden will look, and I'm sure Deputy Little will pitch in, too. Jethro!" I called again.

I glanced over my shoulder at Cass. She looked so out of place in her black designer jeans and tank top, with her purple and black hair matted to her forehead. It was July and we were in the middle of the woods. The thing that I'd learned about Ohio summers was that they were hot and humid. If a cold front wasn't coming in, the temperature sweltered in the mideighties. That wouldn't be so bad, except for the 80 percent humidity on top of the heat. "Maybe you should go back to the car and call Aiden. I can keep looking," I said.

"Oh, so you want me to let you get chopped up into bits alone? What do you think I could say to Hot Cop if that happened? Nothing. Nothing at all. He would surely ask why I hadn't gone into the woods with you. Being from New York City is not a good answer." She swatted at the air. "Neither are the bugs. I swear, I will never complain about the cockroaches in the city again." She froze. "Do you think there are ticks out here? If I find a tick on me, you will never hear the end of it."

I didn't doubt for a minute that was true. "Just stick to the path and don't touch anything."

"Path? This little deer trail does not qualify as a path."

There was a snap like a twig breaking somewhere in the woods.

"What the heck was that?" Cass asked in a hoarse whisper.

"It was probably a deer, or it could have been Jethro. Let's go look."

"I don't want to meet a deer in the woods. I've seen those videos on the internet where a deer goes all kung fu on an unsuspecting hiker. I can't have a deer kicking me in the face. I've spent a fortune on my skin."

"I haven't heard of any kung fu deer here in Holmes County." I quickened my pace toward the sound. I prayed it was Jethro. If it turned out not to be him, I promised myself that I would go back to the car and call Aiden. It was going to be a very difficult call to make. How many girlfriends have to tell their boyfriends that they've lost their mothers' pigs? I bet I was the one and only.

I came to the edge of a tiny clearing. There was a stream running through it. I froze, and Cass's nose ran into my back. "Geez, let me know when you are going to hit the brakes like that."

"Wait," I hissed. "That sound wasn't Jethro."

"How do you know that?" she hissed back.

"Because Jethro and deer don't wear clothes." I pointed into the woods at a yellow T-shirt that moved back and forth.

"Oh great," Cass whispered back. "There's a hunter out here thinking that we are deer and he's going to shoot us dead!"

"It's not deer season," I said as calmly as I could, but I wasn't feeling all that calm.

"Hello poaching? This really isn't how I wanted to die, Bai." She squeezed my arm so hard, I was certain there would be a bruise later.

"You are the problem! We lost both of our stills and it's all because of you!" a voice rang out in the silent wood.

I put a finger to my lips, hoping Cass would get the hint. This wasn't a time for talking.

"I tell you, I didn't kill her. I would never kill anyone, not even to save the still. I'd just move. Why don't we move it altogether? We could go to Wayne or Knox County and start over. It's not that far," a different, high-pitched voice said.

"We can't do that," the other voice said. "We have customers who need us here. If we don't deliver, they will find us."

"Do you think one of the customers killed Leeza?" the high-pitched voice whined.

"Maybe. But it was a dumb move for you to dump her body at the church without telling me. You should have buried her and been done with it."

"I couldn't treat her like that," the first voice said. "I knew she would be treated with respect by the church, and it would warn the reverend to keep his mouth shut in the future."

"You may have wanted that to happen, but all you did was get the sheriff's department involved. Now they've called in BCI, too. We are in so much trouble," the second voice said. "And she owed me money."

I felt a bug on my ankle, but I was too afraid to swat it away for fear of drawing attention to our hiding place in the trees.

"That's why we have to leave this area," the second man said.

"I already told you, we can't."

Cass looked at me with eyes as wide as saucers.

I made a motion that I was going to walk on a little farther to see if I could get a peek at who was speaking.

Cass shook her head, but I went on anyway. I slipped behind a large oak tree. The tree was so thick, it could have hidden me twice over. I peeked around the tree. There were two men standing beside what looked like the site of an accident. Pieces of metal lay everywhere, as well as a blown-out copper barrel.

One of the men picked up a piece a metal and then tossed it into the creek at his feet. "Let's salvage what we can and get out of here and start over. We will have to find a new place. Harvest Woods is no longer safe for us."

"It's a shame," the second man said. "The spot was perfect—plenty of cover and a water source."

"The bugs are hell," the first man said.

"True." The second man swatted at the air.

I blinked when I realized that the man with the high voice was Gabe from the winery, and the other man with him was Jonathan Troyer.

There was a snuffling sound at my feet, and I looked down to see Jethro looking up at me with a terrified expression on his face. I bet he was sorry he'd run off.

"Jethro," I whispered and inched toward him. "Come here, buddy."

The little oinker squealed.

"What was that?" the Amish man shouted.

Gabe raised a gun and shot it into the trees. That was all the motivation I needed. I grabbed the pig and ran.

CHAPTER THIRTY-TWO

Holding Jethro to my chest in a death grip, I ran after Cass through the forest. I prayed that she knew the way back to the car because all critical thinking seemed to have flown out of my head as soon as I heard the gunshot.

I ran straight out of the forest and into Aiden's arms.

"What are you doing here?" I gasped.

"I'd like to ask you the same thing," Aiden said.

Two deputies ran into the woods with their guns drawn. Behind the deputies' car was a BCI van.

Aiden stepped back. "What are you doing running through the woods with my mother's pig?"

It was a fair question.

Cass popped out of the woods and then doubled over to catch her breath. "I've never run that fast in my life. Not even when I'm trying to catch the subway."

"I never knew you could run so fast," I admitted.

"Hey, with the right motivation, like being shot at,

I can do just about anything," she said, then panted, "Aiden, great timing. How did you know we were here and needed backup?"

"Backup?" Aiden asked with a scowl. "Deputy Little drove by and saw your car parked outside of Harvest Woods. When he didn't see anyone by the car except Puff the bunny, he thought it would be wise to call it in."

I bet. Deputy Little knew if he didn't call it in and something happened to me, he would have to contend with a very angry Aiden. Poor guy.

"Now, I will ask again. What were you doing here?"

"We didn't plan to go in the woods," I began.

"That's right," Cass said. "We were just looking at them."

Aiden arched his brow. "Looking at them?"

"That's right," Cass repeated. "We wouldn't have gone in at all if he"—she pointed at Jethro—"hadn't run into the woods in the first place."

Aiden ran a hand down the side of his face.

The driver side door of the BCI van opened and a woman in a pantsuit got out. She had a badge on her belt and I bet a gun under her jacket. Another state agent wearing all-white coveralls opened the side of the van. All sorts of gadgets and tools appeared. Camera, shovels, rakes, vials, and gloves, just to name a few.

The woman walked toward us and nodded to me. "I take it that this is the girlfriend, Deputy Brody."

I straightened up and immediately bristled at her tone. "I'm Bailey King." My tone implied *who the heck are you?*

She nodded. "State Agent Robbie Bent. I work for

the Ohio Bureau of Criminal Investigation. We are here about the illegal still."

Aiden frowned. "Agent Bent and her partner are helping us on this case."

She nodded. "Or it could be that you are helping us, Deputy Brody, but let's not get in a dispute about that."

Deputy Little came over to us. "Sir, the other two deputies caught the men at the still."

"Good," Aiden said. "Were they the ones who fired the shot?"

Deputy Little nodded. "Looks that way, sir." He licked his lips. "The still is . . . well . . . All I can say is it looks like someone blew it up."

"Blew it up?"

"Yes, sir," Deputy Little said. "There is metal everywhere. The suspects claim they found it that way."

"Take them to the station. I believe we might just have found the location of Leeza's murder," Aiden said.

Deputy Little nodded and walked back to his cruiser.

Agent Bent left us then and went back to speak to the man in the coveralls. I guessed that was the partner Aiden had mentioned. The second BCI grabbed a shovel and strapped a backpack on his back. He and Agent Bent followed another deputy into the woods.

Aiden turned to Cass and me. "I want both of you to go home."

I opened my mouth to protest.

Aiden cut me off. "I will get your statements later. The first thing I need to do is question the suspects and get the crime scene techs out here to process the scene."

"One of them is Gabe, the young man Aubrey at the winery told you about. The other man is Jonathan Troyer, the Amish man who accosted Reverend Brook outside the church. I left you a voice mail about him."

He pressed his lips together. "I haven't listened to it yet. I was bringing Bent up to speed on the case." He smacked his ball cap on his knee. "If I had listened to it, I would have stopped you from coming here." He rubbed the side of his head. "Go home. You likely caught the killer today. Let me handle the rest."

I wanted to protest, to ask if he really thought Gabe Johnson or Jonathan Troyer could be the killer or if it was both of them. I wanted to know as much as Aiden what those men were up to.

"You have to go back to the village," Aiden said. "You have Jethro with you. I can't have him running around the woods getting lost or compromising the scene, and I can't have you here with BCI. It complicates things."

I frowned because I saw his point. "You will let us know what is going on?"

"I will tell you what I can." He paused. "Later."

That didn't sound very promising, but it was the best I was going to get. I put Jethro in the back seat of my car, and Cass and I climbed in.

As I drove away from the woods, I saw Aiden in the rearview mirror.

Cass and I drove by the Chupp farm on the way back to the village. The Amish families were no longer in the strawberry patch, and I wished I had stopped earlier when I'd had a chance to speak to RJ's wife, not that I knew what I would have said. I wouldn't have wanted to put the woman in a bad place with her husband. In an Amish family, the wife is expected to do what her husband asks of her. If RJ asked his wife not to speak to me, she wouldn't.

As my car passed the farm, RJ Chupp stood in the middle of his driveway with his hands on his hips. I guessed that he had seen all the official vehicles go by his farm on the way to the woods. I didn't stop, but I wished I knew what he was thinking.

"Let's go make candy, Bai," Cass said. Jethro was on her lap and Puff sat at her feet. "It's what we are good at."

I smiled at her. It was amazing that she knew exactly what I needed to hear at that moment.

Back at Swissmen Sweets, Charlotte was all atwitter. "Bailey, I'm so glad you're all right. Aiden was here when Deputy Little called to say he found your car abandoned beside Harvest Woods. I was so worried. I didn't tell Cousin Clara what was going on. There was no reason to upset her, and I fretted enough for both of us."

"What was Aiden doing here?" I asked.

"He said he was looking for you. He said he needed to talk to you."

About the murder? I wondered. Or about Kayla?

"As you can see, Cass and I are fine and in one piece," I said and set Puff on the floor. Nutmeg ran down the steps from the apartment as if he was reuniting with a friend he hadn't seen in years instead of a few hours. He and Jethro bumped noses. I shook my head. "I just wanted to pop in to see if we were all ready for tomorrow."

"Oh, we are." Charlotte patted the red bun at the nape of her neck. "I'm so very excited. It will be the first time I will see fireworks."

"Really?" Cass asked. "You've never seen fireworks before and you are over twenty?"

"My family didn't think going to a Fourth of July celebration was a good idea. It was honoring country over *Gott*. I'm glad that Cousin Clara's district is much more lenient on such matters."

"I'm glad everything's ready. I want tomorrow to go smoothly for us and Margot."

"And for Deputy Aiden," Charlotte added. "He's seemed to be even more stressed than normal."

"Yes, for Aiden, too," I said. "I'm glad that we stopped by so we could set your mind at ease, Charlotte. Get some rest. I think we are all going to need it for tomorrow."

Later that night, I was lying on my couch, tossing and turning. I couldn't get over what a close call Cass and I had had in the woods. Aiden was angry over it. He had every right to be. I promised myself and him—even though he didn't know it—that I would try to do better in the future. I also promised myself I would no longer take Jethro with me any time I was investigating. The pig was a liability in tense situations.

As if he knew that I was thinking about him, Jethro snorted on his towel on the floor and kicked his legs in his sleep.

My phone beeped, telling me that a text message

had come in. I picked it up. The only person who would text me at this time of night was Aiden.

"I'm outside your house. I don't want to wake up Cass. Can you come outside to talk?"

"Meet me in the backyard," I texted back.

Jethro sat up and, in the process, woke up Puff, who had been sleeping beside him on the towel.

I sat up and whispered, "Oh no, neither of you are going out with me, especially not you, Jethro."

The little pig snorted a retort.

I grabbed a blanket off the back of the couch, and with one eye on the animals, I moved through the kitchen and let myself out into the night.

Aiden's form sat at the picnic table in the corner of my tiny yard. The table had been left there by a previous tenant. I never used it, truthfully because I was rarely home. I was either at Swissmen Sweets or in New York. I couldn't remember spending more than an hour or two in my rental house unless I was sleeping. In many ways, it was a place to crash, not a real home.

Aiden held out his arms to me, and I stood in front of him with my blanket wrapped around my body, kimono style. He rested his hands on my hips.

"Don't you have a million questions to ask me?" he said finally when I stood there for several minutes without speaking.

"I do," I admitted. "But I was sort of waiting for you to tell me how stupid Cass and I were today. I thought we could get that out of the way first."

He laughed. "It was stupid, and I'm happy to hear that at least you know you were in the wrong."

"Really, Jethro was in the wrong, but that's neither here nor there."

Aiden shook his head.

"What is it?" I whispered.

"I got a call from Reverend Brook," Aiden said. "He called me while driving my mother to the airport for their honeymoon." He dropped his head. "I can't believe my mother married another drunk like that."

"He's not like your father."

"How can I know for sure?" He sounded as if he might cry.

"You can't," I whispered back and squeezed him tight.

CHAPTER THIRTY-THREE

I rewrapped myself in the blanket but left my right hand out. I sat next to Aiden on the picnic bench. I took his hand in mine. "Reverend Brook is not your father."

"Maybe not, but he's a liar like my father was. He misled my mother, so that she would fall in love with him and marry him. He didn't show her his true self until after they were married. Those were all things that my father did."

"He would never hurt her," I said.

He turned to face me. "Don't you think what he told her today hurt her? He basically told her that he's been hiding his past from her for years . . . years . . . Bailey. I would never do that to you."

Kayla's pretty face popped into my mind, but I pushed it away. This wasn't the time to bring her up. I didn't know if there ever would be a time.

He turned to me with bloodshot eyes. "I feel exhausted. This case is getting to me more than others have. I suppose because it involves my mother on several levels."

"Reverend Brook's drinking?" I asked.

He nodded. "I was six when Mom got me out of that house with my father, but I remember some of it." He turned away from me. "I remember him coming home wasted. I remember hearing him hit her."

I squeezed his hand. "Reverend Brook would never hurt Juliet. He loves her. That was clear to the whole village even before the two of them admitted it."

Aiden forced a laugh. "You don't have to be in law enforcement long to know that many people who claim to love each other will do horrible things to each other, too."

I didn't know what to say to that. I knew it was true. There was no point in arguing with him.

"I think all you can do is give Reverend Brook time to prove to both you and Juliet that he is the man he claims to be today, not who he was thirty years ago. You can't keep judging people for their past mistakes, especially when they have actively made a change to be better."

"He should have told her. How can she trust him when he kept this secret from her for so long?" Aiden balled his fist. "I know why he did it. He did it because he was afraid that she would stay away from him . . . as she should have."

"It's up to your mother to decide how she will take the reverend's news. Clearly, she has accepted it enough to continue on the honeymoon with him. I still have Jethro. If she was back in the village, she would want her pig with her."

He squeezed my hand and then let it go. "You're right of course."

I squeezed his hand back. "I really think your mom and Reverend Brook are going to be all right."

He turned to me, and the side of his face was illuminated by the porch light. There wasn't enough light for me to see his whole face, just the outline of his features. His cheekbones, strong jaw, and straight nose. It was too dark to even see the color of his blond hair. "I don't know what I would do without you at times. I know we've only known each other a year, but in a lot of ways, it's felt like a lifetime. I don't know what life was BB."

"BB?"

"Before Bailey."

I smiled. "I don't know what life was BA."

The shadow of his mouth curved into a smile, and then it was gone. "We finally know where Leeza died."

"Jethro found the spot?" I asked.

Aiden's jaw twitched. "I'm not going to tell you again what a dumb choice it was to go to those woods."

"Good, and I won't tell you again that we never planned to go into the woods. Jethro forced our hand."

His outline shifted. "It seems he does that a lot."

"True," I conceded. "I'm guessing he and Puff are getting into all sorts of trouble in my house right now because I didn't let them come outside with me. I fear for my throw pillows."

"Whether you found the location of Leeza's death or Jethro did, it doesn't matter. It was certainly at that still. The second one to be found in Harvest Woods." He shook his head. "Had we kept looking after we found the first one, we would have found it.

Agent Bent was sure to point out what a screwup that was on our department's part. The sheriff is furious and blames me for making us look bad in front of BCI."

My eyes widened. "Are there two groups of moonshiners working out of the woods?" I asked.

He shook he head. "No, Gabe and Jonathan claimed both stills. The first one my officers found when Reverend Brook made that anonymous tip was a mock still."

"A mock still?" I asked.

"It had all the trappings of an active still, but it wasn't active. It was a decoy really, to throw off the authorities, and it worked. After, the deputies found that they hadn't gone deep enough into the woods to find the second, real still. Agent Bent claims that her investigators wouldn't have been fooled if we'd brought them on for support earlier. But Sheriff Jackson never would have agreed to that."

I nodded. "What was the connection to Leeza?" I asked.

"It was exactly as Aubrey from the winery said," Aiden replied. "Leeza and Gabe were seeing each other. Shortly after they started dating, he brought her into the business. He thought she was the perfect person to drum up more business for the moonshine. She could gauge which of the customers who came into the winery might be interested. Also, she was a pretty, petite woman. No one would suspect her of smuggling illegal alcohol. The longer her relationship with Gabe went on, the more work she did as a runner, meaning she was the one who picked up and dropped off the moonshine at agreed upon locations."

"Did Stardust Winery know about her side business?"

"I had Little go over there to talk to the owners, and they were shocked. I tend to believe they weren't involved, but of course, I will always keep the possibility that they knew something in the back of my mind."

I sat up straighter on the bench. "So, was the coroner right in guessing the cause of death was from a blast of some sort?"

"Yes."

"After seeing the scene, I can easily believe that, but I still can't get over the fact that no one heard the blast. It must have been very loud."

"I agree, but you have to remember, Harvest Woods is miles from the village, so it would have been unlikely for anyone to hear it."

I thought back to Saturday night and the moment I'd sat up in bed because I had been scared awake by the storm. The thunder and lightning were so close, the next crash of thunder hit before I could even reach a count of three.

"And," Aiden went on, "there are only a handful of Amish farms that might have overheard the blast. It's far too late tonight, but I have deputies lined up to go out and canvass the area again, asking if anyone heard anything."

"How did the still blow up?" I asked.

"Gunshot."

"What? Gabe or Jonathan shot the still?"

He shook his head. "At least they claim they didn't, and I tend to believe them because the explosion destroyed their business. They are both very worried about not delivering to their customers. I can't see them destroying the still and putting themselves in danger. People who buy illegal liquor can be a dangerous bunch."

"Who would want to blow up the still?"

"Whoever did it had every intention of destroying that still. There was a propane tank to heat the water to make the moonshine. The shooter aimed for that. We're guessing the shooter shot off all five rounds from a hunting rifle. Two of them must have hit the tank, but we found three rounds embedded in trees around the area. The three rounds were enough to tell us the location where the shooter was when the shots were fired. The person was about fifty yards away, on a slight rise above the still."

My pulse quickened. "Did you find anything at the spot where the shooter stood?"

He nodded. "One casing. It seems to me the shooter scooped up all the casings after the shots were fired, missing just one."

I nodded, deep in thought.

"That one is all we need," Aiden said.

"Why?" I whispered.

"Because we got a print. If all goes well, we will have the killer in custody before a single firework is shot on the Fourth."

And then this nightmare would be over.

CHAPTER THIRTY-FOUR

My phone rang at seven the next morning. I was up and already at work at Swissmen Sweets. Any candy maker worth her salt was up with the sun. I can't say that I was a morning person, but my career choice certainly forced me to be. I checked the phone screen and saw that the call was from Margot. I showed it to Cass, who was working next to me at the island in the candy shop kitchen. She wrinkled her nose.

Knowing it was better to take the call than ignore it because she would either call back until I caved or just waltz into the candy shop demanding I listen to her, I answered. "Good morning, Margot."

"Well, hello, Bailey. Today is the day! The Harvest Independence Day celebration. Oh my goodness, I can feel it in my very bones that this will become an annual tradition. Did you hear they announced it on a Canton radio station this morning?"

"No, I didn't, but I'm happy to hear that it made the airwaves."

"Made the airwaves? It was much more than that. The host raved about Harvest being *the* place to be this holiday. As you can imagine, I am tickled pink over it."

I could imagine very well indeed.

"Now, I just want to make sure you will be at the celebration."

"Swissmen Sweets will be there," I said, and rolled my eyes at Cass.

"No, no, *you*, Bailey. I need you in particular there. I heard that they found the men behind Leeza's death, so you really don't have any reason to wander off, now do you?"

I wrinkled my nose. "I am planning to be at the booth with the ladies from my shop," I said. "I would be very interested in knowing why you are so keen on having me there. Everyone at Swissmen Sweets does a great job."

"Oh, I know, I know. I wasn't commenting on Clara's work or either of the girls'. I just need *you*."

I frowned, because the way she kept saying *you* was getting a bit creepy. What plans did she have for me? I reminded myself that it couldn't be anything bad, not really. I mean, Margot was a master of getting me and others to do things we didn't really want to do, but she was never a threat.

"All right," Margot said. "I have to run. See you this afternoon. Remember that all booths have to be ready to go by five o'clock sharp. I will not abide lateness."

"We will be there," I promised.

"This is going to be amazing!" she shouted, and then ended the call.

Cass stared at me. "What on earth was that about?"

"Margot has a surprise for me at the Fourth of July celebration and I have a feeling I'm not going to like it."

"I know you're not."

"Thanks," I muttered.

Cass stirred melted chocolate in a stainless-steel bowl. "Let's get these chocolate buggies done," she said. "I think they will be a hit. Maybe JP Chocolates and Swissmen Sweets can collaborate. We would give you credit for the design, of course."

"That would be great advertising for us, and I'd be happy to have info available about JP Chocolates here."

"Excellent." She grinned. "In some ways, it's going to be hard to go back to the city, but I need to take over again at JP Chocolates. Jean Pierre might like playing at being head chocolatier for a little while, but he won't be able to stand it for very long. He much prefers to coach from the sidelines."

I laughed and poured the molten chocolate from the bowl into the waiting rubber buggy molds. I'd had the molds made not long after I decided to move to Ohio permanently and help out with my grandparents' shop. Before I took over, my grandfather would hand-carve Amish buggies from chocolate. His carvings were beautiful, each one different, but they were also time-consuming. When I began helping out at the shop, I slowly started changing how we did some things to make the work go more quickly and to increase orders. I got the chocolate molds made so that we'd always have buggies to sell, and they'd become a popular souvenir item on our website. We'd recently begun shipping and selling our candies online. I had a feeling that side of our business would grow tenfold when the television show hit the air.

I was doing all this slowly, staying within the limits of what my Amish grandmother was comfortable with. Our shop would never be on the scale of JP Chocolates, but I wanted to share Amish candies with the world. *Bailey's Amish Sweets* would air at the end of the week. I wasn't sure that my grandmother was ready for all the attention the show would bring the shop. Of course, she knew I'd been going to New York to film a candy-making show, but I don't think she realized the reach and growth potential it would have for our business.

My phone rang. I hoped it wasn't Margot again.

Cass pulled a tray of chocolate-dipped strawberries from the industrial refrigerator near the back door of the kitchen. "Bai, are you going to get your phone?"

I removed the gloves I was wearing and pulled the phone out of the back pocket of my jeans. The call was from my producer, Linc Baggins, in New York. "This is Bailey."

"Bailey, good, good, I thought you wouldn't answer." He was breathless as he spoke.

"Is everything okay?" Something must have gone awry with the release of the television show and now *Bailey's Amish Sweets* was canceled. I knew it was too good to be true to think I would have my own show on a major cable network.

"Everything is fine!" he shouted in my ear.

I held the phone away from me. Cass and Charlotte were in the kitchen with me, helping prepare all the last-minute details for the Fourth of July celebration on the square that evening. Cass mouthed, *You okay?*

I nodded because I thought I was okay, but I still had no idea why my producer was calling me so early in the morning on a national holiday.

"We must work fast," Linc said.

"Is there anything left to do for the show?" I asked. "I was told everything was complete."

"The network is so excited about the buzz your show has created. They want to throw a premiere party! Now, it won't be a whole red carpet thing, but there will be press and food critics there."

"Wow, that's great news. The show premieres next Tuesday. When will the event be?"

"Saturday. This Saturday," he said breathlessly. "You have to be here. We can't have the event without you."

I raised my brow. It was Wednesday. I bit my lip. Saturday was one of our busiest days, but I would go, of course. It was a once-in-a-lifetime opportunity. "I'll be there." I couldn't keep the excitement from my voice.

"Good, good," he said with a sigh of relief. "And bring Charlotte and your grandmother, too."

"Charlotte and my grandmother?" I asked.

Charlotte, who had entered the kitchen while I had been on the phone, now hung on my every word. Cass mouthed, *What? What?*

I shook my head. Charlotte had gone with me to

New York to film in the past, so I knew she would love the chance to go again, but I couldn't imagine my grandmother in the city. I couldn't imagine her agreeing to go. It was such a non-Amish thing to do, and she would have to fly. She'd never flown in a plane before.

"I know Charlotte would be happy to return to New York," I told Linc.

Charlotte's eyes went wide, and she clapped her hands over her mouth as she jumped up and down in excitement. Cass gave her a high five.

"But I don't know if my grandmother will be able to come," I said.

"She has to come," my producer declared. "Your show would not be what it is without your Amish roots."

"She may not be comfortable with the idea."

"Make her comfortable. We will set you up in the best hotel."

I pressed my lips together. A fancy hotel would only make my grandmother feel more uncomfortable. "I don't—"

"Bailey, I have to go," he interrupted me. "It may be a holiday, but when you're in my field, you never get a day off. I'll have my assistant send you the flight confirmation, hotel, and all the particulars about the event."

Before I could say anything more, he hung up.

"What was that?" Cass asked.

"That was my producer in New York," I said, still a little shocked by the conversation. "Gourmet Television has planned a premiere for my show this Saturday."

Cass set her tray on the large, stainless-steel island. "Bai, this is huge!"

"I know," I said.

"He wants Charlotte to come with me, and of course, you and Jean Pierre will come as my guests, too, but . . ."

Charlotte squealed. "I'm going back to the city!"

"But what?" Cass asked, studying me.

"He wants *Maami* to come. In fact, he insisted that she come."

The kitchen door swung inward. "Who wants me to come somewhere?" my grandmother asked.

I glanced at Charlotte. I knew we were thinking the same thing. My grandmother would never agree to go to New York for the premiere party.

Cass answered for me, telling *Maami* about the party.

Maami shook her head. "I can't go to New York. That is a silly idea, especially not on a Saturday in the summer. You and I can't both be gone on such a busy day, Bailey."

I felt my heart sink because I wanted her to be there. The little girl in me wanted my grandmother, the most important person in my life, to see what I had done.

My grandmother walked over to me and took both my hands in hers. "I'm so proud of you, but I know that you respect my way of life."

"I do," I said.

"You and Charlotte can go. It would be *gut* for you. Emily and I can manage the shop."

"Oh, thank you, Cousin Clara." Charlotte clapped her hands.

"I would love it if you could come," I said, even though I knew there was no point. "My producer will cover the flights. We could stay with Cass if you don't want to stay in the hotel." I glanced at Cass, and she nodded.

"It would be a tight squeeze in my apartment," Cass said. "But I would love to have you."

"Oh," *Maami* said, "I don't know if that would be right. It is not the Amish way to go to big cities. There would be many things there I would not be permitted to do."

"Charlotte is Amish," Cass said, "and she went."

My grandmother smiled at her. "*Ya*, but Charlotte is not baptized in the church yet. It is one thing for a young woman who is interested in the world and is on *rumspringa*. It is another for a grandmother who has been a member of the church for over fifty years."

I clenched my teeth, not because I was angry, but to hide my disappointment. *Maami* had given me the answer I'd expected to hear, but that didn't change the fact that I wanted her to come. I wanted to show her what my life in New York had been like. I wanted her to meet Jean Pierre. It was silly to think even for a moment that she would come. She had never visited my father or me in our home in Connecticut during all the years I was growing up. I was always the one who'd traveled to Holmes County.

For a moment, I was that eight-year-old girl again, trying to understand why my grandparents never came to see me. I'd ask my parents, and my father would say that they didn't believe in travel. At eight, I didn't understand it. If *Maami* and *Daadi* didn't believe in travel, why did I travel to Ohio to see them every summer? I asked my father this question, and he always gave me the same answer: "Because they are Amish, Bailey." By that point his tone was exasperated, and I knew better than to keep asking.

I respected my grandmother's dedication to her faith, but at the same time, I still wanted to share the other part of my life with her. Maybe that was the English in me coming out. I wanted her to see what I had created.

It wasn't the Amish way of thinking. The individual wasn't the focus of their faith; the community was. Part of that was keeping the community together, which meant not traveling too far away from home. Charlotte and my grandmother had gone to Pinecraft, Florida, weeks ago on a little vacation I had organized for them. I wanted them to have a break from the store. *Maami* had agreed to that because Pinecraft was an Amish community on the gulf. Going there was within the parameters that her bishop had set for district member travel. A television show premiere in New York was way out of that sphere.

I gave it one more try. "Maybe you can ask Bishop Yoder," I suggested. "Maybe this would be something he'd approve. It's his decision to let you go, isn't it?"

She patted my cheek. "It would be his decision, but I cannot bother the bishop now with so much turmoil in the community over the stills."

I forced a smile, hoping I looked happier than I felt. "I understand." I shook my head. "Let's finish getting ready for the event on the square. If Margot is right, the place will be packed." I started cutting up more chocolate to melt in the double boiler on one of the many burners in the large kitchen.

Cass gave me an understanding smile, and then a look of determination crossed her face. I tried not to worry over what that might mean.

CHAPTER THIRTY-FIVE

Last year, when I moved to Holmes County, I had been overwhelmed by the number of events that were held on the square, and the fact that Margot Rawlings expected Swissmen Sweets to participate in each and every one of them. During the fair-weather months from late April to October, there was an event every weekend, or so it seemed. Now, many months later, I took Margot's requests in stride, and the ladies of Swissmen Sweets and I had moving supplies and candy across the street to the square down to a science. I had invested in two outdoor folding utility wagons with sturdy rubber wheels. They were the perfect addition to the business. When it was late afternoon and time to set up our booth at the Fourth of July celebration, we filled the two wagons with what we needed and were off across the street.

It was a little after four as we began to set up. Emily had gone home to be with her family, but Charlotte, Cass, *Maami,* and I were all going to work at the candy shop tables. I'd told Emily that she didn't have to stay if she didn't want to because we had Cass as an extra set of hands. In the end, she opted to go home. Her choice didn't surprise me a bit. She was still a newly-wed and talked of her young husband constantly, and I knew she didn't want to chance another run-in with her older siblings.

I was also relieved Jethro wasn't there. After the great chase through Harvest Woods the day before, I thought it was better to leave him and Puff home. Because I knew Nutmeg would hate the idea of being separated from his friends, Charlotte had taken him to my house earlier in the day, too. Now the three animals were surely wrecking my living room, but at least I knew they wouldn't run off or be frightened by the fireworks as they might have been in Swissmen Sweets.

Even though the fireworks weren't to start until after nine at night, the square was already full of lawn and beach chairs as villagers and visitors staked out their spots for the best views of the fireworks.

Thankfully for us, the candy shop booth on the square had a clear view of the playground to the left of Reverend Brook's church. The fireworks were to be shot off from the field behind the playground. We were sure to see quite a show.

Charlotte clapped her hands and then started unpacking the wagons with the rest of us. "I'm so excited. It's been quite a day. First, I found I'm going back to New York, and now we get to see fireworks! I don't know what will happen next."

My grandmother watched her with concern etched on her face. It was apparent to all of us, except maybe Charlotte, that she was moving further and further away from her Amish roots. I wondered when she would make a decision about being baptized or not. Bishop Yoder was much more lenient than her old bishop, but I doubted that he would put up with her indecisiveness forever. His wife, Ruth, wouldn't let him.

There were a handful of booths on the square, and all of them tonight were food-related. Margot had made sure that no one was in danger of going hungry while roaming around downtown Harvest on July Fourth.

We made quick work of unpacking our carts and setting up the table. By this point, Swissmen Sweets had done so many events on the square, we had it down to a science.

More and more people came onto the square by the minute, and I realized that Margot had been right. This was going to be one of the biggest events the village had ever seen. There were even more people than had been in Harvest at Christmas, and for that holiday, Margot had arranged a live nativity, including a camel named Melchior.

As the vendors set up, Margot marched back and forth in front of the line of food booths with her clipboard at the ready. I had seen her high-strung about an event before, but nothing like this. "Quickly, quickly," she called. "All the food services must be open by five," she shouted on her last pass, and then she glared at the one empty table in the line. I frowned. I saw all the regular food vendors present. I couldn't guess who else she expected to be there.

"Yikes," Cass said. "Someone is going to get a tongue-lashing when they show up."

I nodded and frowned. Swissmen Sweets had been doing a brisk business ever since we'd unloaded the wagons. Both the chocolate-covered strawberries and the marshmallow sticks were a huge hit. They did so well, I knew I would have to add them to the summer menu. Strawberries and marshmallows were the perfect summer treats. The chocolate-covered frozen bananas that Charlotte suggested did well, too.

Margot stomped over to me. "Have you seen the Chupps?"

I blinked at her. "The Chupps?"

"Yes." She tapped her clipboard. "The Chupps. I'm asking you about the Chupps. They were supposed to be in that empty booth right over there, selling their berries, and they aren't here. It's after five. I told them to be here at four sharp. This is not acceptable. I knew that I shouldn't have added a new vendor for such an important event, but RJ Chupp was insistent that they could deliver." The eraser of her mechanical pencil hit the clipboard at an increasingly rapid rate. "This will be the last time I go against my gut when it comes to village events. If they don't show, do you know who will look bad?" she asked.

Before I could answer, she went on, "*I* will look bad. I make promises to the village council and to the public about who will be here, and if someone doesn't show, that reflects badly on me and gives the impression that I have poor judgment." She pointed the end of her pencil at her chest, as if to drive the point home.

I held up my hand. "Margot! Take a breath. You are going to make yourself crazy."

"And everyone around you, too," Cass whispered as she handed another customer two marshmallow sticks decorated with red, white, and blue stars.

Margot froze with her eraser over the clipboard. I took the opportunity to speak. There was a good chance it wouldn't last long. "I didn't know that the Chupps had a booth on the square, and, no, I haven't seen them. However, I know that their berry farm is very successful. They will be here if they said they would. Maybe they are caught in traffic. The streets into the village are backed up because so many people are trying to reach the square."

She sniffed. "They should have left earlier, then. I can't have unreliable merchants at my square events! They are too important."

"No one is going to die if they don't have more berries to eat," Cass said as she filled a plastic container with chocolate-dipped strawberries for another customer.

Margot glared at her. "How would you know? You're from New York."

Cass rolled her eyes and looked as if she was about to make another sarcastic comment when a man in the crowd caught my eye.

"No need to panic anymore," I said. "I think they're here." I nodded across the square. RJ Chupp pushed a cart of berries through the crowd, followed by three children, including Essie. Along with the children came the petite woman who I assumed was RJ's wife. She walked a few steps behind RJ and did her best to keep the three small children together. It appeared to be a challenge as they bounced about and pointed out all the patriotic twinkle lights in the trees. The woman held the hand of the youngest girl. She was the little one I had seen in the window. Each child carried something for the booth. The youngest one held a sign that read, "Fresh Berries."

Margot put her hands on her hips and pointed at the empty booth nearby. RJ Chupp locked eyes with me for just a moment. His face fell into a scowl before he continued on to his empty booth.

Margot marched over to help them get settled or to lecture them about being so late. I wasn't certain which.

Charlotte handed another customer several patriotic marshmallow sticks. "Thank you so much." After the man left, she turned to me. "What are the Chupps doing here?"

I shook my head. "Margot said that they have a booth to sell their berries."

Charlotte nodded as if that made perfect sense, but I found the Chupps' presence suspect as well. I couldn't put my finger on the reason why.

There wasn't much time to talk after that. The square filled up with villagers and visitors alike, and it seemed that everyone wanted candy from our booth. All four of us were working nonstop.

"I'll take two marshmallow sticks," a deep voice said. I looked up. I was currently squatting beside one of the coolers we had brought to the event, counting how many strawberries we had left. They were getting low.

When I looked up, I was shocked to see Sheriff Marshall Jackson staring down at me. The sheriff was a large man, and his stomach hung over his utility belt. He didn't wear a hat over his buzzed gray hair, and a pair of sunglasses poked out of the breast pocket of his shirt. The sun was well on its way to setting for the night. When it did, the fireworks would begin.

The sheriff wore his department uniform. I guessed

he wore it because it gave him the air of authority he enjoyed. I jumped to my feet like a jack-in-the-box. "Not a problem."

Charlotte put two marshmallow sticks in my left hand. Bless that girl for acting so quickly. "That's six dollars," I said.

The sheriff eyed me coolly as he removed six singles from his wallet and set them down one by one on my table. I held out the cellophane-wrapped sticks to him, but he made no move to take them from my hand.

Instead, he leaned on the table between us. The folding table groaned under his weight, and I prayed it would hold. "I heard that BCI is on my case because of you."

I swallowed and dumbly held the marshmallow sticks up a little higher, as if he hadn't been able to see them before. I held them right in front of his face.

With one finger, he lowered my hand. "What do you have to say about that?"

"I have nothing to do with BCI being here."

He leaned forward, and the table creaked. "Oh, I know; Aiden is behind that." He lowered his voice so that I was the only one who could hear. "I know he's out for my job. He feigns loyalty to me by not running against me, but then goes behind my back by pulling in the state. I don't need their help to keep the Amish in line."

Beside me, Charlotte shivered at the way he said "Amish." To be honest, it shook me, too.

I held the marshmallow sticks in his face again. "Your sticks, sir."

He glared at them and then at me. "Aiden Brody had better be careful. If he pushes me too far, I could ruin him."

"I'm sure he knows plenty to ruin you," Cass said sweetly.

I blinked at her. I hadn't even known she was listening.

The sheriff curled his lips at her. "Who are you?"

Cass shrugged. "Probably no one who matters to you because I can't vote in this county."

"I'm guessing you're right about that," put in a woman's voice.

Behind the sheriff, BCI Agent Robbie Bent strolled up, and she took the marshmallow sticks from my hand. She wore a T-shirt, jeans, and sneakers. "If the sheriff won't take those, I sure will. My kids will love them." She grinned at the sheriff. "Thanks for the treats, Marshall."

He glowered at her and then stomped away.

Agent Bent watched him go, shaking her head. "He makes people in law enforcement look bad." She nodded to me and walked off.

Cass blinked at me. "What on earth was that?"

I shook my head. I wished I knew, because I had a feeling it would come to a head at some point, and my fear was that Aiden would be caught in the middle of the power struggle between the sheriff and BCI.

CHAPTER THIRTY-SIX

By the time the sheriff and Agent Bent left our booth, it was well after eight. The crowd was beginning to get anxious for the fireworks to begin and had settled in their seats. Our sales became fewer and farther apart.

A small band was in the gazebo playing patriotic music. Everyone seemed to be having a wonderful time. Every so often, I caught a glimpse of Aiden as he patrolled the square. I bit my lip when I thought of what the sheriff might have in store for him. I wasn't sure Aiden even knew the sheriff was at the celebration tonight. There were so many people on the square and spilling over onto the side streets around the village, it would be easy to miss someone, even someone the size of Sheriff Jackson.

Deputy Little was there, as were two other deputies, but I imagined there might be even more officers moving around the village. I knew the department was stretched thin tonight. Aiden said that Independence Day was one of the worst days for accidents in the county. People took risks, and they drove drunk.

I noticed that every time Aiden tried to come to the Swissmen Sweets booth to say hello, we were swamped with customers. I was relieved that he had been nowhere in sight when the sheriff came to my table.

Finally, as it drew closer to the time for the fireworks, Aiden made it to our table. "You have a second?" he asked.

Maami smiled. "Go, Bailey. We're fine."

I thanked her and followed Aiden a few feet away. "Something wrong?" I wondered if the sheriff had said something to him, too.

He made a face. "Kind of. I told you we found the shell casing with the fingerprint on it."

I nodded, and then my face fell. "You didn't find a match."

"No, that's not it. We found a match right away."

"What? Who is it?"

"Bryan Hershberger."

"An Amish man," I said. "I don't think I know anyone by that name, but Hershberger is common, of course."

"Very common. Here's the thing . . ."

"What?" I leaned in.

"Bryan Hershberger died five weeks ago in a drunk driving accident. That's why we have his print. We don't usually have Amish fingerprints if they haven't committed a crime."

I stared at him. "A car hit him?"

Aiden shook his head. "He was driving his buggy drunk and ran into a tree. I pulled out the case file, and it notes there was moonshine in his buggy. Gabe, who is still in custody, admitted that it was moonshine they'd made and that Bryan had been a customer. He didn't know Hershberger was dead, or so he said."

"My grandmother mentioned that accident to me, too." I stared at him. "So you have to find a dead guy?"

"Or someone who has access to his hunting rifle. We're tracking down his family right now. He didn't have much. He never married. His parents are both long dead. Agent Bent is very keen on closing this case tonight."

"I just saw her a while ago. She got some marshmallow sticks." I took care not to mention the sheriff. I would tell Aiden about it eventually, but when we were alone. The crowded square wasn't the right place to relay the sheriff's threat. "She looked like she was off duty. She wore jeans."

He laughed. "Bent is never off duty. She's here on the case whether she looks like it or not."

I shivered.

Aiden's radio crackled. "I'd better take this. It's going to be a long night. Don't tell anyone about the shell casing. I probably shouldn't have told you. Agent Bent and Sheriff Jackson would not approve, but I did because you have to watch your back, Bailey. Whoever did this went to a lot of trouble to blow up that still using a dead man's gun."

I nodded, and he walked away, speaking into his radio as he went.

Back at the booth, I was lost in thought as I took my spot. Who would have access to a dead Amish man's rifle? And it couldn't be coincidence that he'd died in a drunk driving accident after drinking moonshine from the still that had been blown up.

I reached under the table to pull more chocolate-covered strawberries from the cooler to set on the table when the bandstand music stopped in the middle of a song.

"Bailey King. Bailey King. Can we have Bailey at the gazebo?" Margot held up her bullhorn to her lips and shouted my name over and over again.

"What the . . ." Cass started.

From the gazebo, Margot waved at me. Immediately, my face turned bright red.

"Bailey, would you come to the gazebo, please. Don't be shy." Margot looked around. "Everyone, I think she could use some clapping for encouragement."

It began slowly at first, but then the applause grew. Beside me, Cass started to clap, too.

"What are you doing?" I hissed.

"Go find out what she wants," *Maami* said. "She's not going to leave you alone until you do."

This was very true. I stepped out of the candy booth and walked over, waving as I went because it felt worse to walk there and pretend that everyone wasn't staring at me. Out of the corner of my eye, I spotted Kayla standing a few feet away, glaring at me. It was nice to know that I had an official enemy in the village.

"Everyone, Bailey King from Swissmen Sweets!" Margot cried as I reached the gazebo.

I walked up the gazebo steps. "Margot, what on earth is going on?"

She smiled and lowered her bullhorn. "You will see."

I didn't like the sound of that.

She lifted the bullhorn back up to her lips. "Everyone, this is our Bailey! Even though Bailey hasn't been a member of our community for a long time, the King family has been a part of Harvest for generations. The family candy shop, Swissmen Sweets, right across the road there, is an institution in Harvest! It draws people from all over to our lovely village. If you're from around here, you will likely know it, but if not, you must stop by before you leave." She took a breath. "I want to tell you all that our village will be even more famous in the coming weeks because of Bailey. She's going to be more than just our local candy star. We will have to share her with the world."

I tried not to look as nervous as I felt. It was almost dark now, just minutes away from the fireworks display. I looked out into the audience and saw every eye focused on me. It wasn't a comfortable spot to be in. My eyes found Aiden's in the crowd. Relief swelled through me. He was still there. He smiled at me and gave me a thumbs-up. Immediately, I felt calmer. I also reminded myself that as embarrassed as I was standing next to Margot in the gazebo, she was trying to be nice in a way that benefitted both of us.

"We want all of you to tune in next Tuesday— that's less than a week from today—to Gourmet Television at eight p.m. to watch the premiere episode of *Bailey's Amish Sweets.*" She nodded, as if answering an unspoken question. "That's right, Bailey has a television show coming to cable TV that will feature her family's Amish candy-making recipes, Swissmen Sweets, and our adorable little village. Can you believe it? Bailey is going to be famous and take Harvest with her."

The crowd clapped. At least, most of them did. I spotted Bishop and Ruth Yoder in the crowd with other members of my grandmother's district. Ruth folded her arms. I guessed that she didn't take the idea of Harvest being famous as a good thing. I also knew that she and Margot were always at odds, so anything the village event planner endorsed, the bishop's wife was likely to dislike.

The singer from the band handed Margot a plaque. "That's why today, I present Bailey King with this commemorative plaque." She held it up so that everyone could see it. "This is to recognize her contribution to the betterment of Harvest, the town we all love."

She handed the plaque to me. I read it, and to my surprise, tears sprang to my eyes. "Thank you, Margot. This is so kind of you."

She handed me the bullhorn.

I stared at it. "You want me to speak into this?"

She nodded.

I sighed and held up the bullhorn near my mouth. "Thank you, everyone. I love Harvest and the people here." I took a breath. "When I moved to the village to help my grandmother with Swissmen Sweets after we lost my grandfather, I never thought I would find the place where I truly belonged. I have met so many wonderful people." I made eye contact with Aiden when I said this. "And I feel lucky to be sharing this place with the world. My television show came about because of this village. It was the compelling people like you that the producer met in Harvest who made him want to pitch a television show featuring this village. I hope you all will tune in on next Tuesday, and thank you again." I handed the bullhorn back to Margot.

"We are so proud of you, Bailey!" Margot said. "Now, the fireworks will begin in about fifteen minutes. I know you are all excited about that. I'd just like to take this time to tell you about the other exciting events we have coming up in the village for the remainder of July and into August. You will not want to miss a single one!"

I quickly made my way down the gazebo steps and walked to the side, relieved that I was no longer the center of attention. I held my new plaque to my chest. I planned to hang it in the front room of the shop—with my grandmother's blessing, of course. No Amish business wanted to look like it was bragging.

I stood and listened as Margot announced the upcoming events on the square for the remainder of the summer. A hand tapped me on the shoulder, and I turned around with a smile, expecting to see Aiden behind me. The smile fell from my face. It wasn't Aiden at all, but the small Amish woman with glasses who I had seen with RJ Chupp and his children.

"Can I talk to you?" she whispered.

I stared at her.

"Follow me. Please. It's about Leeza." She walked away.

I frowned, and then followed her to the other side of the green.

CHAPTER THIRTY-SEVEN

I didn't think this small Amish woman could hurt me, but I still had some trepidation about following her to the other side of a large oak tree on the edge of the square. I peered around the side of it to make sure no one else was there, lying in wait for me.

The petite Amish woman was alone.

I stepped around the tree and waited for her to speak first.

She wrung her hands. "I'm sorry to have pulled you away from the festivities, but I needed to talk to you, and I can't have my husband, RJ, see me speaking with you. He wouldn't like it."

"What's your name?" I asked.

She blinked. "I'm so sorry. I'm Mary Chupp. RJ is my husband." She squeezed her hands together tightly. "Elizabeth, or Leeza, as she was called by the *Englisch*, was my sister-in-law." Her breath caught. "I'm sorry to have taken you away from the gazebo like that, but I thought this was the only way we could speak without RJ seeing."

"You wanted to talk to me about Leeza?" I asked.

Mary looked over her shoulder again. "I know your grandmother, Clara. She has always spoken so highly of you. As have others in the Amish community. They say you have been able to help them solve many problems. They say you have found killers in the past."

I nodded. This was all true. For good or for ill, I had been able to help other Amish people who had become embroiled in murder investigations. Partly this was due to my innate curiosity. Partly it was because the Amish began coming to me to help after I solved a couple of murders.

"I wonder if you could do that now for Leeza." She paused. "For our family. I don't think RJ will find peace until the death of his sister is solved. He is a stoic man, but he is broken up over her death. I beg you to find out what happened to Elizabeth. I think it would give my husband great peace of mind to know. I know that he spoke poorly of her, but that stemmed from hurt. He was hurt that she couldn't stop drinking. He was hurt that she was finally forced to leave the Amish faith because she refused to change her ways. I think he always hoped she would come back to the faith before . . ." She swallowed. "Well, before it was too late." She dropped her eyes. "Now, it's too late."

Far too late.

"She was trying to change because she wanted to be reconciled with your family."

She gasped. "Everyone was right. You do know everything that it is happening in the community."

"Not everything," I said. "If I knew everything, I would know who killed Leeza."

She swallowed.

"Tell me about Leeza's visit to your farm."

"How do you know of this?" She twisted the end of her apron in her hands and blinked at me from behind her thick lenses.

"Aubrey," I said.

She looked down. "Yes, you mean the *Englisch* girl from the winery. She came to my husband and told him that Elizabeth was working at the winery. He was furious. He has no tolerance for the use of alcohol. He saw what it did to his sister and how it tore his family apart."

"What happened, when Leeza—I mean Elizabeth—came to speak to him?"

She twisted her apron again. "She came the day after her friend. It was too soon to come after RJ learned about the winery. If she had waited a few more days or even a week, he would have cooled down. He wouldn't have been happy with where she worked, but he might have been more open to hearing her story." She looked at her hands, which were tangled up in the cloth of her apron. "But she did not wait. She told RJ that she was no longer drinking, and he said that didn't matter as long as she sold alcohol. He said, too, that he had seen her with the men who were known to sell moonshine in the community. He told her that was unforgivable, that people like her ruined *gut* men. He told her never to come back, never to speak to him again or try to speak to anyone in the family."

My heart hurt for Leeza. No matter what she may have done to help Gabe, her moonshiner boyfriend, RJ's rejection had been terribly harsh. It was no wonder that she began drinking again. It would have been a miracle if she had been able to resist it.

"She left then, and I never got a chance to speak to her. I wanted to so much, but I was afraid. My husband was so angry, and I had to keep the children quiet so they would not make him angrier."

I stiffened. "Are you afraid of RJ?"

"He would not hurt me or the children, if that's what you are asking, but he does have a temper, and his temper was boiling over what he saw as another betrayal by his sister."

I frowned. I wanted to believe Mary, but I wasn't sure I did. RJ appeared to be a stern man from the outside. I could only guess what he was like at home with his wife and children.

"Now that Elizabeth is dead, RJ is feeling guilt."

I wasn't surprised to hear it. It wouldn't have taken much imagination on his part to realize that his reaction and banishment of her was what had led her back to alcohol.

"Finding the killer will bring him some peace."

"How can I help?" I asked. "The police are already looking for the person who killed her. It may even be one of the two men they arrested yesterday."

"*Ya*, I saw they found the still. My husband was speaking about it with some elders from our district early this afternoon. That's why we were late coming to the festival." She took my hand in hers. "I don't believe those men were responsible for Elizabeth's death."

"The men running the still?" I asked.

She nodded.

"Why do you say that?"

"They have done a great many things wrong, but they weren't the ones who killed Leeza."

"Who did, then?"

She dropped my hand and bit her lip. It was as if she were trying to decide whether or not she should say anything more. "It was an Amish person," she whispered, and then looked around to see if anyone might have heard her.

The sky grew darker by the second, and then there was a high-pitched, whistling sound, followed by a bang, like a gunshot, as a firecracker exploded in the sky. The people on the square cheered.

I removed my phone from my pocket. It was ten to nine. The fireworks would begin promptly at nine. I guessed this was a test firecracker we'd just seen.

Mary shivered. "That reminds me of the night of the storm."

My brow went up. "You mean Saturday night? The night Leeza was killed?"

She nodded.

"Do you know something about that night?"

She didn't say anything.

"If you don't want those moonshiners to be falsely accused, you will have to tell me what you know."

She seemed to realize she was wrinkling her apron. She dropped her hands to her sides and stretched out her fingers. She winced as she moved her hands.

"I went out to the strawberry patch in the storm. I normally wouldn't have done that, but RJ wasn't home. He had been working at a farmers market in Wayne County, and he got caught in the storm. He stayed with friends who lived near there. It was just my three children at home the night of the storm.

"Earlier in the day, the children and I had been working in the strawberry patch, and we had left tools there. I knew if I left them in the rain all night, they would be ruined. The children were in bed and seemed to be sleeping through the thunder. I thought that I would have to go out and gather up the tools. I wanted to pick them up, dry them, and put them away so that my husband wouldn't know how careless I had been with them.

"The storm was fierce, and when I first went out the door, I questioned myself. I wondered if I should wait and move the tools after the storm had passed, but then I knew that RJ would come home and be very upset to see his equipment treated so carelessly if he found any damage."

I nodded. "So you went out into the storm anyway."

She smoothed down her apron. "*Ya.* I went out. The rain was coming down sideways and the thunder and lightning were so close." She swallowed.

"Were you more afraid of your husband than the storm?" I asked.

"RJ is a *gut* man."

I realized that she hadn't exactly answered my question by saying that, and again I worried about Mary and her children.

"I went out into the storm, and I made it to the field where we had left the tools. They were just where I expected them to be. It was just a small rake and a mallet for staking some of the plants. I picked both up and was about to go back to the house when I heard a buggy on the road. I froze. Because I thought it was my husband. I knew how furious he would be, catching me out in that terrible weather, and with his tools, too.

"But soon, I knew it wasn't our buggy. It was going too fast. The buggy went by just as there was a great flash of lightning. I was able to see the driver. There was just the edge of a bonnet."

"A bonnet? It was a woman in the buggy?"

"Men do not wear bonnets," she said, as if that were answer enough.

My brain was whirling. Could a woman have blown up that still and killed Leeza? Could an *Amish* woman have done it?

She paused. "Ten minutes later, as I walked back to the house, I heard the still explode."

"You believe whoever was in that buggy blew up the still?"

"I do. I didn't see anyone else go down the road. When I overheard the district elders tell my husband how someone with a gun blew up the still by shooting the propane tank, that was my thought right away."

"Why didn't you go to the police then?" I asked. "You need to tell them, not me."

"I'm afraid. We Amish are taught not to depend on the *Englisch* authorities. We are meant to be separate." She shivered and picked up the edge of her apron again, as if it was the only security she had to hold on to.

There were so many things I could say to that, but I wisely held my tongue. Insulting her strongly held belief system was not the way to convince her to trust me.

"By telling you," she said, "I hope the murderer will be caught, and my husband will never know that I was involved. Please don't tell him."

I frowned. She sounded so much like Leeza's

friend, Becca Stout, when she said that. Mary might not want her husband to know, but there was nothing I could do if he found out. For one, I had to tell Aiden. If Mary was questioned by the sheriff's department, I don't know how she could keep her husband from finding out.

"Leeza's friend, Becca, asked me to do the same thing."

She stared at me. "Becca who?"

"Becca Stout. She asked me to help find Leeza's killer and not tell the sheriff's department about her."

She stared at me. "Becca is no friend of Elizabeth's. She's never been a friend of Elizabeth's."

I shook my head. "Becca claimed to be her best friend. She was the one who told me that Leeza had stopped drinking for a while. I thought the two were still in contact even after Leeza left the district."

"Who told you that?" she asked.

"Becca."

"She lied to you. She hated Elizabeth for leading her brother astray."

"How did Leeza do that?" I asked.

She licked her lips. "When my sister-in-law was still a member of the district, Becca's brother courted her. She introduced Bryan to alcohol during that time. He never drank as much as she did, and he was better able to control his behavior. Everyone in the district knew he had a drinking problem just as bad as Leeza's, but because he didn't disrupt the district by acting out like Leeza did, the church elders ignored it. Leeza was shunned. Bryan never recovered. He never married and continued to drink in secret, though we all knew."

She pressed her hands together. "And then a little over a month ago, he got into a drunk driving accident with his buggy. He ran off the road into a tree. The horse wasn't seriously hurt, but he was killed. Becca blamed Elizabeth for this."

"You think Becca blew up the still because of her brother's death?"

She nodded.

I shivered. If Becca hated Leeza for leading her brother astray, it was no wonder she'd told the bishop Leeza would never change her ways. "What is the name of Becca's brother?" I asked, even though I was sure I knew. It was the name Aiden had told me just a little while ago.

"Bryan Hershberger," she said in a quiet voice. "Before she married, Becca's name was Becca Hershberger."

The enormity of what I had done in not telling Aiden about Becca earlier hit me. I had kept what I knew about her to myself because I thought I was protecting her and respecting her beliefs as an Amish woman who did not want to disobey her husband. I had been fooled. I would not be fooled like that again. "I will have to tell Deputy Aiden Brody about this, and when I do, he will want to talk to you."

She shook her head. "I can't talk to the police."

"Aiden is kind," I said. "He wouldn't make you do anything that you don't want to do, but he also has an obligation to find out the truth and solve this crime. It's not just for Leeza, but to protect others in the community. If Becca killed someone, she's unstable and might hurt herself or someone else."

She dropped her gaze. "I know this. It is why I have come to speak to you. You tell the police, but I will not speak to them."

The sun had completely set by this point.

Mary looked over her shoulder as the crowd got ready for the fireworks to officially begin. "I am putting this into your hands. I don't know what else to do. You can't know how hard it has been for RJ since we learned that Elizabeth was killed. He hoped that shunning would eventually bring her back to our faith. That's why members are shunned, why shunning is placed on a church member in the first place." She swallowed. "It's to remind them of what they are missing in community life. When they no longer have access to the church or their family, they come back."

"But she wasn't baptized. I thought Amish were only shunned if they left the church after baptism."

She shook her head. "Like all things in our faith, it is up to the bishop how he will handle the sinners in the church." She looked at her hands. "We are all sinners, of course, but what I mean is the unrepentant. Elizabeth was like that. She needed her drink so badly that she couldn't see how it hurt her family or herself. Even—even if she didn't ever come back into our community, I wished that before she died she would realize her mistake and try to make it right. That she would give up her drinking. I am grateful to hear that she tried to do that."

I took a breath. "I don't know if it will be helpful to you or not to know this, and it's up to you if you want to tell RJ, but Leeza—Elizabeth—was seeking help for her addiction to alcohol. She began going to a community center to get free addiction counseling."

Mary clasped her hands in front of her. "I'm glad. Hearing that does bring me comfort, and I know that it will bring RJ comfort, too, when he's ready to receive it. At the moment any word about his sister is not welcome."

I nodded. RJ had to accept his sister's fate before he could forgive her.

"We can't know the ways of the Lord," she said in a whisper. "We cannot know if she found peace in heaven or paid for her sinful ways." She took a breath. "It might not be the lesson of my bishop, but I like to think that *Gott* knows Elizabeth's heart. He knows what she would have done with her life if she had not died. He knew the direction in which her life was going before it was cut short. I—I don't think he would punish her because her life was cut off by someone else and she ran out of time."

"I don't think that either." My voice was as soft as hers.

"I have always believed—I have always hoped that in the end, *Gott* would be compassionate. Some men of the church think *Gott* wants to punish us for our misdeeds. That's not been what I have observed in my life."

"It's not what I have seen since I moved to Ohio," I said. "I don't know much about faith." I paused, wondering if I was sharing too much with her. "I didn't grow up in the church. My father fell away from faith after he left the Amish. But from what I have seen since I moved to Amish country, the God of my grandmother, your God, is compassionate."

There were tears in her eyes. "*Danki*. We can only know for sure when we accept our heavenly reward ourselves someday."

I hoped that day was a long way away for both of us. I wasn't ready for the end of my story yet.

"Now, I must go back to my husband." Without another word, she walked away from me just as the fireworks display began in full.

CHAPTER THIRTY-EIGHT

In the sky, the fireworks popped and exploded into a beautiful array of bright red, blue, yellow, and green. The crowd in the square cheered at every blast. There was a bombardment of light and sound above our heads as the fireworks whizzed and boomed. The display was grand. As expected when Margot was in charge of anything, the fireworks were bigger and better than anyone could have thought possible in such a little village.

I couldn't appreciate it, though; I had to find Aiden to tell him what I had learned from Mary. I couldn't believe that I had been so blind when it came to Becca. I'd thought that she really had been Leeza's friend. It would be even more heartbreaking if Leeza had wrongly thought the same.

I spotted Aiden across the square, but as I got closer, I realized he wasn't alone. Kayla stood next to him. She looked up at him. Her lovely face was illuminated by the light of the colorful sky. Aiden looked down at her, but I couldn't read his expression. I froze and took two steps backward, knocking into someone. It was a large man, who glared at me. "Watch where you're going."

"I—I'm so sorry." I stumbled away from him in the direction of the candy booth.

Why was Kayla there? She'd told Aiden she wasn't going to give him another chance. Had she lied?

Cass, Charlotte, and my grandmother sat on folding chairs in front of the booth, so that they could watch the display, too. There was an empty chair for me.

"Bailey," *Maami* said. "Where have you been all this time?"

"Greeting her adoring fans now that she has a big, fancy plaque," Cass teased.

I stared down at the plaque in my hands; I hadn't realized I was still carrying it. "Does anyone know where Deputy Little went?" I asked. I took care not to make eye contact with Cass. If she saw my expression, she would know something was wrong.

"I saw him on the corner of Apple and Main Street," Charlotte said.

"Great! I have to tell him something about the case."

Cass jumped out of her chair. "Why don't you just tell Aiden?"

"Um, I didn't see him," I lied. "It will be quicker to tell Little because we know where he is. Let me run over there now. I'll go do that and be right back." I hurried away from them before anyone could get a close look at my expression.

"Bai! Bailey!" Cass called behind me.

I just kept walking, as if I couldn't hear her call my name between the noise of the crowd and the fireworks going off.

I held the plaque to my chest as I hurried through the crowd and across Main Street. Without stopping, I ran to the corner where Charlotte had seen Deputy Little. My shoulders sagged when I got there and found he was gone.

I shook my head at how stupid I was being. I just needed to tell Aiden, whether Kayla was there or not. This wasn't about me or my feelings. This was about Leeza and finding the person responsible for her death.

Before I returned to the square and faced Aiden and Kayla, I stopped by the shop with the intention of leaving my plaque there. I unlocked the front door and went in.

I walked across the room and set the plaque on the counter. Under the kitchen door, I could see a light in the kitchen. I frowned. I guessed Charlotte had left the light on when she'd run over to the shop to pick up something for the booth. I shook my head and pushed in the door.

I was just about to reach in toward the switch and flick off the light, when someone on the other side of the door grabbed my wrist and pulled me into the brightly lit kitchen.

I stumbled into the room, and my hip connected painfully with the large island before I could right myself or realize what was happening.

I gripped the counter to stop myself from falling over and looked up to find Becca Hershberger Stout in front of me, holding a rifle pointed at my chest. "Becca, what are you doing?"

"Don't play dumb with me. I know what Mary told you. I heard her!"

My blood ran cold. "Where's Mary? Is she all right?"

"She's fine, or she will be after I get rid of you. Two murders will be enough to shut her up for *gut*. She likes to pretend, but she's not that brave. After I take care of you, she will never try to be a hero again."

"She's right, then. You killed Leeza. You killed her because you blame her for your brother's death."

"Yes, I blame her, but I didn't plan to kill her. I was just getting rid of the still and she happened to be lying nearby. She was drunk, of course. I think she must have gone there to get more 'shine. I didn't see her until the still exploded and lit up the woods." Her hands shook.

I didn't like the shaking hands because I was afraid she would slip and fire the rifle by accident.

She glared at me. "The still was an abomination and it had to be removed. Do you know how many times I have asked the church elders to take care of it? How many times I told them that it was leading our young men astray with the devil's drink?" She continued to shake. "But they did nothing. I had to take the matter into my own hands. I decided to do it months ago."

"You wanted to make the moonshiners pay. You wanted to kill them?"

"I never wanted to kill anyone." Her face was pale. "You don't know how hard it is for me to have to kill you. I didn't want to kill anyone, but I decided to destroy the still. I knew where it was from my brother. He loved moonshine. That's what he was drinking the night he died. He told me once where the still was. I knew I could find it, and I knew I could destroy it. My brother taught me how to shoot. But I had to wait for the right conditions. I needed a storm to cover the noise of the blast and put out the fire. If only I'd been able to destroy it before my brother's accident, maybe he would still be alive today. After his death, I was more determined than ever to do away with it, but Saturday night was the first time conditions were perfect."

She took a breath. "I didn't know Leeza was there that night, but when I saw she had died in the blast, I found it fitting. She was the reason my brother was dead. He never would have taken a drop of alcohol if it had not been for her influence. He was wooed by a devious woman. It's not my fault she is dead, but it is just."

"It is your fault. You took the shot at the still. You could have reported it to the sheriff's department. They would have arrested the men running it."

"The Amish cannot trust the *Englisch* police."

"So instead of doing that, you killed a woman."

"I told you, I didn't know she was there!" she shouted again.

Outside, the fireworks continued. I didn't know if anyone on the square would hear me if I screamed. The crack and boom of the fireworks was so loud, drowning out any other sound. It was just like the night Leeza died. Other noises were going to cover the sound of the gunshot.

I inched away from Becca toward the wall.

She held up her gun. "Stop moving!"

I froze. "Becca, you killed Leeza by accident. I'm sure if you tell Deputy Brody, he will have sympathy for you. The sheriff's department was looking for that illegal still, too."

She leveled the gun. "Do you think the *Englisch* police care at all about the Amish? If you do, you're a fool."

My eyes fell on the fire extinguisher I had installed on the wall just days before.

"Now, I have to do this quickly before the fireworks end. I need the noise." She leveled the gun, and I dove for cover, grabbing the fire extinguisher from the wall as I went.

A shot rang out, but the bullet hit the front of one of the mixers across the room.

I pointed the fire extinguisher at her and fired flame retardant on her face. Becca screamed and dropped the rifle on the tile floor. She covered her eyes. It gave me just enough time to blast her again.

She bent down to search for the gun. I swung the extinguisher at her.

She fell into the island just as I had and gasped for breath. I grabbed the gun, choking on the white cloud from the fire extinguisher. I stumbled out into the main room. The cloud gushed out after me. I ran for the front door and fell onto the sidewalk, holding the rifle.

"Get the gun away from her!" someone shouted.

The gun was ripped from my hands. I continued to cough and gag.

"Bailey!" Aiden knelt next to me on the sidewalk. "Bailey!"

"Becca is the killer." I coughed. "She's still in there. Fire extinguisher. You have to get her out. She could suffocate."

Behind me, I was conscious of officers running into my beloved candy shop. Despite everything, I hoped Becca would be all right.

Overhead, the fireworks continued to color the sky.

EPILOGUE

"And this is our star!" Linc Baggins announced as I stepped onto the carpet outside the small New York theater where they would be premiering the first two episodes of *Bailey's Amish Sweets*. Linc had claimed that the premiere wouldn't be a big red-carpet event, but this seemed pretty red carpet to me. I walked on the gold carpet runner along the sidewalk, leading Jethro by a blue leash that matched my dress. Because, of course, Jethro had to be there. He had made several appearances on *Bailey's Amish Sweets*, so Linc called me the day after the Fourth and asked me to bring him along. Juliet was sad to miss Jethro's big television debut because she was still on her honeymoon with Reverend Brook on Prince Edward Island, but he accompanied me with her blessing.

Cass, Jean Pierre, and Charlotte were a few feet behind me. My grandmother wasn't there, much to Linc's dismay. At least he didn't hold her absence against me. I thought that Jethro, who the photographers absolutely loved, made up for that.

Someone shoved a microphone in my face. "Your show is going to be a hit," the reporter said. "Can you tell us what gave you this idea?"

I blinked at him. The truth was, *Bailey's Amish Sweets* hadn't been my idea. It was Linc's, who'd been inspired after he visited my candy shop in Holmes County. I forced a smile. "The producer, Linc Baggins, and I came up with it together." I thought that was a fair answer.

"You are being too modest," Linc shouted. "Now, everyone, we need to get inside for the premiere. The show will air in five minutes."

It felt strange to be ushered into a theater in New York City to watch the premiere of my television show when just days ago I had been held at gunpoint in the middle of my kitchen at Swissmen Sweets. Thankfully, no one had been hurt in that incident. Maybe that wasn't completely true. Becca had a nasty bruise on her side from where I'd hit her with the fire extinguisher.

At least I knew she was out of the hospital now. Aiden had texted me that she was in jail, but he wasn't sure what charges would be brought against her other than attempted murder for what she tried to do to me.

Aiden and I hadn't spoken much since the Fourth. Somehow, I had been able to make myself scarce. First, it was because Cass was leaving, and then it was because I needed to have the shop cleaned after the incident. I also had to get ready for this trip to New York. I hadn't made the time to talk to him about

Kayla. I trusted him, but I wished he would be open with me about what was happening. I decided I would deal with it after the premiere.

Jean Pierre slipped his arm through mine. "I'm so very proud of you. I always knew you were destined to be a great candy maker, but you have surpassed my wildest dreams."

Jethro trotted along in front of us and into the building as if he owned the place. From the reaction of the New Yorkers fawning over the pig, you would have thought he did.

I kissed my old mentor's wrinkled cheek. "Wait until you see it, Jean Pierre, before you say how great it is."

He sniffed. "I don't need to see it to know it is magnificent, just as you are."

I laughed.

I was about to go into the theater when I spied a tall blond man across the room. He watched me intently and my heart skipped a beat. I waited for Linc to go into the theater before I left the line of people and went over to Aiden.

I stared up at him. "What on earth are you doing here?"

Aiden kissed me on the cheek. "I saw you on the red carpet. You were amazing, radiant. The camera loved you. I think even the reporters were charmed."

"Are you talking to me or Jethro?"

The little pig looked up at him.

Aiden laughed. "He wowed the crowd, too."

I smiled. "Aiden, what are you doing here? You said you couldn't come because of the murder case."

He smiled down at me. "I made an exception. Besides, the culprit has been found. The paperwork I have left to do for the DA can wait one more day."

"When did you get here?" I asked.

"Just as you were in the middle of your interviews," he said with a smile.

"But how did you get here?"

He smiled. "I called Cass, who put me in touch with Jean Pierre. He was more than happy to send over his plane for my last-minute trip."

I shook my head. I should have known Cass and Jean Pierre were in on it. I would owe them one. I was so thrilled to see Aiden. I hugged him. "I'm so glad you came!"

"You sure?"

I knew what he was asking. "I'm sorry if I've been . . . distant."

"I know you're upset about Kayla," he said. "You don't have to worry about her. I've told her I'm not interested in anyone but you. I'll keep telling her until she leaves me alone."

I shook my head. "I'm sorry I didn't just ask you outright."

He tucked his finger under my chin and lifted my face. "Don't be. I should have told you about her long ago. Honestly, I thought I would never see her again. Now let's get inside. I don't want to miss the premiere."

"Me either," I said with a grin and pulled on his hand. Jethro seemed ready to go, too.

"I am so proud of you. You are an exceptional person, Bailey King. You are an entrepreneur who has big plans to succeed, but at the same time you care about others. You don't know how rare that is in the world."

I swallowed hard.

He stepped back. "Before we go in, I have one more surprise for you." He stepped aside, and my grandmother in her Amish dress and prayer cap came from around the corner. She held her plain black bonnet in her hands. Her eyes were wide as she took in everything around her.

"*Maami?*" My mouth fell open. "You came?"

"*Ya,*" she said, as if she could hardly believe it herself.

"But the shop? It's a Saturday in the summer and Charlotte and I are both here."

"Emily is back watching the shop. Her husband is pitching in as well. Aiden said we could come and go home the same day, so I talked to my bishop and got special permission to be here. I will be back by Sunday service. Won't I, Aiden?"

Aiden nodded with a giant smile on his face.

"I'm so glad you're here." My voice caught.

"I am, too. The more I thought about it, the more I knew your *daadi* would want me to be here. I told the bishop that, and he understood." She smiled, and her blue eyes filled with tears.

There were tears in my own eyes, too.

She wrapped her arms around me. "You live a little bit in two worlds, respecting the Amish for me. I can live a little bit in two worlds for you, too."

I hugged her back. "*Danki, Maami.*"

Charlotte's Easy Marshmallow Sticks

Ingredients:

three marshmallows per skewer
wooden skewers
chocolate chips
decorations of your choice such as sprinkles,
   M&Ms, Reece's Pieces, nuts, etc.

Directions:

1. Put three marshmallows on a wooden skewer.

2. Melt chocolate in a double boiler.

3. Dip marshmallows on the skewer into the melted chocolate and spoon chocolate over them to make sure they are fully coated.

4. Put the different decorations on plates, one for each type.

5. If you choose, decorate with sprinkles, M&Ms, or any of the other decorations: roll the marshmallow sticks through the decorations while the chocolate is still warm.

6. Let cool.

7. Enjoy!

If you enjoy Amanda Flower's Amish Candy Shop series, be sure to check out her Amish Matchmaker Mystery series too! Please read on for an excerpt from COURTING CAN BE KILLER, available soon.

CHAPTER ONE

"This is the very best day of my life," my dear friend Lois Henry proclaimed as she wove up and down the aisle of the Harvest Village Flea Market. "Look at all this stuff! I should have brought more cash. Do you think some of these booths take plastic?"

It wasn't a question that I could answer because I was Amish and had never owned a credit card. If I bought anything on credit, it was store credit from an Amish merchant I knew well.

"I knew I should have gone to the ATM," she grumbled as she rooted through a patchwork purse that was big enough to carry a toddler. "I might have a few more bills at the bottom of this thing, but sorting through it is like digging to the center of the earth." Her cheeks flushed red under her makeup from the exertion.

If the purse and makeup weren't clues enough, the spiky purple-red hair and chunky, brightly colored costume jewelry would tell any passerby that

Lois Henry was not Amish, nor had she ever been tempted to convert. In fact, the very thought that Lois would have considered the Plain life was downright ludicrous.

My friend certainly stood out in the crowd of mostly Amish shoppers. I caught more than one Amish merchant giving us the once-over as we walked by. I guessed that she and I made an odd pair. We'd been that way since we were girls. Lois was the flamboyant *Englischer*, and I was the sedate Amish woman. To be honest, it might not look like it, but I get into my fair share of trouble, too. I'm blessed enough to have Lois, who is willing to join me down those troublesome paths.

Lois, bless her, was oblivious to the suspicious glances from a few of the Amish men we passed in the market, or maybe she just plain didn't care. I suspected it was the latter. Lois had never cared what anyone thought of her. When we were children growing up on neighboring farms, I had been jealous of her exuberant determination to go after whatever it was she wanted. When I was young, I associated her behavior with being *Englisch* because Lois and her parents were the only *Englischers* I knew. I have since learned that her *Englisch* upbringing had very little to do with it. Her devil-may-care attitude came from her and her alone.

She yanked on my arm. "Holy smokes, Millie, do you see that? That chair is just like one my mother had when I was growing up." She pointed at an orange molded plastic chair. "I have to see if I can snap it up."

I glanced around the market. "I think you have a

gut chance. It doesn't appear that anyone else is looking at it."

"They may just be playing it close to the vest. I can't be the only one here who knows to act cool when negotiating a deal." Lois came up with a fistful of bills from the bottom of her purse. "I knew there was more in here. My granddaughter Darcy is always telling me to get more organized, but then I wouldn't find surprises like this twenty-dollar bill at the bottom of my bag."

"Act cool?" I asked.

She tried to smooth the crumpled bill the best she could. "Yes, when we talk to the vendor about the chair, we must act like we don't want it."

"But you do want it." I adjusted my grip on the shopping basket I had brought with me. As of yet, I hadn't added anything to it. Truth be told, I hadn't come to the flea market that day to shop. I was looking for someone.

She clicked her tongue. "Millie Fisher, you would be the world's worst gambler."

"Considering I am a sixty-seven-year-old Amish woman, I choose to take that as a compliment."

She shook her head. "Just know I won't be taking you on my next trip to the Rocksino in Cleveland. You would completely ruin my luck."

I patted the prayer cap on the top of my snow-white hair. "I thought you gave up on gambling after you pushed your fourth husband into that hotel swimming pool."

"I took a break, yes, after that little incident." She finished smoothing the bills and tucked them into the pocket of her teal jacket. "However, in this life one should always be willing to take a chance and roll the dice." She grinned. "That sounds like one of the Amish proverbs you recite all the time, doesn't it?"

"It doesn't." I shook my head. "Not at all."

She winked at me and wasn't the least bit offended by my remark. I wished that I could be as easygoing as Lois, but on this special errand it was impossible. I turned back to the vendor she had pointed out.

She grabbed my arm and spun me in the other direction. "Don't look at him. If you do, he will know that we're interested in buying something from him."

I sighed and smoothed the sleeve of my plain green dress. "Do I have to remind you that you were pointing at him a moment ago?" Even shopping with Lois was an adventure. "Besides, why do you want that chair?" I asked. "It's orange. It doesn't go with a single item in your house."

She laughed. "Nothing in my house matches, and that's just how I like it."

That was the honest truth.

"Because I might have trouble acting cool, why don't you speak to the man about the chair, and I will keep looking for Ben," I said.

Finding Ben was the real reason we were at the Harvest Village Flea Market that day. I had been worried about the young man, and because I was the only one in the village who knew him well, I felt responsible to make sure he was all right.

"Good deal," Lois said. "By the time you find Ben, I will have that chair in my possession for half of what it's worth."

"Why don't we meet at the livestock judging area? I would like to know how the goats are getting on for my great-nephew Micah," I said.

Lois laughed. "Sounds like a plan."

I knew she would come away with the chair. I only hoped she didn't come away with a new husband, too. Lois had a talent for collecting those as well.

With Lois occupied, I continued my search of the flea market for Ben Baughman. Ben was a nineteen-year-old Amish man who had recently moved to Holmes County from Michigan. I had known him since he was a child; he came from the same community in which I had lived for ten years while taking care of my sister while she was ill. Ben had been a nearby neighbor in Michigan, and a thoughtful one, too. He was *gut* to both my sister and me and came over as often as he could to help me with the chores. He never let me pay him, and I was grateful for it. Taking care of my sister Harriett had been meaningful but hard work.

A few months ago, after my sister's death, I moved back to Holmes County, Ohio. To be honest, I didn't expect to see Ben again, as I had no desire ever to return to my sister's community and I could see no reason he would come to Ohio. However, a month ago I received a letter from Ben. He said that he was planning to move to Holmes County so that he could find work in a larger Amish community. His Amish district in Michigan was very small, and most of the men worked with *Englischers*. Not that there was anything wrong with that, but Ben said he wanted a more authentic Amish life and believed he could find that in Holmes County, where the Amish population was so much larger.

I told him he was welcome to come and I offered him a room in my little house until he got on his feet. I didn't think he stayed with me for even a week. He had been determined to make a life of his own and found a basement room for rent.

Behind me, I heard Lois's voice carry as she haggled with the antiques vendor over the chair. By the sound of it, the seller was already beginning to waffle on his price. I had expected nothing less.

I scanned the large barn for any sign of Ben. I was in the middle of a crush of shoppers and merchant booths that sold everything from produce to furniture to old toys and guns.

I also wondered if I'd chosen the wrong day to be looking for him. Perhaps I'd come on a day Ben didn't have to work. He was a guard of sorts for the flea market. In the last few weeks there had been a series of robberies. Many of the vendors had been hit. When they threatened to leave for the sake of the safety of their goods and their families, the owner had posted a job for an after-hours guard. I had seen the job notice on the community bulletin board at the Sunbeam Café, which Darcy Woodin, Lois's granddaughter, owned and operated. Lois worked there part time, but her hours seemed to be irregular at best. She only worked at the café when she was bored or when Darcy was desperate for a second set of hands.

When I saw the posting, Ben had just moved to Ohio. I told him about it, and he applied and got the job right away. I thought I had done my duty and everything was settled. What I didn't know was that he was going to meet his match at the flea market and that would lead to complications.

I spotted Ben beside the baked goods stand. It was the end of September, so the stand was heavy on apple tarts, pumpkin pies, and sweet potato cookies. He wasn't alone. He was speaking with a woman in a flowered blouse, a long skirt, and a prayer cap. I knew right away that she was Mennonite from her almost-Plain dress and cap. She handed Ben an envelope. He nodded, folded it twice, and tucked it into the pocket of his navy work shirt.

The woman walked away, and Ben smiled as I approached him. His straw-colored hair stood on end despite the strict Amish bowl cut he adhered to. A dusting of freckles danced across his face. He might be nineteen, but when caught in the right light he could pass for twelve. He certainly didn't look like someone old enough to be a night guard or to be falling in love and considering marriage.

He smiled wider, and I saw the gap between his two front teeth that also added to his youthful appearance. "Millie, it's so *gut* to see you. Do you need to do a little shopping at the flea market? You will be hard-pressed not to find what you need here. It seems that everything is for sale."

I shook my head. "I'm not in the market for anything in particular right now, but I know Lois will do enough shopping for both of us."

He laughed. "This doesn't surprise me. I'm on the way to my second job. I just . . ." His voice trailed off as he looked across the flea market.

"What job is this?"

"The lumberyard," he said. "Wait, no. Today it's stocking the Harvest Market. That's where I need to go next. My lumberyard job is on opposite days from the market. Eventually, I will get it all straight. In a week it will be habit, knowing everywhere I need to go and when I need to be there."

I frowned. "How many jobs are you working exactly?"

"Four." He paused when he saw the look on my face. "It was five, but I dropped one. Five was one too many."

"Four sounds like too many, too," I said, concerned. "Especially if you are forgetting where you need to be."

"It's worth it . . ." He trailed off and looked at the orchard stand. Now I knew why he was standing at this part of the flea market. He had the perfect view of the apple orchard stand and the lovely young woman selling the apples. Tess Lieb.

"How's Tess?" I asked.

His face broke into a smile that was made even more endearing by the gap in his teeth. "She's wonderful. Oh, Millie," he said to me quietly in Pennsylvania Dutch. "She's my match. I just wish her father could see that. I am working so hard to prove to him that I'm the right fit."

Tess was an eighteen-year-old Amish woman who lived with her parents and younger siblings on their vast apple orchard just outside the village. This time of year, her family's orchard stand did a brisk business as both *Englisch* and Amish wanted to buy the crispest, best apples.

September was the height of business for the Liebs. In the fall, the orchard was a hive of activity as the apple picking season went into full swing. They sold apples to wholesalers, at the local markets, and even from the orchard itself with a you-pick-your-own grove of trees.

Tess and her siblings were spread out with their apples all over Holmes County, but Tess seemed to always be at the flea market, where Ben had first laid eyes on her.

Across the flea market, Tess handed an elderly man his quarter-bushel bag of apples. As she accepted his money, her eyes strayed in Ben's direction. When their eyes locked, she blushed. If not completely in love, she certainly was enamored with Ben's attentions. It was my job as a matchmaker to recognize whether Ben and Tess were a perfect match or whether it was just Ben's wishful thinking. Affection or not, it made no difference if her family was against the match.

Tobias Lieb, Tess's father, stepped into the apple booth and glared at Ben before speaking harshly to Tess. She dropped her eyes and began bagging more apples.

Ben looked away with a sigh. "As you can see, Millie, I have gotten nowhere with her father. I don't know why, but he seems to dislike me even more than he did weeks ago. I only want to prove to Tess's father that I am ready to settle down," he went on. "I know I am young yet, but I can provide for the family I want to have. I will be twenty next week," he added, as if this gave emphasis to his argument.

"At twenty, you will still be a young man with your whole life in front of you. Give it time," I said, ready to share the wisdom I'd come to the flea market to impart in the first place. "Nothing lasts forever, not even your troubles," I said, reciting an Amish proverb.

He frowned at me. "Where's this coming from, Millie? I thought you would be on my side about this."

I sighed. "I received a letter."

"A letter?" he asked. "Who from?"

I glanced at the apple booth and then back at Ben. "From Tobias." I swallowed. "And it was about you."